The Second Biggest Nothing

T0275428

ALSO BY COLIN COTTERILL

The Coroner's Lunch
Thirty-Three Teeth
Disco for the Departed
Anarchy and Old Dogs
Curse of the Pogo Stick
The Merry Misogynist
Love Songs from a Shallow Grave
Slash and Burn
The Woman Who Wouldn't Die
Six and a Half Deadly Sins
I Shot the Buddha
The Rat Catchers' Olympics
Don't Eat Me
The Delightful Life of a Suicide Pilot

The Motion Picture Teller

The Second Biggest Nothing

COLIN COTTERILL

Copyright © 2019 by Colin Cotterill

Published by
Soho Press, Inc.
227 W 17th Street
New York, NY 10011

Library of Congress Cataloging-in-Publication Data

Cotterill, Colin, author.
The second biggest nothing / Colin Cotterill.
Series: A Dr. Siri Paiboun mystery; 14

ISBN 978-1-64129-191-0
eISBN 978-1-64129-062-3

1. Paiboun, Siri, Doctor (Fictitious character)—Fiction.
2. Coroners--Fiction. 3. Laos—Fiction. I. Title
PR6053.O778 S43 2019 823'.914—dc23 2018057751

Printed in the United States of America

10 9 8 7 6 5 4 3

With my endless thanks to Tim, Martin, Bertil, Ernest CB, Howard, Mac, Dr. Leila, David, Kate, Bob, Shelly, Lizzie, Rachel, Ulli, Geoffrey, Magnus, Dad, Dr. Margot, Juliet, Cara, Shona, Scott, Pary and my wife and best friend, Kyoko.

In loving memory of Saigna.

The Second Biggest Nothing

TABLE OF CONTENTS

CHAPTER ONE
A City of Two Tails

Dr. Siri was standing in front of Daeng's noodle shop when she pulled up on the bicycle. It was a clammy day, but his wife rarely raised a sweat even under a midday sun. She leaned the bike against the last sandalwood tree on that stretch of the road and patted Ugly the dog. Siri shrugged.

"So?" he said.

"So what?"

"What did she say?"

Daeng pecked him on the cheek and walked past him into the dark shop house. He trotted behind.

"She said I have the body and constitution of a sixty-nine-year-old."

"You are sixty-nine."

"Then I have nothing to be disappointed or smug about, do I? I'm fit and healthy. I'm a nice, average Lao lady with supposed arthritis. She did, however, mention that most people my age in this country are dead. I think that's a positive, don't you?"

"But what about . . . ? You know?"

"She didn't say anything," said Daeng.

"She what?"

"Didn't mention it at all. She obviously didn't notice it."

"What kind of a doctor doesn't notice that one of her patients has a tail?"

"I've told you, Siri. You and I are the only people who see it."

"What about the shamans in Udon?"

"They didn't see it, Siri. They visualized it. Not the same thing."

"It's a physical thing, Daeng. You know it is. I can feel it."

"I know. And I like it when you do."

"But now Dr. Porn would have us believe that it doesn't exist, which means I must be senile," said Siri.

"It means we're both senile."

"Then, by the same account, if you don't have a tail, then obviously my disappearances are a figment of my imagination."

"Not at all," said his wife dusting the stools to prepare for the evening noodle rush. "All it tells us is that nobody else notices you're gone."

"I've disappeared in public before," said Siri with more than a touch of indignation. "Haven't I disappeared in the market? At a musical recital? In a crowded—"

"Look, my love," she said, taking his hand, "there is no doubt that you disappear. There is no doubt you cross over to the other side and learn things there and return and tell me of your adventures. There is no doubt you are possessed by a thousand-year-old Hmong shaman and communicate through an ornery transvestite spirit medium. There is no doubt that you see the souls of the dead just as there is no doubt that I have a tail that I received from a witch in return for a cure for my arthritis. But, for whatever reason, nobody else bears witness to our little peculiarities. And perhaps it's just as well. The politburo would probably have us burned at the stake for occult practices if anyone reported us. Even Buddhism makes them queasy. Imagine what they'd do if Dr. Porn wrote in her official report, '. . . and, by the way, Madam Daeng appears to have grown a tail since her last checkup.'"

"You're right," said Siri.

"I'm always right," said Daeng. She squeezed his hand and smiled and returned to the chore of readying her restaurant. She was startled by the sound of hammering from the back room.

"What's that?" she asked.

"Nyot, the doorman," said Siri.

"He's still here?" asked Daeng. "How long does it take to put in a door?"

Mr. Nyot, the carpenter, was busy hanging. Following the previous monsoons, the door had changed shape and would no longer close. Daeng was not afraid of intruders. Ever since it was installed when the shop house was rebuilt, that door had never been locked. Nobody could remember where the key was. There were no security issues in Vientiane. The Party wouldn't allow such a thing. All the burglars were safely behind bars on the detention islands. The ill-fitting door banged in the wind and Mr. Nyot had promised them a nice new door at a special price. But it was also a special door. Daeng went to inspect the work.

"What's that?" she asked, pointing at the missing rectangle of wood at the base.

"It's a dog entrance," said Nyot.

"It's a hole," said Daeng.

"Right now it may look like a hole," said Nyot, "but over there I have a flap with hinges that I will attach shortly."

"That's not what I ordered," said Daeng.

"Maybe not. But this door is five-thousand *kip* cheaper than the next in the range. And I did notice that you have a dog outside that seems unable to enter the building."

"That dog has never entered a building," said Daeng. "Not because it's unable to but because it has some canine dread of being inside."

"Well, when it gets over its fear this will be the perfect door for it."

She couldn't be bothered to argue and the saved five-thousand *kip* would come in handy even though it was a tiny sum. But she was sure that when the wind blew from then on, the dog flap would bang through the night and the hinges would creak and they would miss their old one. She was very pessimistic when it came to doors.

Siri laughed at their exchange as he wiped the tabletops with a dishcloth and thought back to his last contact with Auntie Bpoo, his unhelpful, unpleasant spirit guide. It had been a while. She had him on some kind of training program. He'd passed "taking control of his own destiny" and "awareness," and he was ready for the next test but for some reason she'd gone mute. He attempted to evoke her often, but the channel was off air. Often, he wished his life could have been, not normal exactly, but more under his own control. Daeng was saying something behind him.

"What was that?" Siri asked.

"I said the ribbon was a nice touch," said Daeng.

"What ribbon's that?"

"You didn't decorate the dog?"

"Not sure I know what you're talking about."

"The ribbon, Siri. You didn't see him out there? Ugly has a rather sweet pink bow on his tail."

"Nothing to do with me," he said walking to the street.

Ugly was under the tree guarding the bicycle. Sure enough, he was wearing a ribbon with a silk flower, and from the rear he looked like a mangy birthday present.

Siri laughed. "This looks like the work of a certain Down syndrome comedian I know," he said.

"Can't blame Geung and his bride this time," said Daeng. "In case you haven't noticed, we're doing all the noodle work here. He and Tukta won't be back from their honeymoon for another week. And Ugly was not so beautifully kitted out when I left this morning. Don't take it off. He looks adorable."

Siri was bent double inspecting the dog's rear end. There was more of a sausage than an actual tail so it was surprising the decorator had found enough length to tie on the bow and that Ugly would allow it.

"It appears to have a message attached," Siri said. "There's a small capsule hanging from it. Lucky he didn't need to go to the bathroom before you noticed it."

"A message?" She smiled. "How thrilling."

Never one to pass up a mystery, Daeng joined her husband on the uneven pavement. Ugly seemed reluctant to give up his treasure. He growled deep in his throat.

"Come on, you ungrateful mongrel," said Siri. "Who do you think pays for your meals and applies ointment to all your sores and apologizes to the neighbors for your indiscriminate peeing?"

It was a compelling argument and one that Ugly obviously had no counter for. He held up his haunches for his master to remove the capsule. It was a silver cylinder about the size of a cigarette. Its two halves could be pulled apart. Siri had seen its kind before but he couldn't remember where. Inside was a tight roll of paper, which he unfurled.

"Unquestionably a treasure map," said Daeng.

"Only words, I'm afraid," said Siri. "And handwritten."

Still pretending that his eyesight was as good as it had always been, he held out the slip at arm's length and squinted at the tiny writing. He would blame that arm for its shortness rather than admit to any deficiency in his eyesight. The note was just within range.

"It's in English," he said.

"What a shame," said Daeng.

He read it aloud with what he considered to be an English accent.

> *"My dear Dr. Siri Paiboun, it has been a while. By now I'm sure you have either forgotten my promise of revenge or have dismissed it as an idle threat. But if you had known me at all, you would have realized that my desire to destroy you and your loved ones is a fire that has burned in my heart without end. After such a long search I have found you and I am near you. I have already deleted one of your darlings. Before I leave I will have ruined the life you have established just as you did mine. I have two more weeks. That should be more than sufficient."*

It would be several hours before Siri and Daeng could fully appreciate the seriousness of their note because neither of them understood English. They knew French and could read the characters and they could guess here and there at meanings. But the languages were too far apart to cause either of them to panic. That would come later.

CHAPTER TWO
The Glory of Totalitarianism

At the end of 1980, Vientiane was a city still waiting for something to happen. It had waited through the droughts and floods, through the flawed policies, the failed cooperatives, the mass exodus of the Hmong and lowland Lao and, more recently, ethnic Chinese business holders across the Mekong. It had waited for inspiration, for good news, for a break. It had been waiting for five years but still nothing of any note had happened. So, what better way to celebrate five years of Communist rule than by inviting a large number of foreign journalists to observe the results of all those things that hadn't happened? There were those who argued that *nothing* was a good thing. For thirty years the Lao had been waging a war against their brothers and against the foreign powers that put them in uniforms. Wasn't *nothing* better than that?

It was what they called "a cocktail reception" even though none of the glasses being carried around on silver trays contained anything more exotic than weak whisky sodas and room temperature white wine. The hostesses who carried the trays wore thick makeup, military uniforms and uncomfortable boots. They smiled in a way that suggested they were under orders to do so. They did not enter into conversation with the already soused foreign journalists because they could not. They were from villages in distant provinces and even fluency in the Lao language was beyond their linguistic ability. And they had been warned by their superiors about these men from the decadent West and the shady East who bit the heads off babies and had sexual organs the size of ripe papayas. The girls trembled at every flirtatious glance, each beckoning whistle.

In its day, the nightclub of the Anou Hotel had been a gloomy cavern of nefarious goings on. When first the French, and then the American soldier boys played there, it was a mysterious grotto, so dark you couldn't see the age of your dance partner, so heavy with marijuana smoke you couldn't smell the fluids that had soaked into the carpets the night before. But on this evening, this glorious evening that marked the fifth anniversary of the founding of the People's Democratic Republic of Laos, the lights were all on, and there were no secrets. The gaps in the parquet tiles on the dance floor had been filled with cement and painted brown. The table vinyl curled up at the edges, and the light-blue paint peeled from the beams.

But, as Comrade Civilai said, perhaps this was the symbolism the Party wanted to pass along to the world. The decadent past had fallen into ruination. The last altars to the gods of depravity were crumbling and turning to dust.

"Or," Civilai added, "perhaps there was no other venue with a functioning sound system and a full bar."

Since he left the politburo he'd not been sure of the motives behind Party policy. Perhaps he never had.

Intimacy was obviously another government plot to

endear itself to the outside world. There really wasn't a great deal of space in the Anou. Sixty-four foreign journalists—all male—were shoulder to shoulder with Russian interpreters, most of the resident diplomatic community, selected aid workers and donors and the UN, even though nobody was ever really sure what the latter did to earn their living in Laos. All of the ministries were represented, each minister and vice minister with his own aide to help carry him back to the Zil limo at the end of the night.

Comrade Civilai—wearing cool, *avant garde* sunglasses—was there because of his distinguished service to the cause of communism in Laos and his apparent undying loyalty to the politburo. Chief Inspector Phosy was there because, despite several attempts to oust him by those who had become accustomed to graft and corruption, he was still the head of the police force. His wife, Nurse Dtui was there because it was a perfect opportunity to practice the foreign languages she'd taught herself with little or no benefit thus far. And Dr. Siri and Daeng were there because it was walking distance from their restaurant and a nice evening. They hadn't been invited, but no scruffy sentry with an unloaded AK-47 was going to turn away such a distinguished white-haired couple.

This small group of friends and allies sat at a table near the exit. They'd tired of attempting to snare any of the reluctant hostesses and instead had relieved the open bar of a half bottle of Hundred Pipers. With it they toasted anything that came to mind: to the miracle that they were all still alive, to Geung and Tukta on their honeymoon at a small vegetable cooperative outside Vang Vieng, to the peaceful, almost ghostly quiet streets of Vientiane, to the dizzying figure of 15 percent Lao literacy announced that afternoon, and, finally, to friendship. The bottle was approaching empty. Civilai had made more than his usual number of bladder runs to the bathroom because he'd hit a bad patch of stomach troubles following experiments with Lao snails in fermented morning glory sauce. The comrade was a pioneer in the kitchen and pioneers stepped on their own rabbit traps from time to time.

"What I don't understand . . ." said Siri.

"There must be such a lot," said Civilai, returning from the crowded toilet.

"I'm serious about treating this condition of yours," said Siri.

"I'm not letting you and your rubber glove anywhere near my condition, thank you, Doctor," said Civilai.

"Then, what I don't understand," Siri tried again, "is the significance of five years. Nine I can appreciate. Always been a lucky number. And ten has some decimal roundness to it. But five?"

"Well, young brother, it's quite simple," said Civilai. "The government is celebrating five years because, despite all its mismanagement and false hopes and poor judgment, it's still here. They never expected to make it this far."

"Who's going to kick them out?" said Daeng.

"Exactly," said Civilai. "That's the glory of totalitarianism. You can screw up for five years and admit you have no idea what you're doing and you wake up the next morning and you're still in power. You can experiment all over again."

"If you weren't suffering from dementia I'd arrest you for treasonous rhetoric," said Phosy.

"Look around, young chief inspector," said the old

politburo man. "Point me out one minister or vice minister here who isn't demented. All those grenades exploding too close to their brains."

"Uncle Civilai, you seem particularly nasty tonight," said Nurse Dtui. "Is it the snails?"

They charged their glasses and toasted to the snails.

"In a way, yes," said Civilai. "I'll tell you, sweet Dtui. Today, with no warning, no request, no discussion, I received a copy of the speech they expect me to give to all these pliable journalists at the end of the week."

"You could always say 'no,'" said Siri.

"And then what? They'd give the same script to some other doddery old fool to read the lies."

"So what are you planning to do?" Daeng asked.

"Harness the power of redaction," said Civilai.

"You'd get two minutes into the speech and they'd drag you from the podium," said Phosy.

"But what a glorious two minutes they would be," said Civilai.

"Except the simultaneous interpreters will be reading the original script," said Daeng. "The old king tried to change his abdication speech, and the radio station brought in an actor to read the Party version."

"An actor we could sorely use right now," said Siri, anxious to change the subject.

"I still have the floor," said Civilai.

"Oh, right," said Nurse Dtui, ignoring him, "your movie. I was going to ask about that. Don't you have a cast yet?"

"I feel nobody takes me seriously anymore," Civilai grumbled.

"The Women's Union has brought together a vast gaggle of would-be performers," said Siri.

"All we're missing is a functioning camera," said Daeng.

"The camera is functioning," said Siri, "and we are on the verge of acquiring a world-class cinematographer to operate it."

"Here I am about to re-educate the planet," said Civilai, "and you dismiss my plan out of hand."

"Perhaps we aren't yet drunk enough to take you seriously," said Daeng. "Another bottle might persuade us."

Civilai huffed and the hairs in his nostrils flapped. He walked off to the bar with a heavy smattering of umbrage and a noticeable stagger.

"He's not really going to sabotage the speech, is he?" Nurse Dtui asked.

"He's a politician," said Siri.

He'd planned to say more but realized that short phrase said it all.

"And the camera story?" asked Phosy.

The camera in question was a very expensive Panavision Panaflex Gold which had become 'lost' during the shooting of a film called *The Deer Hunter* in Thailand. Through the rice-growing underground it found its way to Laos and into the spare room on the upper floor of Madam Daeng's restaurant. Until then, all it lacked was someone with the ability to turn it on. But that small setback to the filming of Dr. Siri's ambitious Lao spectacular was apparently resolved.

"Our cinematographer has arrived and will begin his duties this weekend," said Siri with a smile. "Daeng and I and various relatives went to the airport to greet him and make sure he didn't change his mind and get on the return flight."

"And by 'cinematographer,'" said Daeng, "what Siri

means is a young boy with a certificate in film production and no experience."

"Yet more experience than all of us in the operation of a camera," said Siri. "I was born into a generation of candles and beeswax lamps. Electricity entered my life late. It wasn't until I arrived in Paris that I discovered the magic of *volts* and *ampères*. But by then I had decided to dedicate my life to medicine. If I had not, who's to say by now I wouldn't have been the one to invent the cassette player and the Xerox machine?"

"Is he legal, this camera person of yours?" the chief inspector asked.

"He's Lao," said Siri, "the cousin of Seksak who runs the Fuji Photo Lab. He's harking the call of the Party for its lost sons to come home to the motherland to share their new skills and savings."

"He left in the '75 exodus?" Dtui asked.

"Before," said Siri. "He made an orderly exit about ten years before with his father. Dad had a scholarship from the Colombo Plan. His wife died in childbirth, so it was just the two of them. They moved to Sydney. Bruce went to—"

"His name's Bruce?" said Dtui.

"His father renamed him when they got there," said Siri, "perhaps in an attempt to hide him amidst all the other Bruces. The boy had studied with the Australians here and become proficient in English. He sailed through high school and entered college."

"Why would he ever want to come back?" Phosy asked.

"His cousin believes he was disillusioned with the decadent West. His father had been killed in a car accident in Australia and Bruce was homesick. Missed his distant family. When our government announced we'd welcome expatriate Lao with no hard feelings, he was only too keen. His cousin told him about our film. He read my script and was delighted to join us."

"Can you afford him?" asked Dtui.

"Said he was happy to do it for nothing."

"Must be mad," said Civilai, returning with another half bottle of whisky, which he plonked down on the table like a memento of war.

"You could talk the crutches off a legless man," said Daeng. "How do you do it?"

"Those young fellows just need to know who's boss," said Civilai. "Look important. Don't say anything. Walk behind the bar. Pick up the bottle. Simple."

He sat at the table, his revolutionary fire apparently doused.

"And speaking of who's boss," said Daeng, "where's Madam Nong this evening?"

"My wife does not enjoy watching me drink," said Civilai. "She seems to think I devalue myself when I allow alcohol to make decisions for me."

"Whereas Madam Daeng here knows only too well that I am at my brightest and most perceptive with the Hundred Pipers playing the background music," said Siri.

"Sadly, as the music grows louder and the perception reaches a crescendo, the passion is known to wane," said Daeng.

There was a long silence at the table.

"We all know this is Daeng making a joke, right?" said Siri.

"I'm not so sure," said Dtui.

"Daeng, tell them," said Siri.

Daeng looked around the room.

"Daeng?"

The embarrassment was blurred by the voice of somebody leaning too closely into a badly wired microphone. Like announcements at the national airport, nobody knew exactly what had been said. But it was the signal for Siri's crew to down their drinks and head to the exit. It was speech time and their finely tuned instincts naturally sent them in the opposite direction.

It was only a short walk to the noodle shop, but Siri must have told them a dozen times that his wife was joking about his waning ardor. Still she kept mum and they were all shedding tears of laughter by the time they reached the closed shutter. High in a tree opposite perched Crazy Rajhid, the Indian. They could only see his silhouette against the moon, but it was obvious he was as naked as on the day he was born. They waved. He ignored them. He still believed that if he kept perfectly still he was invisible.

It was the time of the evening when the dusty streets were usually deserted and no other sound could be heard: no television, no radio, no hum of air-conditioning. But on that evening their drunken voices were carried across the river to Thailand to show the enemy that socialist Laos could still have a good time once in a while. In an hour, when the curfew took hold, their voices would be silenced too, but right now was as good a time as any to stand on the riverbank and yell abuse. It was nothing personal, just a friendly diatribe against a nation with an ongoing animosity toward their inferior northern neighbors. It was therapy.

Once in the restaurant, Madam Daeng made a batch

of noodles to soak up the whisky and put something in everyone's stomach for the ride home. Only Civilai, still blaming the snails, forwent the meal.

"I think we need to approach the girl," he said.

"What girl's that?" Phosy asked.

"The blonde," said Civilai. "Acting second secretary at the American embassy. Looks gorgeous. Speaks fluent Lao. She was standing at the bar. I've met her at a few functions recently."

"He has these hallucinations," said Siri.

"In a room with two hundred men you really didn't notice one attractive woman?" Civilai asked.

"Even in a room with two hundred women I'd only notice Daeng," said Siri.

Daeng smiled and squeezed his hand.

"I was making all that up about his ardor," she said.

"At last," said Siri. "Why do you feel the need to approach the blonde, Civilai?"

"She has acting experience," said Civilai. "We need her for the film."

"In what role?" Siri asked. "Ours is the story of the nation through the eyes of two young revolutionaries not unlike ourselves. How many pretty blonde Americans featured in the birth of the republic?"

"We could write in a part for her," said Civlilai.

"As what?"

"I don't know. She could be the CIA."

"All by herself?" asked Siri.

"Why not?"

"I think you'll find most women in the CIA back then were making coffee and typing," said Madam Daeng.

"Look, it doesn't matter what she does," said Civilai.

"How many commercially successful movies have you seen that didn't have a glamour interest?"

"I believe we have one or two beautiful Lao women in major roles," said Dtui.

"That is admirable," said Civilai. "But if we're aiming at the international market . . ."

"Lao women aren't attractive enough?" said Daeng.

"They . . . you are lovely in the domestic sense," said Civilai, "but we need sexy. We need . . . we need a Barbarella."

Only Siri and Civilai knew who Barbarella was, and Siri wasn't about to disagree with his friend's choice. There followed a testy five minutes as the old boys tried to define sexy and explain why even the most attractive Lao in her finest blouse and ankle-length *phasin* skirt would not qualify. They dug themselves deeper into the muck with every comment. The discomfort was only eased when Civilai felt the need for one more visit to the toilet.

"Time for us to go pick up Malee," said Dtui. She stood to leave. "She's with a neighbor and they'll want to get to bed."

Despite his lofty position, Chief Inspector Phosy and his wife were still billeted at the police dormitory until their modest government house was completed. To his wife's mixed disappointment and admiration, he'd refused to move into the palatial two-story abode of his predecessor.

"Come husband," she said.

"I'm fine to drive the Vespa," said Phosy.

Dtui twiddled her fingers and he handed her the key. She knew that if he felt the need to tell her he was fine there had to be some doubt. Even in the carless streets of the capital there were potholes and sleeping dogs, and her husband had worked thirteen hours that day. He'd be safer on the pillion seat. They'd started toward the street when Siri remembered his letter.

"Oh, wait," he said, and pulled the folded paper from his top pocket. "A quick translation and you can be on your way."

He explained how the note had been attached to Ugly's tail sometime that morning. Nurse Dtui, hoping for a study placement in America, had put in many hours to learn English. In'75, armed with a scholarship and high hopes, she'd watched the Americans flee, and, like their Hmong allies, Dtui was stranded. She looked up from the words with an expression of horror on her face. Her English was competent enough to read Siri's letter and good enough for her to realize the menace it contained. She called Phosy back from the street and had the team sit once more around the table beneath the buzzing fluorescent lamp while she translated. Siri and Daeng appeared to be unmoved by the content.

"You don't seem that concerned," Phosy told them.

"It wouldn't be the first threat we've received," said Siri.

"Almost a weekly event," said Civilai.

"Well, I'm your friendly local policeman," said the chief inspector, "and I'm not going to let you laugh this one off. It isn't just a threat to you, Siri. The writer is promising to hurt your loved ones and that includes everyone at this table."

"I don't love him," said Civilai. "I'm not even that fond of him. That should let me off the hook."

"Ignore him," said Daeng. "He's having one of his difficult years. Go ahead Phosy. What do you suggest?"

"First, I suggest we look at the letter for what it does, not just for what it says."

"What's that supposed to mean?" said Civilai.

"Well," said Phosy, "the fact that it's in English sends a message in itself. As Siri doesn't speak the language I doubt he's antagonized too many English speakers in his life. And, even if the writer knows more than one language, why would he choose English for this particular threat?"

"I'm assuming you'll just be asking a batch of questions and have us fill in the answers later," said Civilai.

"I think that's a splendid system," said Madam Daeng. "Continue, Phosy."

"Secondly," said Phosy, "why does he only have two weeks to complete his mission? If he lived here there'd be no restriction."

"So, he's a visitor," said Nurse Dtui.

"On a visa," said Siri. "We aren't that generous in the immigration field."

"And we just left a room full of foreign journalists who are in town for exactly two weeks with nice fresh correspondent visas in their passports," said Phosy. "Any one of them could be our writer. Even the Eastern bloc boys would have a grounding in English."

"We can't interrogate all sixty-four of them," said Daeng. "We need to eliminate some."

"Well, he's certainly not Vietnamese," said Dtui.

"How do you know?" Siri asked.

"He gave Ugly a break," she said. "They still eat dogs over there. No Vietnamese is going to balk at slicing up a flea bitten mongrel if it serves a purpose."

They heard a low howl from the street. It might have been a coincidence but Siri doubted that.

"Okay, there are four Vietnamese journalists," said Daeng. "That takes us to sixty."

"Not much of a help," said Civilai.

"We need to start with the threat itself," said Phosy. "Siri, the writer made a promise that he would have his revenge. That his lust for vengeance is still burning inside him. I'm guessing that when he made that threat initially you would have sensed that it was more than just words. You would have seen him as capable of following through with it. It would have frightened you. For some time you would have been looking over your shoulder. On how many occasions have you experienced that type of fear in your life?"

All eyes turned to Siri. He looked up at the lamp and seemed to be fast-rewinding through his seventy-six years. He sniffed when he reached the end.

"Twice," he said.

"Then, that's—" Phosy began.

"Better make it three times," said Siri. "Just to be sure. Three times when I truly believed the nasty bastard meant what he said and had the resources to keep his promise. I'm not given to panic, but I confess to missing a few heartbeats on those occasions."

"Then that's where we start," said Phosy. "Who's first?"

CHAPTER THREE
Paris, 1932

I was sitting at an outdoor table in front of the Café de la Paix. I was alone, but I told the waiter in his long white apron that I was expecting someone. He was surprised to hear French from my lips. They usually were. He was unnecessarily polite. All the other tables were occupied by French sophisticates. White people as far as the eye could see. Dapper men with pencil mustaches and straw boaters. *Vogue* magazine women with bangs that restricted their vision to lap level. White silk dresses billowed in the wind. Champagne bubbled. You'd never have guessed France was in the middle of the Great Depression.

There was a sort of upside down racism in Paris those days. The French military had recruited thousands of Chinese for the war effort, and most of them had been killed in battle: ravaged by Spanish flu or just left to die slowly from neglect and hunger. They were expendable and soon forgotten. Their story would never have been released by the government but the bolshie French press got wind of it and exposed the disgrace in its national newspapers. The government had no choice but to apologize and thank the Chinese for their contribution to the Allies' victory over the Germans.

As I had an Asian face I got a lot of looks of remorse during that period. Those "we're sorry for what we did to you" looks. The looks never became words or actions, but I did get the odd smiles from pretty ladies in white. It was May and *la mode* of spring was the tennis look. The temperature was taking its time to catch up to the season. Hundreds of inappropriately dressed people sat shivering at their tables or walking briskly along the boulevard. Three ladies at the table beside me were cradling their coffee cups to keep their fingers warm. I smiled at them. They looked at one another before smiling back. As I was no slave to fashion, I wore mittens and a muffler.

I'd arrived in Paris on a steamer in 1924 at the age of twenty. Unlike the other Asians on board, I didn't have to shovel coal or stagger from the galley to the state rooms with trays of canapés and champagne buckets. I had a ticket. My cabin was small but comfortable. I was in the enviable position of having a sponsor who had taken it upon herself to turn me from a shoeless waif into a young man of letters. Madam Le Saux, more commonly known as Loulou, had first met me at a temple in Savanaketh. I had been dumped there at the age of ten by an uncaring relative who instructed me to learn all I could, then disappeared from my life. I learned everything the monks had to teach and read the French books in the small library over and over again. By the age of twelve I was bored.

Madam Loulou arrived one day in a yellow Peugot with a driver in a cap. She was tall and slim but for her midriff, where fat had gathered unkindly. She reminded me of a python I'd once seen digesting a pig. Hers was the first

French I'd heard spoken by a native speaker. My initial reaction was amazement at how clever she was to have mastered such a difficult language. Her face was so heavily cased in makeup it took some time for her expressions to match her words.

"Does anybody here speak French?" she called out. Her voice was manly, crumbly at the edges.

Nobody answered, not even the abbot whose French was by far the best at our temple. He slunk back into the prayer hall, took up a broom and started sweeping.

"My word," she said. "They sent me here because your temple has such a fine reputation. Yet I cannot find one person who understands me."

I don't know what possessed my skinny legs to walk me forward, nor how I dared look her in the eye.

"We all speak French, Madam," I said, "but we are embarrassed to attempt it in front of you."

She walked toward me, her heels sinking into the dirt with each step.

"And why would you be embarrassed?" she asked.

"Because we are not perfect," I said.

Despite the tightness of her dress, she crouched and wiggled her index finger in my direction.

"Come here, Little Prince," she said.

I shuffled forward close enough to see the wrinkles under her makeup.

"Only in nature can we find perfection," she said. "Man must settle for 'good enough.' And you are good enough for me. I choose you."

And, just like that, I became her project. She made donations to the temple for extra tuition. She produced excellent counterfeit documents proving my links to the

Lao royal family that gained me entry into the *lycée* in Saigon where she paid my fees. She attended my graduation and presented me with a second-class ticket on the *Victor Hugo* to France. In my pack, I had a letter of introduction from the governor general in Saigon to the director of Ancienne University and enough funds to cover my first-year expenses in Paris. Madam Loulou guaranteed me funds for every year that I achieved excellent grades until the day I became a doctor.

What she didn't guarantee was that she would stay alive long enough to honor that promise. Even as I was journeying across the Atlantic my sponsor succumbed to consumption and was dead by the time I docked in Marseilles. It wasn't until several years later that I learned of the background of my dear Madam Loulou. For many years, my sponsor had been the proprietor of one of the most popular whore houses in Saigon. She had amassed a small fortune mainly from the patronage of French army officers, one of whom was the aforementioned governor general. She had arrived in Vietnam early in the French campaign and in a city with more brothels than drain holes, she quickly made a name for herself. This was achieved, not from the beauty of her girls but from their unique skills. Madam Loulou had trained each one in the ancient art of fellatio. You might say she'd become a celebrity by word of mouth.

Loulou had never married nor produced offspring. She had nobody to share her wealth with. Somewhere along the line she got it into her head that she was on her way to hell: a belief loudly supported by the wives of the officers she serviced. A Catholic priest in Saigon—also a customer—suggested she might readjust her trajectory by saving poor orphans. And, in the shell of a nut, that's what led her to me and twenty other young boys. I still look for her in the back alleyways of the Other World, but I never see my darling Madam Loulou. And that, omitting several years of struggles and humiliations, of poverty, of retaking high school courses and accepting disgusting jobs to keep myself alive in France, explains why I was sitting in front of the Café de la Paix that chilly May morning. I was in my third year of medicine at Ancienne and doing moderately well, "for an Asian." But I'd run into a bad patch of my own doing and I needed counsel.

"Anybody sitting here?" came a voice.

The young fellow leaning over me was dark-skinned with a fine head of black hair greased back. He was dressed like half the men there at the café, and he grasped a tennis racket in his left hand. His right hand he held out to me. I grabbed it, laughed, and shook the hell out of it.

"Sit down, you fool," I said, "before someone challenges you to a game."

Civilai pulled out the chair and apologized in charming French to the three ladies behind him who needed to shuffle slightly to allow him to sit. They smiled. He gestured to the waiter, pointed to my cognac and held up three fingers.

"What makes you think I couldn't beat them?" he said.

"I doubt that racket's ever kissed a ball," I said.

"You're right. But see how impressed everyone looks. A Chinaman trained in the fine art of tennis. They'll go home and tell all their friends we can count to forty."

Civilai was, in many respects, my cultural savior in those tough years. We'd met at the Louxor, a small cinema in La Chapelle, where I worked as an usher and confectionary seller. I'd been there so long most of the patrons knew me by name. Civilai was from a wealthy family and never really had to work for a living. Our backgrounds were so different we really had no right to have become friends, but our love for the cinema drew us together. He told me that he was a Communist. At the time, I really didn't know what that meant. It seemed everyone in Paris had to have a cause. You had to be something other than yourself: a fascist, an anarchist, a poet. So I paid little heed to Civilai's constant references to Karl Marx and Lenin. He told me about his pal, Quoc, a Vietnamese who had great plans to go back to Indochina and rescue the slaves in the French colonies. Together they would establish a Communist state, just as soon as Quoc got out of jail in Hong Kong. He seemed, to my mind, to be spending a lot of time in jail.

As a child at the temple in Savanaketh, I hadn't had many dealings with the French administrators. In fact, I probably viewed them as great white gods educating us natives—through armed force—how to be civilized. I liked their uniforms. It didn't occur to me they were raping our land. We didn't have anything when they arrived and several decades later we had even less and were paying taxes on it. But, to a ten-year-old boy, that seemed to be the way of the world. If you had a big gun you had the right to do what you wanted.

But then, in France *entre deux guerres,* Civilai had become my grapevine to a country I had no other means to communicate with. I had no friends or family back in Laos. Like all the bemused tribesmen and women, who had been corralled together under a Lao flag, I'd been born in a country that I still knew very little about. I'd written

'Buddhist' on the application to Ancienne, but the religion of my birth made no more sense to me than the Catholicism drummed into me at school. At 23 I'd already seen more of France than I had of Laos. Without Civilai I would probably have swallowed the colonial line that the country was working in the tropics to improve the lot of ignorant savages. Were it not for a generous fellationist, I would have been one of them.

"Do you ever order just one drink?" I asked my young friend.

He placed the newly arrived drinks like chess pieces on the checkered tablecloth and pushed one toward me: cognac to queen's pawn two.

"Monsieur L'Usher," he said, "one never knows when one's waiter might be struck down with a heart attack, leaving all those at the tables around his prone body deprived of their rightful *digestifs*. Always order as if these drinks might be your last."

"At these prices they undoubtedly will be," I said.

"Then consider yourself lucky that this very morning a handsome filly at Longchamp caught my eye. She almost begged me to put a hundred francs on her to win. And she did not disappoint me. Consider this afternoon my treat."

I knew there were no races at Longchamp in the morning. With Civilai, there was always a horse, a greyhound or a roulette table keen to cover the costs of our outings. He never once belittled me over my poverty nor offered to pay for my courses or keep up with the rent. My pride remained intact, but I was certain that if a disaster befell me, my friend would be there to help me out. I just had to ask. I never did.

"Salut," he said and clinked my glass with his. We drank

to nothing in particular. "Shouldn't you be in school?" he asked.

"I don't go to as many classes as I used to," I said. "I work better from books. I tend to pick out the best lectures to attend. I went to one this morning on diacetylmorphine."

"Sounds fascinating."

"It was," I said. "It was one of those moments when you can be sure the world has just made another one of its serious mistakes."

"Like assassinating Archduke Ferdinand?"

"Potentially much worse than that," I said.

"Then tell me all about dicey mental morphine," he said.

"Diacetylmorphine is a pain reliever ten times more powerful than morphine. Morphine was first extracted from opium in 1805. It served us well medically, but it tended to be addictive. Scientists, searching for an alternative, synthesized diacetylmorphine, and it was an immediate success. The Bayer Company began mass production. Countries around the world hastily approved this new 'non-addictive' painkiller, and soon it was more popular than sex. And for good reason. A year after its launch in North America, 200,000 people had become addicted to this super drug that Bayer had named heroin. It was immediately banned worldwide for anything but medical or scientific use.

"But, of course, as soon as the drug became illegal, all the criminal networks went up a gear. The Chinese gangs already have refineries. The Corsicans are building labs right here in France under the noses of the *gendarmerie.* The lecturer believes that in the next decade heroin will outperform opium as the addiction of choice worldwide. It's less bulky and easier to hide."

"And this is what they're teaching you at medical school?" Civilai asked.

"You can pass on the information to your boss."

"Quoc? Why would he be interested?"

"Some of the most successful revolutions and coups in history have been funded by the drug trade. It's how the French maintain their presence in Indochina. You and your Communist buddies could get in on the ground floor."

"Siri, communism is all about empowering the workers, not debilitating them. When we take over from the French, the first thing we'll do is burn their opium crops."

"I admire your faith," I said, even though I didn't give it much of a chance.

"So anyway, what brings me here?" he asked.

"My postcard, I presume."

"It gave up so little information."

"I didn't want the French postal service to be the first to know."

"Excellent. I have an exclusive, and you want my advice."

"More, your blessing," I said.

"Oh, no."

"Oh, no, what?"

"I sense a liaison."

"More than a fling," I said. "I've asked her to marry me."

Civilai whooped and held up four fingers to the waiter.

"Does she know you have fifty centimes to your name?"

"She does. But she also has fifty centimes to hers. So between us we have one franc, which is the beginning of a fortune."

"Have I met her?" he asked.

"Yes, on your last trip to Paris. You and your Mademoiselle Nong joined us for the matinee of Mata Hari at the Louxor."

"Not the Lao beauty with the tight sweater?"

"The very same: Bouasawan."

"Why would a girl whose figure outperforms every erotic postcard on sale along the banks of the Seine agree to marry you?"

"I'm a catch," I said.

"You do know she's a Communist?"

"So are you."

"No, I mean she's a *Communist* said very loudly. I recall she discussed her motivation with Nong that day. She came to Paris for the sole purpose of joining the Party. She'd already memorized the manifesto before she arrived. She signed up with the CPF even before she registered at Ancienne. Nong believed she was a fanatic."

"Passion is a wonderful thing."

"I hope she can find time for you amid her obsession."

"This from a man who's leaving in a week to muster a proletariat and turn Indochina red?"

"I'm enthusiastic," he said, "not fanatical. I like to call myself a middle-path socialist. I appreciate the concept and the potential of communism. I think it could work to unite our people against the French. But I don't decorate my apartment with hammer and sickle wallpaper. I don't send photos of myself in a swimsuit to Lenin."

"You know she doesn't do any of that."

He was starting to irritate me.

"Don't get defensive, little brother," he said. "I'm just offering my opinions."

While the waiter was putting the new glasses on the table, Civilai knocked back the drinks he already had.

"How can I not be defensive when you disparage my choice of bride?" I said.

"Look, Siri, she's gorgeous. She'd make any man's heart turn somersaults. And there is no doubt she's intelligent or that she loves her country. I see no problem with her whatsoever. The only problem I see is you."

"I'm not good enough for her?"

"Like me, she obviously recognizes just how good you are. You are unique and supremely talented. But you don't believe in what she believes."

"I believe."

"You don't."

"I do."

"Convince me."

"What?"

"Convince me that you share her passion."

The cognac had warmed my blood and was making me disagreeable. I took off my muffler. I hadn't been planning to tell him but he'd left me no choice.

"I've joined," I said.

"Joined what?"

"The Party."

"Nonsense."

"It's true. I went to a few meetings with Boua and thought, well, this isn't so bad, is it? And I decided that, with a bit of work, this communism thing has a chance. So I paid my dues and got my card. I can show it to you if you like."

"I don't want to doubt your motives . . ." he said.

"I love her, Civilai. I've loved her since the first day I saw her in class. She's the most . . . the most substantial Lao woman I've ever met. She has dreams. She has unselfish ambitions. She smells nice. She can change the world, and I want to be beside her while she's doing it."

"Then all I can say is congratulations," said Civilai, and, as a fitting subject break, a coal cart was pulled over by a fat policeman right in front of us because the horse wasn't wearing blinkers. In protest, the horse shat all over the boots of the policeman who arrested the driver. He in turn protested that it was the horse that did the damage, not he. Some of the more intoxicated onlookers applauded the horse.

To my mind, our conversation became a little less amicable after that. We didn't part on the best of terms. If we'd known how long it would be before we'd meet again, we'd probably have drunk one more glass for the road, said *au revoir* with a handshake and wished each other luck. In retrospect, I wish we had because then I would have been late for my appointment and not become embroiled in one of the most unpleasant events in French history. Instead, still miffed about his comments, I told Civilai I had to leave in a hurry to pay a visit to the Hotel de Rothschild, where there was a sale of secondhand medical textbooks. But I made the mistake of mentioning that the main event of the book exhibition was its opening by the president, Paul Doumer, himself. I knew that would irritate him.

It was as if I'd pushed down on the detonation plunger of Civilai's personal TNT. He launched off on a tirade against the fuzzy-bearded gentleman that, were it not in Lao, would have shocked and offended all those around us. Drinkers tutted their disapproval at the volume, but Civilai ranted on. Doumer had been the Governor General of the colonies in Indochina. His were the taxes that drained the lifeblood out of the villages. His were the laws that favored the French over the natives; favored the lowlanders over the tribes people. His were the policies that made a success of their investments for the first time, all on the back of local suffering. More investors came to take the gamble that led to more pillaging and looting. When the Lao proved too backward and lazy to absorb this development, Doumer carted in Vietnamese administrators and laborers by the thousands. There were probably more Vietnamese in the country than Lao at that time.

And what funded all these grandiose projects? *La grande comtesse d'O.* Doumer took over the opium monopoly and used the profits to supplement the modest funds he received from France. It was not a new policy. He was merely continuing a historical precedent in the third world. But he was good at the game. His chemists processed raw Indian resin using a technique that made the opium burn faster, thus increasing the demand. He imported impure opium from China for the poor addicted coolies. While the world was seeking bans on the opium trade, Doumer was embracing it. So successful was his policy in the Far East that he returned to France a hero, and his rise through the political ranks was inevitable.

And in Civilai's mind, I was on my way to stand meekly in a chilly street alongside the type of people who adored celebrity. We would applaud as he arrived and applaud as he left, and we would go home and tell our loved ones how close we'd been to the great statesman. That could not have been further from the truth.

"I hope you two have a very good time together," said Civilai, throwing down his last cognac and leaving me with three untouched glasses of my own. His chair bumped our neighbors' table as he stood and he bowed in apology. He picked his way through the diners and stood at the border of the sidewalk. He looked back at me, winked and smiled before joining the passersby. On the table he'd left some bank notes and an unused tennis racket.

Of course, I'd heard a lot about Doumer from the newspapers and the orange box speakers in the parks of Paris. I needed textbooks, but that wasn't my only reason for attending the event at the Hotel de Rothschild. Even before I learned that it was true, I'd always believed that you could look into a man's eyes and see his soul. I wanted to see the face of a man who'd been so adept at shifting and shuffling human cargo that he'd been able to change the destiny of a people. The French had killed thousands of us in the name of advancement. Yet, there in Paris, the colonial overlords were saints, sacrificing their valuable time to bring peace and hope to the poor nations. I needed to learn from Doumer—the great magician—how he'd pulled off this trick.

The previous year I'd gone to see the colonial exhibition. I was one of the nine million people who queued to see an interpretation of life in the French controlled territories. Grinning Africans in ostrich feathers danced comically. The scent of homemade coconut sweets wafted through the crowds. On the Lao stage a handful of bored non-Lao actors were threshing rice and pounding in an endless loop. A black-and-white film showed scenes of jolly villagers welcoming men in uniform, working beside them in the fields, drinking together. Of native girls learning from a white woman in crinoline how to use a steam iron. Every country had its film and none of them made mention of the schools poor local children weren't allowed to attend or the slave porters carrying a new officer's household goods, or natives being whipped for insulting an administrator. In fact, the actors at the colonial exhibition were all having such fun you'd want to hop on a steamer and join them. The French Communist Party ran an alternative exhibition showing the depressing truth of colonial occupation, but, naturally, very few people attended. Reality was such poor entertainment.

Getting from Café de la Paix to l'Hotel de Rothschild would have only taken me ten minutes on the Metro. It was cheap and reliable, but I always felt the tentacles of claustrophobia squeezing my chest when I was under the ground. Whenever possible, I would walk. Paris was a beautiful, vibrant city, and it felt disrespectful to be slinking around beneath her. The cool wind was at my back as I started off along rue Auber past the Grand Hotel. The edifices always felt like the faces of ornamental canyons around me. Ladies wrestled with their parasols. A man chased his boater. Remembering the horse at La Paix, I kept one eye to the ground when I crossed to Boulevard Haussmann. The trees there had been trained to lean away from the buildings, which made it appear that the apartments were lounging back against the grey sky. I passed the depressing, windowless Chapelle Expiatoire and—cognac and wind assisted—I reached rue Berryer in twenty-five minutes.

Any hopes I may have had of strolling up to the president as we perused the book display, looking into his soul and inviting him for a chat and an absinthe were thwarted when I turned the final corner to see that a large crowd had gathered opposite the hotel. Two *gendarmes* stood in the road in front of the onlookers motionless but for their black capes flapping like bat wings. There was no rope barrier, but the crowd comprised mainly elderly ladies and families with children holding small tricolors. An enterprising shoe-shine boy was taking advantage of the boots on display. The policemen had apparently assessed the danger level and decided there was no threat, so they had their backs to the crowd.

It was very orderly and I could have probably slotted in amongst the old ladies, but I actually wanted to look at the exhibition and pick up a few bargains before they let in the public. Fortunately, we "Chinese" were at our most popular, so I ignored the police, who ignored me in turn, and entered an alleyway beside the hotel. I emerged at a rear door whose sign read TRADESMEN AND HOTEL EMPLOYEES ONLY. This was no fluke. Three months earlier, Boua and I had entered the hotel through this door whilst gate crashing a wine-tasting event. We had become quite competent at enjoying free French hospitality. On occasions, we'd even been able to convince people that we were the Japanese ambassador and his wife. Why not?

For a presidential visit I'd expected security to be tighter on this occasion, but the commissionaire's table inside the door was unattended. I was able to walk through the busy kitchen and the chambermaid's quarters unchallenged. Nobody knew what to say to me. And suddenly, there I was in the grand ballroom, which that day looked more like a book emporium. Men in monocles and tailcoat suites fussed over last-minute preparations, and hotel staff stood at attention in a line receiving their final in-house briefing. I was able to browse at leisure and even paid for and put aside my book selection at one of the secondhand booths.

A bell chimed from the direction of the reception area, and the staff hurried to the front of the hotel. I followed them because I admit I had become infected by the atmosphere. I wasn't even an employee, but I'd been there long enough to want the hotel to do its very best—even for a bastard like Doumer. I needn't have worried. The welcome committee was regimental. Everyone knew of his or her function and where they should stand. Except me. I retreated behind one of the stone pillars and from there I could see through the two enormous glass doors and beyond them I witnessed the arrival of two motorized police vans. The rear doors were thrown open and a dozen *gendarmes* stumbled out of each. Some took up positions on the hotel steps. The others wrestled open the doors, secured them in the open position, and spread themselves around the foyer. If they were armed, their weapons were well concealed. But I suspected there were more qualified plain-clothed officers strategically dotted around. One, quite obviously a military man with a crew cut and the nervous twitch of a security guard on alert, was in place behind the next pillar. I smiled at him and he ignored me. I'd expect nothing less from my bodyguard.

It was a very long, tense ten minutes before the President's Citroën arrived. An aide hurried to open the rear door but the president was already halfway out before he got there. I'd seen Doumer on newsreels at my cinema. He was a portly man with a fancy white beard, and I had a theory that this was what Father Christmas did for the other eleven months of the year. I couldn't help smiling at that thought as he stopped on the top step, turned and waved at the grannies and the bemused children. He entered the hotel and the male staff members leaned forward into a respectful bow. The women curtsied. There was silence apart from the manager welcoming the President on behalf of the hotel and the Fund for Wounded Soldiers.

A table had been set up in the foyer with the types of political books a president would have been expected to read. But I saw him as more of a detective fiction type. I was already an aficionado of Simenon and I decided that would be my opening gambit:

"I'm sure you'd prefer the exploits of Inspector Maigret," I would say.

I was practicing my pronunciation of that line and Doumer was alone at the table waiting for the photographer to adjust his lens. Doumer would laugh at my impudence and confess that he was indeed a crime novel fan. Leap forward five months and we'd be at his gentleman's club sorting out troubles in the Far East fairly and sensibly with not a shot fired.

I took a step forward but it seemed that by doing so, I broke some invisible thread and threw the ordered world into chaos. A shout came from the kitchen. It was a foreign language, but I wasn't alert enough to say which. A plate smashed. The kitchen doors flew open and a ruddy-faced man ran into the reception area. He had the build of a pasta chef and wore a suit so tight that it could only have been a relic from his slimmer past. A large serviette covered his right hand and forearm. It made him look like a waiter and perhaps it was that image: the head waiter emerging angrily from the kitchen after some unforgivable culinary incident that prevented the security detail from moving. We were a still photograph with only the man in the tight suit animated. He looked around the room, caught sight of Doumer, and staggered toward him.

He shouted again. This time I recognized his language as Russian. Then in French he said, "I do this in the name of the miserable ones who wait in Russia."

Then, like a birthday party magician, he pulled back the serviette to reveal an FN1910 pistol. I recall that he fired five shots, but I still don't know how many hit Doumer. Enough to make him dead, I could see that. He fell backward onto the book display and his blood ruined a number of first editions. By the time everyone realized what had happened, it was too late. I looked back at the security man behind the pillar. He had his gun drawn and aimed at the assassin, but he hadn't fired. In fact, I saw him look left and right, then return his pistol to his inside pocket. He watched the *gendarmes* tackle the gunman to the ground. He observed as the President's waistcoat changed from grey to crimson. And I couldn't be sure amid the chaos, but I fancied I saw the young man smile. I remember he had almost perfect teeth, which was quite unusual in those days.

He walked calmly to the hotel entrance and into the street. It was odd. Perhaps I was one of the few people there who didn't really care that the President had been shot. That's why I noticed him. Why had he not intervened? If he was a bodyguard, why was he leaving?

I wasn't yet doctor enough to offer to tend Doumer's wounds. He had a team of surgeons to care for him but none of them would make him any more alive. So, in pursuit of my own curiosity, I followed the short-haired man. He casually crossed the street and melted into the crowd even though the road had been cleared of traffic, and it would have been easier to walk there. I stayed with him. When he got to the first corner he turned, knelt, and pretended to be tying a shoelace. Even if he'd seen me I doubted he would have considered that I might be following him. You tend to notice only what you expect to be there.

He cut into a narrow lane with art and craft stalls on either side and picked up his speed. He stopped briefly at a stand with a display of ornamental mirrors, and there he made his second check for prospective followers. I'd put on a woolen hat I kept in my pocket and was almost beside him as he scanned the crowd through the mirror. If he'd looked to his right we would have met eye-to-eye. But he did not. Once he was through the maze of vendors he turned on to the boulevard at Faubourg Saint-Honoré, and I could see his shoulders relax. Now that we had distance between us I felt more comfortable. He sauntered along the northern pavement and I kept to the south side. We passed the saddlers and trunk stores, and he paused calmly to admire the fashions displayed in the windows of the high-class stores. Everything was going fine until he passed the foolish stone balloon monument and descended into the Metro at Ternes.

This was a problem, not just because of my claustrophobia, but because I had paid my last franc for the books at the hotel. I had nothing left for the Metro. But I was determined to stay with my man until I could work out what the hell had happened at the hotel.

The underground walkway to the station was long and tiled. Every sound echoed. My man wore shoes with metal tips. A blind person could have followed him. But the workday was not yet finished, and there were few people traveling. He was heading for a labyrinth of tunnels on the way to the platforms, and I had to stay close to see which he took. At each level and with each turn he could be there waiting for me. I was close enough to see him hand his 70 centimes to the kiosk cashier and receive his ticket. He showed it to the guard when he passed the gate.

I had neither ticket nor coins, but I had an ethnic brotherhood. The cashier was dark as cocoa, possibly Moroccan. I hoped he might have attended the colonial exhibition. I stood in front of him with the hangdog expression I used to get extensions on my essays.

"I have no money, brother," I said.

He could have told me to go jump in the Seine, but he cocked his head to one side, smiled a splendid set of teeth minus one at the front, and tore me off a ticket from the roll.

"Your lucky day," he said, "but don't try this shit again when I'm on duty. I got to cover shortcomings."

I could hear the metallic rattle of an East-West line train in the distance, but I couldn't tell in which direction it was headed. I ran past the guard and stood considering the options. There were two staircases. I chose west because my own instinct would have been to double back across the city. The stairwell seemed to go all the way down to Hades. I hit the empty platform after the passengers had boarded. The station assistant normally closed the metal gate when a train arrived, but it was open. Someone had failed to shut a door correctly, and the assistant was running along the platform blowing his whistle. It gave me time to look at the faces through the smoky glass of the windows. I reached the third carriage, and there I saw my man. He looked at me directly but with no sign of recognition or interest.

I walked to the fourth carriage, where the assistant was having trouble with the door. One of the hinges had dropped, and it took two people to lift it back onto its frame: the man outside, the train guard inside. We left the station seven minutes late.

At Courcelles I stepped off the train but my man did not. I climbed back on. The same happened at Monceau, and, by then, I had a sort of working hypothesis of what I'd witnessed at the Rothschild. My man was clearly not a part of Doumer's security detail, but he was armed and in a position to see all that happened. Even after the assassin had removed the serviette from his forearm, a good five seconds passed before he pumped his bullets into the president. My man's weapon was unholstered and aimed at the shooter, so why had he not fired? And why did he smile?

I was left with only one conclusion. The slurring Russian had been recruited by someone to shoot Doumer. Perhaps he had some grievance against the president about his treatment of Russians. He was clearly unstable but passionate. Someone had brought him into the hotel, perhaps as a guest. They'd provided him with a weapon and plied him with booze for Dutch courage. Only one thing was missing. The plan had to have a contingency. There had to be a second shooter in case the Russian folded or missed. Once the assassin had discharged his weapon, my man behind the pillar, a marksman, sober, would ensure that at least one bullet hit the target.

But the Russian did not fail. The president was dead, and the second shooter could return to his cabal and make his report.

At Villiers, my man stepped off the train and I was behind him. He was so confident that he no longer checked his back. I still had no idea what purpose my following him would serve. I wasn't yet clear-headed enough to assess what the benefits for France or Europe or the world would be with Doumer dead. I didn't really care. It just annoyed me that any idiot could undemocratically solve his problems with a gun or a sword or a stick of dynamite. Surely we'd progressed far enough from the ape to settle our differences without violence.

By the time I reached street level, I'd lost him. There were no large buildings nearby for him to have disappeared into so fast. It was as if the station had been built in the center of a large field in anticipation of development closing in on it. I could see all around but there was no sign of my man. I was embarrassed. Maigret would have been ashamed of me. I sat on a bench that had the view of just one tree, and I considered my next step. Who should I tell? What exactly would I say? Would anyone believe me? And, at that moment, my man walked out of the Metro exit. Somehow I'd passed him without noticing. The telephone. That was it. He'd stopped in the telephone booth. They were a new item in Paris, so it hadn't occurred to me. I imagined he'd reported that everything had gone according to plan.

He walked past my bench. I squeezed the cap in my hand and concentrated on the tree. I'd been a boxer and wrestler at university. Good in my weight class. But my man had a gun in his inside pocket. A lot of use the old one-two would have been against that. But, as before, he looked straight through me and crossed the park heading east. Perhaps it was there that I learned how to be invisible. I let him get fifty meters ahead then climbed back on his tail. He didn't go far. On Constantinople, he joined the queue at a tram stop. I didn't want to pass him, so I studied the headlines at the news kiosk. The newsagent eyed me with suspicion. The longer I stood there the deeper into me she glared. I had to make a decision. The tram was on its way. If I left it to the last moment and ran for it, I'd draw attention to myself.

Then there'd be another scene when the conductor asked me for money and found out I had none. But, if I didn't catch the tram I'd lose the second shooter.

The tram passed the kiosk. The driver clanged the bell and applied the brake. What if this was my man's final check? What if he left it to the last second before boarding the tram? That way he'd be certain he wasn't being followed. And then again, what if he had no intention of getting on board? And that, as Civilai would say, was the filly I put my savings on. I stood at the kiosk and waited for the passengers to board the tram. My man looked around, put his foot on the running board, then took it off and stepped backward. The conductor asked if he intended to get on, and my man waved him away.

"Hey, China," said the newsagent. "This what you're looking for?"

She reached inside a leather pouch and produced a very racy magazine. Some might have called it downright filthy. But I was a trainee surgeon and I'd seen all those parts before. The tram had pulled away, leaving my man alone on the sidewalk. He crossed the boulevard and walked directly to an expensive-looking apartment building opposite. He opened the main door and before it shut behind him, I noticed the uniformed concierge at the reception desk salute him. He lived there. Damn. I had to admire his audacity. Who would oversee an assassination three Metro stops from his home?

"Bravo," I said, but I wasn't going to let him get away with it. Neither was I likely to walk into a *gendarmerie* and file a report. And I wasn't about to seek help from my new comrades at the PCF. They'd have hoisted the assassin on their shoulders and treated him to a slap-up meal.

There was only one person I thought I could talk to. The following morning, I was due to attend the second lecture of three from an army general called Richard from the French medical corps. It was he who had described the rapidly approaching blight of heroin that morning. I'd been impressed by his distress and concerns about the drug business and his preparedness to accept the blame on behalf of the French government for its involvement in the opium trade.

After his lecture the following morning, I invited him for coffee in the university refectory. I told him what had happened after the assassination of Doumer. He asked why I hadn't filed a report immediately, but I could see he understood. He asked for my address but made no comment as to my actions or suspicions. I thought he might have considered me to be some sort of crackpot. I heard nothing for the rest of the day. I met Boua for lunch and told her I'd been at the book exhibition and witnessed the killing of Doumer. I'm not sure why, but I decided against telling her my theory of the second shooter and about my pursuit of him. It was the first time I'd withheld information from her but would not be the last, and we weren't even married yet. Perhaps I felt she'd consider it her duty to tell her Communist friends and things would have become . . . messy. I wanted to marry her without issues pulling us apart. Even then I was cautious of Boua's hypersensitive buttons and which ones launched missiles.

That evening, two young plainclothes army officers found me at my local café. Boua was at a policy meeting. The soldiers came directly to me even though we'd never met. They sat down at my table, introduced themselves and produced a manila envelope. From it they took two large photographs. Both were close-ups of my man.

"Is this him?" one asked.

"Yes," I said.

"Would you be prepared to act as an eye witness in the arrest of this person?" asked the other.

I said "yes" immediately but after they'd thanked me and left I started to think of all the reasons why I should have said "no." My life hadn't seen a great deal of excitement up until then. I'd studied, I'd traveled, I'd worked in a cinema. But I hadn't lived the adventures I saw on the screen. Then, suddenly, there I was front seat at an assassination and on the trail of a man with a loaded gun. I was playing the sheriff role but I honestly didn't know who the good guys were. What if the military had planned the kill? What if the shooter was a patriot? I knew Doumer was no angel. How dare I condemn his killers? But I'd pushed that wagon up to the top of the hill and those wheels had a habit of building up speed on the way down.

Late that night, I was awoken by the hammering on the door of our tiny apartment.

"Siri," someone shouted, "come and drink with us. We're celebrating."

I could only open the door a few centimeters when the bed was down and through the gap I saw my young military friends. They nodded and gestured for me to come. I told Boua a classmate had just . . . no, I can't remember what lie I told her. But she believed me because I'd been an honest man until then. If I felt any guilt, it was diluted in fear for my own life.

I was driven back to my man's apartment building opposite the tram stop. As we entered, the concierge was being led away. I was told to wait in the foyer. An older military man in a tracksuit silently waited with me. There were no sounds of doors being broken down, no gunshots, no shouted threats. But, ten minutes after our arrival, half-a-dozen soldiers in plain clothes came down the staircase escorting a man in pajamas with a sisal bag over his head. He wasn't cuffed or shackled, which made the situation more tense than was necessary. They stood their prisoner in front of me and pulled off his hood.

He still wore the crust of sleep around his eyes.

"Monsieur Paiboun," said one of the young officers, "is this the man you saw at the Hotel Rothschild pointing a gun in the direction of the President yesterday afternoon?"

I was distraught that he should have used my name. I put my trembling hands in my pockets.

"It's him," I said.

"And did you follow him from the hotel to this apartment at 235 Constantinople immediately after the assassination?"

"I did," I said.

"Should we not ask him why?" said my man.

There were six guards around him. Surely one of them could have told him to stop talking. But, no.

"Because, whoever little Monsieur Paiboun is," he said, "whoever he works for, we will learn of it. When I am released, I shall find him. If they foolishly decide to execute me, my brothers will find him. We will find him and we will take his life apart piece by piece, friend by friend. And when there remains only him, we will take him apart even more slowly and painfully, organ by organ, until there is nothing left. But long before the end he will have regretted this day."

At last the guards took his arms and half-carried him to the street and the waiting van. Before climbing aboard, he looked back at me and gestured a knife across his throat. And then he smiled. And the smile was more frightening than anything he'd said.

CHAPTER FOUR
The Widow Ghost

Siri and Daeng were sitting on their bamboo recliners on the bank of the Mekong looking out to the pinpricks of light on the far bank. Siri had crossed the river in both directions and could have been killed doing so a number of times in any number of ways. But Mother Khong always looked so innocent, as if you could just wade your way through it, pick up supplies on the Thai side and float back over. This time of year it was at its most sly. Escapees often waited for the end of the monsoon floods only to find themselves carried south on the current.

"I can't believe you haven't told me this story before," said Daeng.

"Have you told me all yours?" Siri asked.

"Not yet."

"Exactly," said Siri. "We have a combined age of . . . several hundred years. We need untold stories to entertain each other in our dotage."

"You don't think your involvement in the assassination of a president is a priority A-plus story?"

"I was just a witness. I have many more exciting stories than that. If I'd killed him myself it would have been the first story out of my mouth. I just happened to follow a coconspirator."

"One who promised to take you apart organ by organ. Did you ever find out who he was?"

"There was nothing in the press. No public trial. The only version of events on record is that of the drunken Russian *émigré.* Before his execution at the guillotine he claimed that he was driven in a trance to kill heads of state. Officially, the man I followed wasn't involved."

"And unofficially?"

"I met the army surgeon again a few years later. I was a qualified doctor by then. We were at a reception. He was drunk. He told me more than he was probably supposed to. He said the second shooter was a Corsican. He'd been in North America establishing a foothold for his family in various illegal activities. Some years earlier his two brothers had been in Annam setting up a network to send Chinese opium to Marseille. It was around the time Doumer was in Vietnam trying to find money to fund his projects. For two years he'd bought up the entire opium harvest and it still wasn't enough, so he started to eat away at some of the private contractors who had established networks. The Corsicans had set up such an organization. Doumer made an offer to take over their trade, but the brothers were answerable to the family. They refused him."

"And I bet they had an accident," said Daeng.

"A truck they were traveling in exploded. The authorities said it was a petrol tank leak, but some of the workers said they'd seen men with military haircuts creeping around the night before. Doumer denied any involvement but the Corsicans knew better. The younger brother, my man, was on the boil for a long time. That's why the family sent him to the States. But the Corsicans have short fuses and long memories. He watched the news of Doumer's return to France and fumed when the old man assumed the senate seat for Corsica. There were those who suggested Doumer was merely carrying his opium business home. The family suffered again at his hand and the elders finally gave the green light for the younger brother to return to France. By then, Doumer had become president and the rest we know."

"And you think the Godfathers still have a black list with your name on it, Siri?"

"It's not impossible, Daeng. There are still Corsicans in Laos left over from the opium heydays of the forties and fifties. They're married to Lao women and waiting for opportunities. Any one of them could be related to my man. There could be a contract out on me for old times' sake."

"You see, Ugly?" said Daeng to the dog. "This is what happens when you allow strangers to attach notes to your nether regions."

"And that's odd too," said Siri. "Ugly doesn't let anyone near him. A head pat's the most he can handle. He's not going to stand still for five minutes while an assassin ties a ribbon to his tail, is he now?"

"Yet, he obviously did."

"Curious."

Daeng poured them both a glass of homemade rice whisky, and they let it flow over their palates before allowing it to drop and burn holes in their livers. Around then, someone on the Thai side was apparently blown up by an illegal propane gas tank. They recognized the sound. It happened often.

"What I suggest . . ." said Daeng.

"Yes?"

". . . is that we do absolutely nothing."

"I thought that's what we were doing."

"We don't want paranoia to set in."

"Why does everyone on the planet think I'm paranoid?"

"Exactly. I suggest we just work on the small and solvable problems."

"Such as?"

"I'm glad you asked," said Daeng. "You remember Granny Far from the skirt bank?"

"How could I forget her?" said Siri. "We're keeping her alive, aren't we?"

The skirt bank was one of Madam Daeng's many community projects. More and more women she knew were running into financial strife and were selling what items of value they had to keep their families fed. Many had already sold their silk *phasin* skirts for far less than they were worth. Their family heirlooms were lost forever. Siri and Daeng had come into some good luck as a result of a drug deal that went wrong. They happened to have been in the right place at the right time. It was no fortune. Enough, Siri thought, for a nice little car and sufficient petrol to run it for a while. But Daeng had convinced Siri that they should use that money to set up a loan service. The women could deposit their *phasins* at Daeng's shop. She would give them a fair price for the skirt and, one day, when the spirits were in a more convivial mood, they could pay back the loan and reclaim their goods.

The spirits were obviously in no hurry to heap blessings on the hapless women because Daeng's spare room was starting to look like a fabric warehouse. Mr. Geung, currently doing whatever it was that grooms did on their honeymoons at vegetable farms, was the curator of what he called the *sin* bin. He had no written records but he had a remarkable nose. If anyone returned and claimed their treasure he could sniff it out in no time.

Granny Far had long since lost her valuable *phasin* collection to unscrupulous dealers on the Thai side. But she still had an assortment of chain-link silver belts. Her children and grandchildren, and all but one nephew, had fled to the camps across the river. The anticipated arrival of money from her relatives in third countries had yet to materialize. So, from time to time, the old lady would ride her bicycle over to Daeng's noodle shop, have a bowl of her favorite spicy number two and call Daeng to one side to discuss a little business.

That evening, the business had been entirely different.

"Her nephew," said Daeng.

"What about him?" said Siri. "He's a nasty little shrew if I remember rightly. Did he run off with the old lady's belt collection? Wouldn't put it past him."

"No, he's dead."

"Ah, well. Then I apologize to his spirit for being so negative. Someone shoot him?"

"He died in his sleep."

"Really? How old was he?"

"Seventeen."

"Hmm."

"He'd worked the night shift in the kitchen at the Russian Club," said Daeng. "The curfew's flexible at the moment with all the journalists in town. He came home at two-ish and went to bed. Granny Far tried to raise him at nine but he was dead. No wounds."

"Any vomit—saliva?"

"No."

"Well, I hope our donations to the family were generous enough to cover a nice budget cremation."

"Siri, he's still there."

"Still where?"

"On his bed roll on the floor."

"Why?"

"Because I promised her I'd take you there to have a look at him."

"Oh, did you?"

"Yup."

"You do know I'm not a coroner anymore?"

"It's like riding a bicycle, Siri. You never forget."

"What about my replacement, the good Doctor Mot?"

"About whom you were quoted as saying, 'If they weren't stuck on, he wouldn't know a breast from a buttock'?"

"I did say that, didn't I? What about Dtui?"

"She and Phosy are taking care of their journalist group. And Granny Far specifically asked for you."

"Why?"

"There are . . . unusual circumstances."

The thing Siri liked most about his Pigeon bicycle was its padded passenger seat and the fact that Madam Daeng had to wrap one arm around his waist and push one breast against his back while they were riding together. Whenever he hit a pothole, a spontaneous samba ground them together. There were few potholes that escaped his attention. But Granny Far's house was only ten blocks away along the river. She was on the doorstep when they arrived. Ugly was with them of course. He hadn't expected to be on duty that evening, so he trotted drowsily to the spot where they parked the bicycle and collapsed beside it.

"Lucky it's not been a hot day," said Siri. "Or we should start to get a whiff of the boy by now."

He and Daeng followed Far to a room at the rear of the house, where the nephew lay beneath a grey mosquito net. The youth's face was contorted into a horrible death mask. His hands were poised in front of him as if warding off an attack. And he was wearing a nightdress; a woman's pink, sleeveless nightdress with Disney dalmatians printed all over it.

"I take it he wasn't given to homosexual tendencies?" said Siri.

"No, Doctor," said Granny Far, "he had a lot of young lady friends."

"And he didn't dress in girls' clothes at any other time of the day?"

"No, Doctor," said Far. "Would you like to cut him open now? I have an old plastic table cloth we could put down."

"No need," said Siri.

"Was he poisoned?" she asked.

"No, Granny Far," said Siri. "He wasn't poisoned. He was haunted to death."

"Oh, I say," said the old woman, and she held her palm to her chest. Siri was certain she had some good luck talisman hanging there. He had one too. It could often mean the difference between life and death. He instinctively reached for his own stone amulet beneath his shirt.

"Is there anything we can do?" Daeng asked.

"On the way in I couldn't help noticing the pile of furniture in the yard," said Siri.

"It's all the old stuff," said Far, "and wood from the old trees out back. I loaded it there this afternoon."

"So I take it your temple no longer provides a service?"

"All the monks have gone, bar one," said Far. "And his only functions seem to be grumbling and insulting anyone who wastes his time with dead loved ones."

"So you'd sooner do it here?" said Daeng.

"It's been the family home since the last century," said Far.

They wrapped the corpse in the old plastic tablecloth and carried it to the familial pyre, where they sat the nephew on a chunky Chinese chair. They knew they were supposed to inform the authorities and stand back and watch the cogs turn slowly, but there wouldn't have been much of the nephew left by the time they'd got his file up to date. There'd be the issue of lighting a fire without village headman permission, but Far said she could handle that.

"Doctor, could you say a few words?" said Granny Far, still attempting to ignite her candle with a cigarette lighter.

"What kind of words?" said Siri.

"I don't know. Something fitting."

"I don't know anything religious."

"That's fine."

"How's your French?" he asked.

"Non-existent, Doctor."

"Then here goes," said Siri.

"J'avais auparavant,
Vaincu de la jeunesse,
Autres dames aimé,
Ma faute je confesse."

"That's lovely," said Granny Far. "What does it mean?"

"It is my desire that your nephew finds a comfortable place in nirvana," said Siri.

She offered him a silver belt for his trouble but he refused.

Back at the restaurant they locked up and retired for the night. They lay on the mattress in the familiar spoon position. Daeng caressed her husband's neck as they watched the moon rise through the open window.

"You've heard of that type of thing before?" Daeng asked.

"A lot," said Siri. "But since the beginning of the exodus—thousands of young men fleeing to the West—it seems to happen unsettlingly often. It's almost an epidemic. We hear about it in letters to relatives all the time. But I've never witnessed it first hand before."

"But what causes it?"

"Belief," said Siri. "Or should I say, misbelief. In many ways the young men feel they've failed in their duties as protectors of the family. They find themselves away from their support network. They don't have access to the shaman or to their village spirits or their ancestors. All those paths you could take in stressful times are closed. It makes them more susceptible to the malevolent spirits that have hitched a ride with them."

"But Far's nephew didn't go anywhere."

"But his family did and they took their beliefs with them. He felt he'd failed them by not going with them. He was left alone with the widow ghost who sucks out men's souls when they're sleeping. The Hmong call her *tsog tsuam.* In the beginning, she might make appearances like a movie extra in his dream. She'll have the role of a waitress or a passerby. But then he'll notice her . . . expect to see her.

And with every dream she becomes more prominent. He tries not to sleep but can't fight it. He's heard about her from his friends. He knows she's only interested in young men, so he goes to bed dressed as a woman to trick her. But, by then, it's often too late."

"How does . . . how could she kill them?" Daeng asked.

"The boys believe that she crushes their chests while they sleep. In the dream they're dead, and it's so convincing there is no point in breathing anymore. The spirit then takes the soul as a memento. She exists in many cultures with many names. But when you peel away her disguises and wipe off her makeup it always comes down to that one, same antagonist: *phibob*, the evil spirit that's responsible for most of the damage done to man's mind."

Siri tugged at the cord around his neck and pulled out the talisman from under his T-shirt.

"Feel this," he said.

"It's hot," she said.

"They feel threatened by this kind of talk," said Siri. "We have ours housetrained for the moment. But they continue to live on in the minds of thousands of lonely men around the world."

"How can you fight anything like that?" Daeng asked.

"I think I have an idea," said Siri. "I could—"

Daeng screamed and let go of the amulet.

"Hot?" Siri asked.

"I have an imaginary blister," said Daeng.

"Good, then it seems they know what I'm thinking. I've touched a nerve."

CHAPTER FIVE
Darts and Balloons

"I have so much gas in me Madam Nong has to tie a rope round my ankle and hold on to it so I don't float away," said Civilai.

"Yes, I'm sure we're all fascinated by your flatulence stories," said Siri.

"I didn't say anything about flatulence," said Civilai. "Gas is a different beast altogether. Gas is containable and controllable. Flatulence sneaks out at inopportune moments. You won't be hearing any wind instruments from me this evening. No, Sir. I'll know when it's time for me to empty my gas and I shall . . ."

"Civilai, spare us," said Madam Daeng.

". . . head off in an orderly fashion, open the valve, release the pressure and return with you all none the wiser."

"Except now we'll all guess where you're going and what you're doing," said Daeng. "Even if you're not."

"I'm feeling quite off my food already," said Bruce.

"Ah, Son, you'll have to put up with a lot worse than this before our film is complete," said Siri. "This is just a sort of test."

Bruce, alias Deesabun, had arrived back in Laos the previous week. He was twenty-two with dyed-blond hair, had an earring in his left lobe and carried eight kilograms more than he really needed. He'd been a quick learner in Australia and was already assured a lucrative career in TV production. But in the cutting room at SBS in Sydney he'd seen the conditions in the refugee camps and heard the struggling Lao government's pleas for qualified personnel to come home. His conscience got the better of him. It was a romantic notion to return to the country of his birth with something of value to offer. His cousin at the Fuji film lab had written to him about a group of visionaries who had written a film script. They had a Panavision camera they couldn't operate. They needed Bruce.

Upon his return, he'd met Siri and Civilai who had begun their romance with cinema half a century before in France. He was astounded by the depth and breadth of their knowledge of film. Their script, on the other hand—rewritten by the Ministry of Culture to incorporate Comrades Lenin and Marx, altered again by the Women's Union to raise the profile of women and returned to its original state by its writer, Siri Paiboun—would have been impossible to film in its present state. They had just the one camera, no permission to travel to locations and a budget that wouldn't have paid for sandwiches and lemonade on a B-movie set in Australia.

What they lacked in resources and ability, they more than made up for in alcohol. The first official executive directorial meeting was convened immediately after the evening noodle rush. The tables were clean, the utensils were spotless and a crate of Bordeaux sat at the feet of Madam Daeng, who wielded the corkscrew. The wine was the last from the cellar of the French Embassy, closed for the past two years due to a misunderstanding: the French thought Laos was still a colony.

Bruce was welcomed formally with a toast although Siri noticed Civilai sipped sparingly from his glass. They'd all warmed to Bruce's character—a sort of Lao/Aussie blend that made them smile. Siri particularly liked the fact that their cameraman was not afraid to speak his mind.

"Do you have good news for us?" Daeng asked.

"I certainly do," said Bruce. "I spent the afternoon with your camera, and I'm pleased to say it is now fully functional."

The directors cheered and drank to the victory. Bruce started to explain such things as fuses and batteries but he could see these details were fluttering hopelessly in the air some distance from the old folks' ears. So, he entertained them with other good news.

"I told you I had a surprise for you," he said. "Well, under the auspices of international aid for the third world, I was able to get a donation of a hundred and eighty hours of film and some video equipment. It's all in a crate sitting at the Customs shed at Tar Deua."

They stood with their drinks and saluted their cameraman.

"Excellent," said Siri.

"Our young hero," said Daeng.

Even sickly Civilai drank to the news.

"I just don't know how to get it out of Customs," said Bruce.

"Fear not," said Civilai. "It used to take a week of paperwork, but the process has been streamlined remarkably this past year. The current policy is for them to hold on to everything until someone shows up with an envelope full of money to thank the official for looking after their goods."

"Thank heavens for the return of corruption," said Daeng.

"Simplifies everything," said Siri.

"Ladies and gentlemen," said Civilai, "time is against us. I suggest we read through the opening scenes and put our collective minds together on how to win over the audience from the outset."

"You might have to take off your sunglasses so you can see the script," said Daeng.

"These aren't sunglasses, Madam," he said. "These are ultraviolet, light-sensitive lenses imported from Eastern Europe. Johnny Halliday wears them."

"They're from the morning market," said Siri. "And they have no more UV protection than beer bottles. And I'm sure even Halliday takes his off at night."

"All right, it's an image thing," said Civilai. "I'm looking for a hat to go with it."

Given his bad health, nobody had the heart to talk him out of it.

The script began by switching back and forth between the lives of two teenagers—one poor, one rich, but both causing havoc to the French colonial administration in Laos: a jeep disabled here, a phone line cut there. The military give chase but are always one step behind until they learn of the identity of the two boys. They torture the relatives who refuse to give them up. At last the boys meet for the first time at the port in Da Nang, about to stow away on a steamer to France. Both already heroes.

"Just out of interest," said Bruce, "and it really doesn't matter to me one way or the other, how much of this script is biographical?"

Siri and Civilai looked at each other and smiled.

"I'd say about . . ." Civilai began.

"At least . . ." said Siri.

They looked at Daeng, whose eyebrows were somewhere up by her hairline.

"A substantial amount," said Civilai.

"Wow," said Bruce. "So, the assassination of the French president in the thirties. . . ?"

The old boys laughed.

"Come on, Son," said Siri. "Who'd be foolish enough to admit to something like that?"

"It would be madness," said Civilai.

"Ridiculous," Siri agreed.

"But that reminds me," said Civilai, "I should take a look in the attic."

"For the . . . ?" said Siri.

"We'll need it for the assassination scene."

"You still have it?"

"The gun?" said Bruce. "Wow!"

Daeng smiled and refilled the glasses. Nobody had an attic.

The group sat together for another seven hours: Siri and Civilai attempted to expand the scope and grandeur of their film, while Bruce attempted to bring them all down to earth. But talking about something they loved was one of the happiest nights Siri and Civilai had spent together for a long time. When the tragedies began, Siri wondered how different everything might have been if he'd taken the threat more seriously. But, as it was, that night, with the warm buzz of expensive Bordeaux in their veins, they stood at the end of the meeting and, inspired by their Aussie cinematographer, they hugged. It was un-Lao but surprisingly therapeutic. Siri could feel all the bones in Civilai's chest and commented that it was like embracing a xylophone, but he didn't let go and Civilai was in no hurry to get away. They all felt that they were about to embark on a long hike through beautiful scenery with Civilai stepping into the bushes to throw up from time to time. But that didn't take away the magic. The completed film was in their heads. They'd started writing their Oscar acceptance speeches. This was a great moment and they all knew it.

Bruce was still negotiating with the government for the return of his father's property. In the meantime, he was staying at a guesthouse a few blocks walk away. They pointed him in the right direction and pushed. Civilai staggered to his lemon-colored Citroën. They were more concerned about his walking than his driving so nobody attempted to take the keys from him. He'd be alone on the road and the car barely hit forty kilometers an hour. Civilai, probably legally blind behind his Soviet shades, spent some time searching for the slot for the key, but, once engaged, the engine purred like that of a more impressive vehicle. He wound down the window.

"Little brother," he called to Siri.

Siri walked to the car and Civilai handed him a wad of papers he'd retrieved from the glove box.

"I forgot," he said. "I got the list. Here! Sixty-four journalists, one of whom is probably here for the sole purpose of killing you slowly and painfully and massacring the rest of us in the process. Their CVs, their blood types, their ages and all the way down to their favorite sandwiches. I've called in what few favors I have left to do background checks on them. I have hope we'll find him before he starts slicing slivers of skin off—"

"We can all imagine how he'll go about it," said Siri. "But don't you worry yourself. I have freedom-fighter Daeng and Ugly the Wonder Dog to protect me."

Civilai grabbed Siri's wrist.

"Siri," he said.

"Yes?"

"My little brother."

He didn't let go.

"What?" said Siri.

"I love you."

Even after three bottles of Bordeaux, there were some things men didn't say to each other. Siri could see his own embarrassment reflected in the dark of the glasses. Still Civilai didn't let go. It was as if he was waiting for Siri to say something meaningful back.

"Civilai," said Siri.

The doctor could feel his heart throb.

"Yeah?"

"Let go of my wrist."

"All right," said Civilai, and with two coughs of exhaust from a rusty tailpipe, he was off.

Nurse Dtui, the wife of Chief Inspector Phosy, had what they call an eye for language. She'd studied and absorbed Russian without the benefit of hearing it spoken. She'd learned how to pronounce the words from the six pages at the front of the textbook that laid it all out linguistically like a mathematical table. But that suited her style. She'd done the same with English even though that language was a bugger for inconsistency and exceptions to rules. As a member of the Lao administration team at the Moscow Olympics, she had proven her value as a translator, so it was only natural they'd find a role for her at the fifth anniversary celebration. Interpreters the Pathet Lao could trust were thin on the ground. Those who had learned English from the Americans were either having a dour time up north in reeducation camps or were on their way to the West. German and Russian speakers were starting to return from the eastern bloc with dubious technical skills, but their ability in those languages was a far cry from simultaneous translation. The majority of the press corps in town to cover the celebrations was from socialist countries. The Soviets, like the French before them, were keen to spark an interest in investment in this little landlocked country overflowing with natural resources and potential.

In fact, "potential" rather than "actual" was the adjective *du jour* in Vientiane that week. The organized visits were mostly to demonstration sites: samples of what a successful project might look like with a bit of luck and better handling. The groups were led by Soviet Embassy officials fluent in the languages of the socialist brotherhood and accompanied by Lao minders. The government officials understood little of the live commentaries that endorsed Laos the way Madam Loulou advertised new girls to her regulars: "She may not look like much, but she has hidden promise and a surprise or two."

And all this left Nurse Dtui's little pack of decidedly non-Communist English speakers wondering why they'd been invited at all. She and Phosy had met them that second night at the bar of the Vieng Vilai: the Constellation

Hotel of old. It was there that Air America pilots and CIA spies and USAID workers would gather in the days when the landlords of Sodom and Gomorrah still collected their taxes in Vientiane. The boys would down their cocktails at the Constellation before heading off to the late-night sin spots of the after-hours capital. Those were the days when the options were vast in number and bottomless.

No such choice in 1980. The bar of the Vieng Vilai was something of a graveyard. To order drinks one had to drag the manager from the reception desk. He had the only key to the drinks cupboard. Once Dtui had ordered on behalf of her group, it was obvious the manager wouldn't know an Old-Fashioned from a Vieux Carré. In '75, the hotels had been left in the hands of men who had never stayed in one. Since then, tourism had been nonexistent, and a number of hotels had been converted to dormitories for cadres and their families. The sudden and random government decision to open the city to tourists had thrown the hotel industry into a panic. The managers had no guest relation skills and no foreign languages. They most certainly could not recommend wines or explain the contents of a cocktail.

So, at the insistence of the chief of police, the manager of the Vieng Vilai handed over his keys, returned to his office and left the group to take care of itself. The journalists looked on in admiration as the policeman climbed over the bar and began to hand out drinks. They'd been there dry for three days. Under Phosy's management, there was no tab and no limit. The Australians would have ordered beer had the fridge been plugged in but they settled for tall Cuba Librés without ice. This was a third-world country after all.

They pushed two tables together, raised their glasses to Laos, and Dtui began to recite the welcoming address she'd memorized. Given her limited contact with English speakers, she did a fine job but didn't get very far. They applauded after her third sentence. The other ten would never be heard. During the free-for-all that followed, she realized the limitations of her medical textbooks. She was sadly lacking in vulgarities, recognition of accents, idioms, abbreviations and the words to rugby songs. This shortfall was soon addressed by the journalists as they set about her reeducation.

At one point in the ongoing translation for Phosy, who knew no English at all, she confessed that she had no idea what anyone was saying. And it was at that point that Marvin, a tall, blond Australian leaned forward, and, in fluent Lao, said:

"Perhaps we can help you in that matter?"

There were nine journalists at the table that evening: two Britons, two Australians, three Swedes, a Filipino and a Thai from the *Bangkok Post,* and all of them were competent in Lao. One or two might have been mistaken for Lao on the telephone. Even one of the Swedes, on his first trip to Indochina, had learned enough in the previous month to earn a trip to Laos.

"You see?" said Jim, a worldly Anglo-Australian photojournalist with a younger man's face, "Western newspapers aren't going to waste their budget on sending idiots to copy down whatever the Party tells them."

"It's been over two years since the last foreign journalist was here," said Sixten, one of the Swedes. "The world wants to know what's really going on."

With the bar open and no other guests in the room, the

evening progressed in a more traditional Lao fashion with bonds made and secrets shared. At one point, Dtui and Phosy were behind the bar fixing a round.

"I don't think they know you're the chief of police," said Dtui.

"I didn't tell them," said Phosy.

"They're very . . . open," said Dtui.

"What do you mean?"

"I mean, all that about the world knowing what's really going on," said Dtui. "Shouldn't they be a little bit more careful about what they say?"

"I think they're hoping for a reaction," said Phosy. "Our secret service people can't do anything when the world knows its journalists are here. If anything happens to them it would be a public relations nightmare. It would defeat the whole point of inviting them. They can say anything they like."

The evening turned to night and the guests decided it was time to go to eat. Three restaurants had been set aside for the visitors and they opted for the nearest. Despite a lingering paranoia honed over five years of not knowing whom to trust, Dtui liked the foreigners for their openness. Her favorites were Marvin, the gangly Australian, and Jim, the dirty-mouthed but funny Englishman who had given up his British passport and was currently based in Sydney. She and Phosy knew that the pair were already stoned when they'd first arrived. Perhaps they'd been expecting the worst and put up that marijuana force field to withstand another night of sober cultural pleasantries. Neither of them seemed the worse for wear from their smoking. They held their own in the noisy discussions. Marvin had signed on as a journalist for the *Sydney Morning Herald* but he was, in fact, a Lao scholar: an expert in Southeast Asian history and culture. He had come, as he said, "To see what a mess they'd made of his beloved Laos."

Jim had made a name for himself as a photographer at the height of the aggression in Vietnam. He still carried an interior tiara of shrapnel as a memento. The editor at the *Times* in England had passed on the Lao invitation to him in anticipation that he might get a picture or two that belied the Soviet claims of peaceful community development under its leadership. He'd suggested Jim write a vignette of socialist Laos with himself as a central character: *Sunday Times* magazine fodder.

Jim and Marvin went back a way. They'd shared a house in Vientiane in the sixties. They'd seen the country at its most corrupt and now they were seeing it at its most repressed. Both men were confident that it wouldn't be long before the repression subsided and the corruption made a triumphant comeback. Dtui had immediately recalled Civilai's description of the Customs department at Tar Deua.

"So, my boy, you're a plumber?" said Jim with his arm around Phosy's shoulder as they walked into the street.

It wasn't an outright lie. Phosy was very handy with a wrench and undertook most of the repairs at the police dormitory bathroom. He'd decided nothing would be gained by announcing who he was to the group. But he was with a canny crew of journalistic vagabonds. Jim sniggered.

"Something funny?" Phosy asked.

"Nothing at all," said Jim.

Phosy knew his cover was blown.

"What gave me away?" he asked.

"Oh, I don't know. Perhaps the manager calling you chief inspector?"

"I didn't think anyone heard."

"We're daft. Not deaf."

Phosy raised his voice for the crowd on the grassy pavement.

"Then I want you all to know I'm only here to chaperone my wife, for obvious reasons. I'm not spying. I'm off duty."

"Relax, Constable," said Marvin. "We've been riding around on bicycles all day. Nobody followed us. No guard post stopped us. I got the feeling nobody was interested in us at all."

"I imagine that's what the Soviets want us to write," said Bjorn, the oldest and most opinionated of the Swedes. "How free this place is. No shadowy characters taking notes. No hidden cameras. No bugs in the rooms."

"I got bugs," said Jim. "Big bastards in the bathroom."

"All we get is a jolly drunk policeman and his pretty wife," Bjorn continued. "How can we not write lovingly about this lie?"

"Here he goes again," said Marvin.

"Somebody has to," said Bjorn. "Because this isn't real, is it? The chief of police gives us free drinks. It must be such a liberal place. But it isn't. It's Vietnamese-style repression where you're paper-worked to death. And you Lao have your own style of zero truth. They don't say we can't interview inmates in the reeducation camps, but it will be too difficult to get a flight north at this time of year. We're welcome to speak with the minister who publically criticized the cooperatives, but he's out of town right now. Everything's possible, but nothing's doable. You're all cool about your history as colonized monkeys, but I don't see any French or American newspaper people invited here. You were kind enough to let the Americans keep their consulate open after you took over, but they're down to a diplomatic staff of six, and they aren't allowed to do anything. You nullify your critics with your smiles and your fake indolence."

There was a chilly Vientiane silence in the air for a second until Dtui laughed.

"Well I think I know who's going to mysteriously disappear overnight," she said.

A few more seconds for the chill to melt and the group fell into a swirl of laughter.

"At last, you've met your match, you grumpy old bastard," said Jim to the drunken Swede.

They applauded the nurse, blew her kisses and congratulated Phosy for marrying her. In five minutes most of them were on their way to dinner and Phosy and Dtui were left with Marvin and Jim in front of the dark hotel façade.

"Nice to see you've all got it worked out," said Phosy.

"Ah, don't listen to that flaky old hack," said Jim. "Nobody takes any notice of him. He's been in the region so long he can't see anything beyond his own bias."

"So, you don't agree with him?" Dtui asked.

"Some of it," said Marvin. "I mean, don't get me wrong. We're very fond of this place. We aren't going to belittle you in the press. But really, Dtui, what's this junket all about? The government's got nothing to show us apart from the fact you're still here, still surviving in spite of all those years of war and strife. You're a lesson to the world in tolerance, but I'm not buying the 'land of the free' angle."

"You do know I'm not a plumber," said Phosy.

"No, you're a public servant," said Jim. "And all the scary policies and cloak-and-dagger shit is put together at the Kremlins and the Stasi headquarters of the world, and I'd bet you're no more aware of the dark side of your country than the average farmer. No offence."

Phosy resented hearing it from a foreigner but he couldn't refute it. There were more secret police being trained by the Vietnamese in Laos than there were regular police officers. Even as chief of police, he wasn't granted access to the study venue or its graduates. Half of his investigations of missing persons were stymied with an official "Confidential. Do not proceed."

But he was proud of his country for what it had achieved, and he wasn't about to agree with a foreigner on its shortcomings. They walked the journalists as far as their Vespa and Dtui took the key.

"So, what do you two do when you're riding around on your bicycles?" Phosy asked.

"Observe," said Marvin. "Talk to the ladies in the market. Meet the unexpected character acquaintance from days gone by."

Phosy noticed a brief look from Jim that silenced his friend.

"What type of acquaintance?" asked Dtui.

"Probably one of the old girls from the White Rose," said Jim. "That's where he learned all about balloons and darts, if you know what I mean."

"Not to mention how to smoke ten cigarettes at a time," said Marvin. "And I consider this to be the perfect moment to change the subject. You two wouldn't happen to know of a doctor here in Vientiane called Siri, by any chance?"

"He's our—" said Dtui.

"It's a common enough name," said Phosy. "Why are you interested?"

"Just one of the Swedes was looking for him, is all," said Marvin.

"Do you know why?"

"No idea."

"I'll keep my eyes open for him," said Phosy.

They parted company with handshakes and the confession that the journalists probably wouldn't be catching the following day's 7 A.M. bus to visit the model collective. Dtui drove slowly back along the river road toward the dorm. They passed the Russian Club where the Soviet journalists failed in their attempts at Cossack dancing. They passed Daeng's noodle shop with Ugly on duty outside. They passed the grey padlocked shop fronts and the peeling white colonial buildings. They passed Crazy Rajhid being invisible in front of the Lan Xang Hotel, and they stopped for a while to admire the stars reflected in the water.

"Do they really know more about us than we know about ourselves?" Dtui asked.

"Dtui, when the only information you have about a place comes from the mouths of people who fled that place, you aren't going to hear many positive comments. You'll only get bitterness and anger and misinformation. That's why they were all invited here. To remind them we aren't evil. That we have the same dreams as them."

"What was all that about the darts and the balloons?" Dtui asked.

He looked at her with his eyebrows raised. "Yeah, I didn't get that either," he said.

"We should invite them to Daeng's shop," said Dtui. "I'd

love to see them lock horns with Siri and Civilai. They'd really have something to write about then."

"We'll see," said Phosy.

She kick-started the Vespa. The engine spoke up like the only voice in the whole of Laos. She wondered whether any of the English speakers would make it up in time for the early bus. She knew she wouldn't be meeting Jim and Marvin there. What she didn't know was that she'd never see them again.

CHAPTER SIX
Civilai's Own Brigitte Bardot

Siri's second threat arrived in the pouch of a postal worker early the next morning. The envelope was foolishly small like one of those wedding invitations impoverished couples sent out to save money. There were two stamps, both Lao: one with a picture of Lenin and one with the words *Royaume du Laos* with *Royaume* struck through. The old postman didn't leave. He was dressed in civilian clothes, with an armband and a battered hat as his only uniform.

"What are you waiting for?" Siri asked, "A tip?"

The old man's eyes and nostrils were already feasting on Daeng's breakfast noodles. Like the teachers, he hadn't been paid for several months. The modest Soviet funding hadn't stretched to the end of the year. Moscow and Hanoi were talking about reactivating some of the old opium plantations in order to cover government salaries in Laos. Siri stuffed the envelope into his shirt pocket and showed the postman to an empty stool. One more en-suite bathroom for Siri's charity penthouse apartment in heaven.

It wasn't till after eight, the office workers sated and at their desks, that Siri and Daeng could finally take a break.

"Tell me again," said Siri.

"They'll be back in seven days," said Daeng.

"What could they possibly do for two weeks on a honeymoon?"

"Well, during the day, they're learning vegetable cultivation," said Daeng. "The rest you'll have to use your imagination."

"Can't we . . . you know . . . hire someone till they come back?"

"Why, Siri? Don't you enjoy watching me work?"

"I do my share. And you know I love watching you work. You are the prima ballerina of noodles. But I would love it even more if I could sit at a back table with a strong coffee and a good book. I'm retired."

"You're sounding more like a Mandarin than a forty-something-year paid-up member of the Communist Party. Lording over the staff indeed. Shame on you. It's good for you to labor from time to time. Learn new skills."

"What's wrong, Daeng? Did my table-wiping ability not please you today?"

"What do you mean?"

"You're being grumpy."

"I'm not being grumpy. I am being both angry and anxious."

"Why?" he asked.

"You know why. I saw the postman, I saw the look on your face and I saw you stuff a letter into your pocket."

"Oh."

"Let's see it."

"It's probably just an ad for colostomy bags. They have a mailing list for everyone over—"

"Siri! I have a noodle strainer in my hand. In the

underground, they taught us thirty ways to disfigure a man using a noodle strainer, so don't push me."

Siri fished out the crumpled envelope and tore it open. They sat at the nearest table while Siri scoured the letter. He looked up.

"Well?" she said.

"Colostomy bags," he said.

Daeng reached across and thrust the strainer, missing his already-disfigured ear by a fraction.

"I can't read it," he said.

"English?"

"Same handwriting."

She took the letter from him, nodded, and slid it into her apron pocket.

Dtui was off at some cooperative with her group, so they had to wait until ten to get a translation. Bruce had an appointment to get a Lao driving license at nine. That involved taking his Australian license to the motor registry department, translating it for the clerk, and waiting an hour while she typed up a new one and attached a photograph to it. They insisted on taking the photograph themselves so Bruce arrived at the noodle shop with a license that looked like it belonged to a Solomon Islander.

"Makes your teeth look nice and white though," said Daeng.

"In fact they're all you can see," said Bruce. "They'll have to turn the lights out to ID me."

He was carrying a heavy cloth bag and a clip file. He put the file on the table in front of Siri and Daeng. They looked at it.

"Go ahead, open it," said Bruce with that big Solomon Islands smile.

Daeng flipped open the cover and there at the top was their title page held down with silver clips. They'd given their film the working title *Death to the Oppressors*. Both the Ministry of Culture and the Lao Women's Union had expressed their concerns, but Siri had assured them it was just a temporary filler until they had feedback from their marketing department. But it was *Death to the Oppressors* that stared back at them from the front page of the script. It was the most professional looking thing they'd ever seen: no typing errors, no cross throughs, no smudged or fading ink, no wine stains.

Daeng continued to thumb through the pile: the list of characters, the timeline. By the time the first page of the screenplay showed itself, Siri had already decided to adopt Bruce as his only son and leave him the Triumph in his will.

"How did you achieve all this?" Siri asked.

Bruce, as pleased as a papaya slice, unzipped the cloth bag and produced a clunky mechanical gadget that opened up to look like some science-fiction typewriter. It had a screen like a small television and a keyboard and other knobs and levers that gave the impression it could take off and fly.

"It's called a word processor," said Bruce. "Wordstar—just came out a couple of years ago, but it was already hot in the stores as I was leaving Sydney. The tech boys at UTS put together a Lao script version. You make all your mistakes in the screen here, correct them and print it out at the back. I took the liberty of retyping your script using a screenplay format. I can change it as we go along."

"Siri, you're dribbling," said Daeng.

"It's marvelous," said Siri. "Right, Daeng?"

Daeng wasn't nearly as excited. She was too focused on the letter in her apron pocket. Her instincts were tingling. Her tail was twitching. The two notes might have been the work of a crank—some dark practical joker—but she hadn't stayed alive this long by being complacent. If someone had gone to the trouble of contacting and threatening them, he was a troubled soul and anything was possible. Leaving Siri to drool over his new toy, she took Bruce to a table near the road and made him a coffee.

"Bruce," she said, "I was hoping you might take a look at something for me."

She handed him the letter and leaned back on her chair. He read it, looked up, then read it again.

"What is this, Auntie?" he said.

"One of the journalists was asking if he could help with the script. This is a sort of screen test. We want to know if we can use his idea in our film. Of course, we'd have to translate it, but . . . just see what you think."

The boy read through it again silently to be met by a smile from Daeng.

"I don't believe you," he said.

"Which part?" she asked.

"Any of it. This looks like the real thing to me. Am I wrong?"

"Perhaps you can translate it for me?" she asked.

He huffed and nodded his head.

"Hello, Dr. Siri," he read. *"Let's face it; you wouldn't be afraid of me if I didn't give you a demonstration of my power. Threats without bodies to back them up are meaningless. Don't forget the theme of this maniacal obsession is 'loved ones' although*

there may be one or two collateral victims who fall outside those parameters. Since I arrived, I've been watching you. Clearly, the love of your life is Daeng. Then there's Civilai. We all know how close you are to him. So I've decided the order of departure of those remaining will be your best friend first and then your wife. I doubt you'll consider life to have any meaning once you've lost those two, but don't worry. Your own death will be so slow you'll have plenty of time to contemplate your loneliness.

"The cogs in the clock have started to turn and they are unstoppable. I look forward to watching your futile attempts to undo that which cannot be undone."

Bruce stared at her but her expression gave nothing away.

"Thank you," she said. "I think that was quite convincing, don't you?"

"Madam Daeng, we have to talk ab—" said Bruce.

"Oh look, Comrade Civilai," she said.

Civilai's lemon Citroën pulled up half on, half off the pavement in front of the restaurant. Siri broke away from his word processor trance and came to the doorway to see what was happening. He stood beside Bruce and Daeng. Civilai fought his way out of the driver's door and walked slowly around to the passenger side, using the car to prop him up. He opened the door and out stepped a classical blonde beauty in a sensible blouse and an ankle-length skirt.

"Ladies and gentlemen," said Civilai, "allow me to present Cindy, the new star of our movie."

Things were uncomfortable for a while. Cindy said "hello, how are you?" to everyone in impressive Lao and they all replied politely. Daeng invited their guest in for a cup of coffee. Cindy thanked her and said water would be fine. Coffee gave her migraines. Civilai leaned back against his car looking admiringly at his Brigitte Bardot. He had obviously not heeded the decision of the production committee that finding even a minor role for pretty Cindy would be a push. A starring role would be a feat of superhuman effort. Daeng decided it would be better to break the news to her sooner rather than later. It would probably shatter the girl's dreams but sometimes you had to shoot the pony rather than watch it hobble its way to a slow death. She took Cindy up to the *phasin* skirt room and got straight to the point.

"You're very pretty," she said.

"Thank you," said Cindy. "It has its drawbacks."

Daeng didn't bother to ask what they were.

"I'm afraid you can't star in our movie," she said.

"I can't?"

"No. In fact I can't even imagine a small part for you."

Cindy looked through the window. A flock of terns chose that moment to fly south. The sun reflected silver off their feathers.

"Thank God," she said.

"What?" said Daeng.

"Your Civilai was so insistent," said the woman. "I met him at one of our diplomatic social events. Several of them, in fact. He brought up the movie idea. I was totally against it but our head of mission suggested I cooperate. We can't afford to upset your government given our shaky status here. I've only just arrived so I didn't have much choice."

"You've only just arrived?" said Daeng. "But your Lao is . . ."

"I was an IVS here in '69. I was building latrines and

laying pipes for a year up country. Not everyone bothered to learn the language. Most said it wouldn't serve any purpose once we left. But I loved the sound of Lao and I have an ear for it, I guess."

Daeng looked at the young woman: simple clothes, unfussy hairstyle, straight-talking, obviously older than she looked. She must have known what an effect her looks had on men, men like Civilai.

"Did he flirt with you?" Daeng asked.

"Civilai? Yes, he flirted. He flirted like old men flirt, happy enough with a smile and a blush and a peck on the cheek. Just enough to let him imagine being back there when he was twenty and still available."

"He's been married to the same woman for forty-four years," said Daeng.

"Madam Nong. Yes, I know. He talked about her the first time we met. I got the feeling he was telling me he was happily married just in case I fell head over heels in love with him. He didn't want to disappoint me."

Daeng laughed.

"My Siri leaves it to the last minute to mention he's already taken just to be sure the young ones fall for him, and they do. But he isn't dangerous."

They clinked their water glasses.

"I've read the script," said Cindy. "I got a copy from the Women's Union. My reading's not that clever, but I got through it. A week with my head in a dictionary. But we don't have a lot else to do at the consulate these days."

"What did you think?" Daeng asked.

"Part historical, part political, part magical, part absolutely ridiculous. But what a ride. It would make a great movie."

"You think so? We've only got the one camera."

"I can help with budget."

"You can?"

"Sure. At the consulate we don't have an agenda anymore. But we have discretionary funds. We have a green light to help with education and the arts. No offence, but there aren't that many cultural activities going on right now. Your movie would qualify. What do you think?"

Cindy was invited to participate in the second production meeting that afternoon, and they came up with a budget that wouldn't break the State Department. They had a late lunch together except for Civilai, whose weight seemed to be dripping off him like wax from a temple candle. He settled for water. Bruce offered to take Cindy back to the consulate in the Willys jeep he'd picked up for next to nothing. They could see his pilot light burning just by being around her. He wasn't the best-looking young man to have fallen for her but he had ambition and a sense of humor. She seemed to like him. She screamed as the jeep left the ground and hit the empty road.

Which left Siri, Daeng and Civilai to go over the contents of the letter.

"Bruce didn't believe for a second it was fiction," said Daeng. "We might have to include him in on this."

"I doubt he imagined his return to Laos would be as full of excitement as it's turning out to be," said Siri. "Beautiful blondes and death threats."

"The question is," said Civilai, "when do we start to take it all seriously?"

"As you'll be the first to go," said Siri, "I suggest we stake you out over there beside the road like a house bantam and wait to see what bites you."

"Right," said Daeng, "we lie in wait and catch him in the act of whatever horror he has planned for you."

"I don't feel much peer support in this venture," said Civilai. "Have you alerted Phosy?"

"His people are going through the journalist files you left with me," said Siri. "We don't exactly have anyone at Interpol, so we can't verify that they've all told the truth in their CVs. But he sent copies to all the embassies and asked them to do background checks. They have no obligation to comply."

"I'm not sure I understand the letter," said Civilai. "What is all that about cogs and clocks?"

"My interpretation is that he's already set in motion whatever plans he has," said Daeng. "Either he's already hired someone to do the nasty . . . or there's a bomb in the basement on a timer," said Siri. "Luckily, we haven't got a basement."

"What if it's a riddle," said Civilai. "What if there are clues in his notes that will allow us to stop the ticking clock?"

"I don't get the feeling he's that accommodating," said Daeng, fishing the first note from her apron and turning it over to Dtui's translation. "The only thing that isn't immediately obvious is the line, '*I have already deleted one of your darlings.*' Does that mean he's already murdered one of your loved ones, Siri?"

"A few years back my dog was killed violently," said Siri. "I was very fond of her."

They heard a brief growl from the street outside.

"Siri, you know what I'm getting at," said Daeng. "Your first true love."

"Boua?" said Siri. "I'd prefer not to talk about her."

"Why?" Daeng asked.

"Because whenever I do, you sink into a foul mood for two or three days."

"That's just a woman thing," said Civilai. "Always comparing themselves to their predecessors, even when the ex is dead."

"Shut up, Civilai," said Siri and Daeng in tandem.

"It's true," mumbled Civilai. "Now look what you've made me do."

He headed off to the bathroom for the umpteenth time.

Once he'd gone, Daeng said, "I think we need to talk about her. Even at the expense of my flimsy female attitude. If this note refers to her, it means the killer was around when you were in Vietnam."

"It was suicide," said Siri.

He'd read Boua's suicide note so many times the paper had crumbled to dust. He read the final sentences now in his mind. *Can you ever forgive me for what I've done to you, and for what I have to do this evening? This is the only escape for us two.* Her one true love: communism, had been a disappointment. It had failed her. And once her vision was clear, she could see how she'd ignored and belittled the man who'd stood beside her for better and, decidedly, for worse. Thus, two hearts had been broken and she could not live with herself.

"Or it was made to look like suicide," said Daeng. "There are those who doubted the official report."

Daeng had never seen the suicide note and Siri had never mentioned it. That was the only real secret between them. He felt uncomfortable to be a part of the conversation now.

"By the time you got back to the camp they'd already

cremated her," Daeng went on. "So there was no evidence. Nobody really knows what happened. Around that time was there somebody you upset? Someone who might kill your wife but be prepared to wait twenty-five years to find you?"

CHAPTER SEVEN
Saigon, 1956

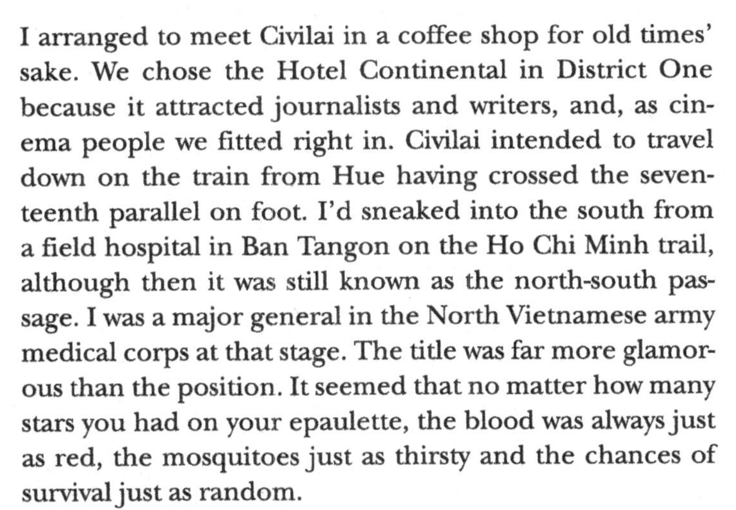

I arranged to meet Civilai in a coffee shop for old times' sake. We chose the Hotel Continental in District One because it attracted journalists and writers, and, as cinema people we fitted right in. Civilai intended to travel down on the train from Hue having crossed the seventeenth parallel on foot. I'd sneaked into the south from a field hospital in Ban Tangon on the Ho Chi Minh trail, although then it was still known as the north-south passage. I was a major general in the North Vietnamese army medical corps at that stage. The title was far more glamorous than the position. It seemed that no matter how many stars you had on your epaulette, the blood was always just as red, the mosquitoes just as thirsty and the chances of survival just as random.

Boua and I seemed to be stationed apart more and more often. She was a lieutenant colonel at the nurses' training facility in Dong Hoi. We saw little of each other. We'd returned to Laos from Paris in '39, still in love, I supposed. Altogether, I'd been in Paris for seventeen years. I loved the place. I'd imagined us with a cottage in Montreuil, three kids, a garden with an apple tree, and a Pomeranian called Loulou. There'd be a back terrace where Loulou and I would sit on Sundays. I'd drink coffee and cognac while Boua baked tarts in the kitchen.

Boua saw something slightly different. She saw hundreds of young Lao and Vietnamese being mowed down by French machine guns, their bodies rotting on battlefields. And over time, Loulou and the kids got fuzzier, and I could think of nothing more noble than returning to our homeland to overthrow the French—the same French who'd taught me and trained me and who'd brought me homemade *petits fours* to thank me for lancing their boils.

By the time we left France, Boua had made me feel so ashamed of my selfish ideas that I'd deleted them. For many years, I swore I'd merely tolerated the bastard French and their capitalist values. The mysterious *petits fours* haunted me in nightmares. When I arrived in Laos, I was every bit as passionate. Boua was passionate for Laos, and I was passionate for Laos . . . through her. Same destination, different route.

I admit I felt the adrenaline pumping as the steamer docked in Singapore, and we travelled north. We were warriors almost immediately. We spent our early years with the ragtag Free Lao militia fighting—or at least frustrating—the Japanese. In Vietnam, the OSS had identified groups of what they preferred to call "nationalists" led by a multilingual patriot called Ho Chi Minh: Civilai's old buddy Quoc after a number of name changes. The Americans provided weaponry and training. With the French off in Europe rescuing their motherland from Hitler, the Viet Minh assumed the mantle of protectors of Vietnam. By the war's end, the Vietnamese and Lao nationalists had accredited ourselves nicely, and we were certain we no longer needed the French. With trumpets blowing and new flags waving, we declared our independence. There was dancing in the streets, but they were slow dances to short tunes.

Pumped up from their victory in Europe, the French returned to Indochina in numbers to resume their usurper role. But the management had changed in their absence. The French set out to nullify all that foolish talk of independence and endeavored to put down the local rebellion, but it was a rebellion that would not lay still. With help from the Chinese, the North Vietnamese grew stronger and their influence spread. The French had a fight on their hands.

The Pathet Lao grew out of the Viet Minh momentum. Boua and I moved to the north of Laos where we trained medics and stitched up young boys who were fighting for the great cause of communism. But I noticed soon enough that not one of them knew, or cared, what communism was; they saw a banner of some sort that stood for equality and self-rule. But I'd lean over my patients by candlelight and listen to their whispered stories. And, without exception, they'd joined the Pathet Lao because they were tired of being shat on. They'd been shat on by the racist French, shat on by the corrupt Royal Lao army, shat on by fate, by the spirits, by Buddha. They just wanted a break from all that shit. And that was when my true passion for my country—a passion a longtime coming—took root. At last, I saw a point. The country boys put on a uniform and picked up a gun not because they stood for something, but because they wanted a fair roll of the dice. They didn't want victory as much as they wanted peace.

In '54 the rebellion of hope spilled over onto the

battlefield, and, in a fight that shocked the world, the French received a drubbing at the hands of a bunch of locals at a place called Dien Bien Phu. Boua and I were in Vietnam by then. We watched the final curtain from a ridge looking down at the despondent French army. I was saddened by the carnage, but I'd never seen my wife so joyful.

The international agreements were signed and the French dragged their feet until '56, when the last of the actors were to leave the theatre. And there I was in the coffee shop at the Continental watching it all happen. They had a parade that passed right in front of me. The drums of the Moroccan Sharpshooters' Band made ripples in my *café au lait.* In their big hats and their snowy-white uniforms and their confident stride, you'd never have guessed the French were the losers. Some of the crowd even cheered them as they passed. With nothing really to show for a hundred years of occupation, it struck me as particularly arrogant that they should hold their heads so high; that they should still be taller and heavier than us.

I'd been there at the café for forty minutes still nursing my cup with no sign of Civilai. I wondered whether he'd been stopped at the border or shot trying to cross it. Those were oddly unpredictable days. It crossed my mind a few times that I was the enemy. The '54 Geneva Agreement had sliced the country in half and we victors had been ordered to keep behind the line that divided a country we'd won. It was like the winner of the Tour de France being allowed to keep only the handles of the trophy.

I'm not sure we really wanted the south anyway. It had been flooded by Catholics escaping some imaginary genocide in the north. The suburban slums of Saigon continued to spread out like an ink blot. It was impossible to know who was from where or to police the mayhem. The South Vietnamese security forces had been trained hurriedly and indifferently by the fleeing French, and the task of supervising a city in transition was beyond them. For a while, anyway, anything was available and possible.

So, there I was, a Lao with no passport, undeniably an enemy agent, drinking coffee in the center of a city in denial. I could feel its incurable tumor. It still wore its foundation and its blush. Its pretty girls still cycled past in their beautiful silk *ao dai,* but you could see the bruises beneath the makeup. The men still strutted, but their heads turned often to look behind them. Saigon was keeping a brave face, but there was nothing holding the skin and bone together. A voice roused me from my thoughts.

"Anyone sitting there?"

I looked up and wasn't at all surprised by what confronted me.

"Did you really travel all the way from Hue with that tennis racquet?" I asked.

"Of course not," said Civilai. "Look around, little brother. French all over the city are trying to sell off their household items before they jump on the boat home. And imagine all those wealthy Catholic refugees who were forced to leave their china collections in the north. They would love nothing more than to pick up a new set here in the south. But, goodness me, they don't even have enough money to feed their fat children. They don't even have a real roof over their heads."

He waved his tennis racquet in the air.

"I picked up this beauty for almost nothing at a yard sale," he said.

Only Civilai would scour the suburbs to set up a joke.

"Sit down before somebody challenges you to a game," I said.

It was good to see him. We shook hands, and the nerves in our palms exchanged a familiar intimacy. We had kept in touch as much as an endless guerilla war allowed. He'd gone his way after Paris, organizing, activating, agitating. He was the only Lao on the central committee of the Workers Party of Vietnam. I'd seen him on the stage in Tuyen Quang when our Free Lao movement was hijacked by the Vietnamese-designed Pathet Lao movement. He was already a celebrity then, a visionary, a revolutionary, a genius but still an idiot. We'd reunited by chance at seminars and in bunkers. Whenever there was a lull in the fighting we'd go out of our ways to meet up and see a film or two. That war would never have been the same without Civilai. I was always glad he wasn't dead and he assured me that the feeling was mutual.

The note that had brought me to Saigon had been written in Lao and was, wisely, cryptic. He knew I'd come. He ordered a pitcher of beer from the one nervous waiter. Cafés in Saigon were bombed from time to time just to keep the enemy on their toes. It would have been an ironic end to our relationship to be blasted by a North Vietnamese hand grenade. The waiter knew that thanks to the influx of refugees he could be replaced. We, on the other hand, could not.

We drank our long-dreamed-of cold beer and caught up on the previous four months. I told him about the delta. He told me about Hanoi. We followed the progress of the drug trade. The Golden Triangle was producing half the world's opium, and the French, who had distributed the drug to fund their occupation, were now trafficking the product to pay for their withdrawal. As was our tradition, I asked him about his wife, Nong, who was teaching at Ai Quoc College, and he asked me about Boua. His marriage always seemed happier than mine, and I found myself inventing a perfect relationship to tell him about. I'm sure he knew I was lying.

"So, why are you here?" he asked, which surprised me considering he'd invited me.

"Because you need me?" I said.

He'd lost some weight and some hair since last we'd met. Jungle life took its toll on all of us one way or another. I'd long since forgotten the joy of hearing a solid stool thundering down to earth at our outdoor latrine.

"You are quite correct," said Civilai. "There was sympathy within my group when I told them of my findings. But when I asked for a team of commandos to accompany me here, they pointed out quite rightly that they were more likely to throw themselves under a tank than to accede to my request."

"Given the title of our assignment," I said, "you don't see it as a little ironic that two Lao would take it upon themselves to carry out a mission on behalf of the Vietnamese?"

"Let's just say that if we're successful—and I really hope we are—our little country will be owed a great debt of gratitude. One that I shall claim back over and over until the favor bucket is dry."

"How dangerous do you consider this to be?"

"At the very least we could be tortured and shot."

"In that case I doubt one jug of beer will be enough," I said.

Half an hour later we walked, perhaps a little unsteadily, the four steamy blocks to the National Museum of Saigon. We stood admiring its grand pagoda-like façade. There was a thick layer of gravel on the driveway, and we each selected the best specimens and put them in our trouser pockets. We paid our *piasters* to the indifferent young guard at the desk and put our names in the visitor's book. It hadn't been signed for four days. Oddly, considering what we were about to do, we gave our actual names. Civilai took time to write a comment.

We looked at the little map on the central beam and made our way to the north gallery. The guard didn't follow us, and there were no attendants in any of the rooms. So, there we stood in the middle of the Ly Dynasty: the golden age of Vietnamese art. Its ceramics were praised and sought after throughout the world and rightly so. The pots in front of us were elegantly slender with their emerald and light-green glazes and their distinct motifs. Every one of them was a work of art and literally priceless.

"They're beautiful," I said.

"Hard to believe they're over nine hundred years old," said Civilai.

"Hard indeed," I agreed.

"I'm guessing that the big grey-green one up there on the shelf will be the loudest," said Civilai.

"You think they'd mention volume in the tourist guide book."

"Perhaps nobody's ever tried to get a sound out of them before," said Civilai.

"Then let us be the first," I said.

I pulled a medium-sized hunk of gravel from my pocket, took aim and chucked it with all my might. Somehow, I managed to miss the largest pot, but I did smash its neighbor to smithereens.

"That's the one I was aiming at," I said.

"Liar," said Civilai.

"Can you do any better?" I asked.

"I believe so."

He walked forward, stepped over the red rope, grabbed two particularly elegant pieces of pottery and smashed them together like cymbals. The sound was far more pleasing.

"I didn't know that was allowed," I said, and I joined him on the illegal side of the rope. We did a good deal of smashing. I was just about to drop kick a potbellied antique when the gallery attendant arrived, still wiping baguette crumbs from his lips. He stood in the entry way, eyes huge, mouth agape. My kick took out a whole line of finely tapered pots, the shards of which landed at his feet.

"What are . . . what do you think . . . ?" said the attendant.

"Destroying priceless artifacts," said Civilai, anticipating the question. He went to the wall and elbowed the glass on the fire alarm. The building rattled from the sound. But the curator and his secretary had already arrived in the gallery from the other direction. The curator staggered backward. The secretary, a plump young man in steamy glasses, screamed and ran back along the corridor, probably in search of a telephone to call the police. The guard arrived. Nobody dared approach us maniacs. I sat cross-legged on the ground, attempting to make a paper airplane from a quite lovely sixteenth-century watercolor, while Civilai attempted to lob his gravel into the last pot standing. We had destroyed no fewer than eighteen priceless artifacts.

It was clearly the first crime scene the new South Vietnamese police force had had to deal with. The officers who arrived had no idea what to do. Officially, the commissioner general was the go-to person for matters of national importance. But he was due to leave in three days, and all he dreamed of was a trouble-free period in which to pack, to drink his way through as much of the wine cellar as possible, and to disconnect tactfully from his mistress. All of his duties were handed over to the commander-in-chief, General Jacquot, who, in turn, passed these last-minute annoyances on to the prefect of the Saigon-Cholon region, Monsieur Blazer. He too had planned to escape peacefully yet there in his anteroom stood two anarchists who had dared to ruin his orderly exit by destroying national treasures.

Blazer was still the prefect, and he could have ordered us executed there and then. It would have been a profound statement to make before launching a career in domestic politics. Exactly the kind of gesture he needed. But he seemed confused by our nonchalance.

"What do you have to say for yourselves?" he asked.

"They destroyed millions of francs' worth of antiques before our very eyes," said Marchant, the curator. He'd followed the police van to the prefect's house on his motor scooter. He was a sweaty, shifty-looking man with oily hair and an unimaginative body.

"I rather thought I was addressing these two villains," said Blazer.

"But I . . ." Marchant began.

"Your negligence at letting this happen I can deal with later," said the prefect. "Right now, I'm interested to hear the motivation behind this hooliganism."

He walked up close to us and I wouldn't have been surprised if he considered himself to be a threatening force. He came near enough for me to smell the wine on his breath, and I'm sure he could smell the beer on mine. He was tall and wide at the shoulders like a coffin standing on end. It was midday but he was in a dressing gown with a cravat. On his feet were the most outlandish carpet slippers. Were this a movie, the costumes department would have been chastised for its unlikely choices. It was hard for us to keep straight faces at such a sight.

"Do either of you speak French?" he asked, slowly.

"I did pick up a little at the Sorbonne," said Civilai.

"Are you mocking me, Monsieur?" he asked.

Civilai went on to list the years of his studies, the distinctions, and finally, the honors degree in Law. I had no doubt he was more qualified than the balding fellow standing in front of us. He turned his gaze to me.

"And you?" he said.

"Siri Paiboun," I said. "Merely a surgeon with a degree in medicine from Ancienne."

"I can check all this," he said. But we doubted he'd wait for the boat to come back with the answer to his inquiries.

"They should be executed immediately," said the curator, who appeared to be in an advanced state of agitation. Blazer ignored him.

"If you are truly academics," he said, "the act that you perpetrated today is even more inexcusable. You should be ashamed."

"And yet we aren't," I said.

"Then are you both mad?" he asked.

"Well, yes," said Civilai. "I would have to say we are mad in many ways. Only madmen would enter enemy territory and advertise their presence here in such an outlandish way. But we stand here before you with spines unbent and sanity unquestioned."

The weight of it all seemed too much for the prefect, and he sank into an overstuffed velvet armchair. All the rest of us, including half a dozen police, two French military types, three men in ties and a token woman, were left standing.

"Then I shall give you three minutes to explain yourselves before these gentlemen take you into the yard and shoot you," said the prefect. "I can think of no good reason for what you did at the museum."

"There is none," said the curator.

"Siri?" said Civilai, very generously considering this was his project.

"Very well," I said. "It's all very simple really. If we asked for an appointment to see the prefect on the week he was about to leave the country, the appointments secretary would have laughed at us. So, we had to find some subterfuge that would guarantee us instant access."

"What?" said Blazer. "You destroyed a museum exhibition in order to get an audience with me? That is indeed insanity."

"I don't know," said Civilai. "It worked, didn't it?"

"If I were armed I would shoot them both here and now," said the curator.

"Blood is a terrible stain to get out of a carpet," said Civilai.

"See?" said the curator. "They're making fun of you, Sir."

"In fact, we're only ridiculing you, Monsieur le Conservateur," I said. "We have the utmost respect for the prefect."

"Monsieur Blazer, surely you can't—" the curator began.

"Monsieur, could you stop talking?" said the prefect. "You're making my headache worse. All I need to know is what our maniacs here considered so important to say that they would cause mindless vandalism in order to say it."

"Perhaps we could sit with you over a glass?" said Civilai.

"Don't push your luck," said Blazer.

"After we've told you our story, you'll wish you'd made us comfortable," I said.

"Perhaps a spot of lunch," said Civilai.

The prefect laughed. "Of all the audacity," he said. "You'll stand, you'll remain in irons, and you'll have less than a minute to come up with a story."

"A firing squad is all they deserve," said the curator.

The prefect called to the sergeant at arms. "Escort Monsieur Marchant out of the room, Sergeant."

Two guards approached the sweaty man.

"In fact, it might be circumspect for the curator to stay," I said.

"Is this some sort of ruse?" said Blazer. "Is this the commander-in-chief playing a practical joke on me? A jolly deception as a farewell souvenir of Indochina?"

"I hear the commander-in-chief has no sense of humor," said Civilai.

"That's true," said the prefect. "Well then, for heaven's sake tell me what it is you have to say. Be brief. My lunch is waiting for me."

"Then, simply, the method we used to attract your

attention and the reason for wanting to do so, are one and the same," I said.

"I don't understand," said Blazer.

"On the black market in Europe, the Ly Dynasty ceramic and watercolor collection would be worth well over a hundred million francs to a collector," I said.

I reached under my shirt and every gun in the room was raised in my direction. I put up my hands.

"With your permission, Sir," I said.

The prefect nodded and I reached beneath my belt and pulled out a shard of pottery that had not been discovered when we were frisked.

"This," I said, "is a memento from our rampage this morning. The Ly collection is nine-hundred-and-sixty years old. This shard is two months old. From a distance, the pottery looks exactly the same. You only really notice the difference when you handle it."

"As we did," said Civilai.

"Nonsense," said the curator.

"Fakes are heavier than the originals, they're fired higher, and they have a sort of soapy feel to them. Antique ceramics are made of clay, and clay always has some impurities, often iron, but the collection in the gallery this morning had no rust spots at all. The exhibits on display at the museum comprised very clever fakes."

"Now I've heard everything," said the curator. "You think I wouldn't know the difference between genuine and fake earthenware?"

"You certainly would," said Civilai. "There's no doubt you knew that the ceramics in the museum . . ."

The curator walked swiftly toward the door. "I won't stay here to be insulted," he said.

"Stop him," said Blazer.

Two of the guards took Marchant by the arms and marched him back into the center of the room.

"How dare you treat me like this," he said. "I have some very influential friends in parliament, I'll have you know. You will certainly regret this."

"I've found from experience," said the prefect, "that people who actually have influential friends have no need to remind anyone of the fact. Go ahead, Doctor."

"You should find the originals in warehouse eleven at the airport," I said. "The crates are marked 'REPATRIATION32B.' According to the bill of lading the trunks contain household goods belonging to some of your senior people. You'll be looking specifically for crates eighteen, nineteen and twenty on the manifest."

"Have your people open them carefully," said Civilai. "We don't want any accidents. The names of the three army officers who colluded with the curator here and the names and addresses of the potters and painters recruited into the scheme are in a large envelope tucked into the back of the visitor's book at the museum. I was afraid it might have been confiscated and lost during my arrest."

"Or ripped apart in a hail of bullets," I added for effect.

The curator said nothing.

"How could you know all this?" asked Blazer.

"The Vietnamese who work under the curator and at the airport are no fools," said Civilai, "although their superiors treated them as such. The Vietnamese staff discovered the plot to replace the collection with fakes, but, given the influence of those involved, they didn't know who to tell. That's why they contacted us."

"And who are you exactly?" asked the prefect.

"A group of patriots who merely wish to protect Vietnamese culture," I said. "When all this colonial malarkey is out of the way, this will be a single nation again with a common history. It's probably best if you don't know any more than that."

We'd decided nothing would be gained by telling him we were Lao Communists.

"Naturally we'll have to verify these claims," said the prefect. "And while we are doing so, I shall keep you all here under guard. These are serious accusations and I cannot proceed without recommendations from my superiors. I shall return when we know more. In the meantime—I don't know—make yourselves comfortable."

There followed a peculiar hour during which Civilai and I sat on a divan and Marchant took the velvet chair. Each of us had an armed guard at our back. We had a front-row view of the curator passing through various shades of anger and into the vivid hues of fear. We had not been banned from speaking, so Civilai and I caught up on the films we'd seen on our respective 8mm show nights and the duties of our wives. We weren't careful about what we said. It was rare for foreign experts to come to the colonies and bother to study our languages. We were all supposed to speak French, so it didn't occur to us that the curator might be a linguist.

Much later, we went back over our conversation from that hour and began to question how much information we'd given away—if we'd mentioned places or names or whether we'd said anything in our own language that could have led to us being traced. Because, just before Blazer returned, we witnessed the look of Satan in the eyes of the curator. He leaned forward, and in fluent Lao, he said:

"Monsieur Civilai, Dr. Siri, you may be feeling smug about this victory. But it is only temporary. What you did today promises to ruin me financially and professionally. The prefect will not find the local artisans on your list because obviously I could not allow them to live given what they knew. I found I am something of an architect when it comes to murder. There will be nothing to tie me to the deaths of a few old potters. I will not be executed—our government cannot afford such a scandal—but when I return to France, my life will not be worth living. The only thing that will keep me sane from now on is the thought of finding you both and your charming wives and your children and doing to you all what you did to the pots. I shall crush you and destroy you, and I shall enjoy every second of your pain. It will be the fulfillment of my life's ambition to see you suffer."

We ate a late lunch at the prefect's table as we celebrated the rescue of Vietnamese national treasures. We drank probably the most expensive wine I'd ever tasted, toasted again and again by a late visitor, General Jacquot. It was true he did not have a sense of humor, but he had a remarkable capacity for wine. With such a victory under their belts thanks to us, the future of both men in national politics was assured. Whenever we met after that we drank to our success, but I never did forget the threat or the cold look of hatred on the face of the man who made it:

"I shall crush you and destroy you, and I shall enjoy every second of your pain. It will be the fulfillment of my life's ambition to see you suffer."

CHAPTER EIGHT
The Succubus Conductor

"So, if I'm reading this addendum to the screenplay right," said Bruce, "at a crucial moment in the battle, you and Civilai rip . . ."

"The two characters who may or may not be me and Civilai," said Siri.

"Right, anyway, these two characters rip off their shirts, grab the nearest machetes and charge down into the valley to confront the French forces at Dien Bien Phu."

"That's correct," said Siri.

"Why would you . . . they do that?"

"Good question," said Daeng.

"I mean, why machetes?" said Bruce. "There were guns everywhere."

"And why rip off their shirts?" said Daeng.

"It's cinema," said Siri. "It's symbolic."

"It's symbolic of insanity," said Daeng.

"I'm afraid I have to agree," said Bruce. "The movie's already two hours too long. Can't we just stick to the original script?"

"Things were getting dull," said Siri. "I wanted to inject a John Wayne moment."

Bruce seemed to be finding it harder to keep his team in order and focused. Civilai was taking more and more time off, and Daeng seemed preoccupied with other matters. Only Siri showed an unwavering commitment to the project. But then even he disappeared. Bruce turned toward the street for a second when a rare car went by, and when he looked back, Siri was gone.

The doctor found himself on a film set he recognized but couldn't immediately name. He was standing before a throbbing pink spaceship in a landscape of dry ice. He resented the fact that he was still not in control of these spiritual summonses. He knew who had called him to the other side and that he'd have to put up with more of Auntie Bpoo's mood swings. The old transvestite was his spirit guide. It was she who should have been at Siri's beck and call, not the other way around. Aladdin didn't have to go spelunking into the lamp to get things done.

"All right, I know you're here," said Siri. "Let's get this over with. I have a film to make."

"Huh," came a familiar voice. "That's one little chicken that won't ever make it out of the egg."

Bpoo appeared from behind the spaceship. She was finding it hard to walk in her skin-tight silver spacesuit. She'd gained a lot of bulk since their last meeting. She reminded Siri of a big balloon baby wrapped in tinfoil. Despite her weight, she left the ground and floated in her personal zero-gravity zone. She removed one of her gloves and lowered the zipper at her chest. Siri recognized the scene. It was Jane Fonda's erotic striptease from the beginning of *Barbarella.* The Fonda version had been one of his most memorable soft-porn moments in cinema, but he really did not want to watch the Auntie Bpoo interpretation through to its climax.

"What's all this supposed to mean?" said Siri.

"You should know. You're the host."

"*Barbarella,*" said Siri. "1968. Is this a new test?"

"No, I just took a fancy to the costume. You know I'm naked underneath?"

"That's what I'm afraid of. But I'm going to have to stop you there. Our relationship is about to change. I don't have to put up with your idiosyncrasies anymore. I realized something the other day that explains everything about you. I understand why you're such a grump."

The spirit guide dropped to the ground like a suet pudding.

"You really know how to hurt a girl," said Bpoo.

"All these exotic locations, all the symbolism, all the drama and acting and cross-dressing, I get it now."

"I doubt you're that clever."

"No, you're right. It should have occurred to me a long time ago, back when you were still alive and making do with three dimensions. I should have seen it then."

"Are you telling me the offspring of a celebrated shaman has finally had an insight? The wait has been excruciating. Oh, Great Seer, what can you tell me?"

Sarcasm was rampant in the otherworld.

"The dress-ups," said Siri. "The tutus and stilettos and halter tops, the entire wardrobe that doesn't fit you. Clothes that you hate wearing. You have no choice, do you?"

"I have no idea what you're talking about."

"Don't you? I think most of your life, even into death, you've been stalked."

"Gibberish."

"The *phibob* found your weakness a long time ago. Somewhere back in your history when you were still a normal, polite young man with a real life, maybe even a career. The malevolent spirits decided to turn you upside down by visiting you in your dreams as a succubus. She became your lifelong nemesis."

"You should stop now, little doctor," she said.

Her spacesuit was liquefying and dripping off her like leaks in a gargantuan thermometer.

Siri continued, "You were so desperate to get her out of your life you started to sleep in a nightdress to persuade her you weren't male. You'd heard the rumors that she only took the lives of men. And it probably worked for a while, but she followed you, even into the daylight hours and haunted you. So you began dressing as a woman all day, all night, afraid to let down your guard even for the briefest time."

"This is a bad talk," said Bpoo.

"Of course your friends and neighbors ostracized you. They thought you'd gone mad. And you got to the point where you had no friends. You weren't homosexual or actually interested in cross-dressing, so those communities didn't want you. And you'd never attract a wife looking the way you did. So you became a bitter loner: miserable and obnoxious."

"No."

"And there you are now in the otherworld, still petrified to let down your guard. Still unpleasant. Still looking over your shoulder all the time. Because you're in their realm now, so there's no sleep for you. No rest. And you know the funniest thing about all this?"

"Make me laugh."

There was no scenery now. The spaceship was gone. They were facing each other in a green-screen room both dressed exactly the same in Siri's unfashionable attire. They were sitting on plastic bathroom stools.

"The *phibob* have only one weapon," said Siri. "All they can do is put their fear into you: the fear of death, of helplessness, of worthlessness. None of it is real. They plant an idea into you and sit back and watch you self-destruct. Ghosts don't kill people. People are eaten from the inside by their own terror. You've been living this lie all your life. Still, in the afterlife, you continue to be afraid even though they have no physical control over you. You are drowning in your own imagination. You still shroud yourself in all this symbolism because you think it puts them off your trail, but they aren't there, Bpoo."

"Is this you attempting to take control over me?" said the transvestite.

"Ah, so that's why you're being so defensive about it all. I have never and will never have control over you," said Siri. "But at least now I understand you. I'm sorry that you've spent so much of your life hiding and depressed. I'm sorry for all the times I've been rude to you. I've decided to go out of my way to like you. In fact, you've inspired me to put together a plan."

"To save me?"

"No, you're on your own. But I think I can save the boys your succubus has on her list. I might need a little help with that."

CHAPTER NINE
Collateral Deaths

"Oh, Siri, you made me jump," said Nurse Dtui.

"He sneaks up on you, doesn't he?" said Daeng.

Siri was back in the restaurant, but the sun was on its way down, and Dtui and Phosy had arrived in his absence. Bruce was still leaning over his processor.

"But where did you come from?" said Dtui. "I'm sure you weren't there when I came in."

"They used to call it 'out of thin air,'" said Siri. "But the air got thicker, and you have to fight your way through the pollution. Actually, I was in the bathroom. How's the screenplay coming along?"

"Well, when you ran off to wherever you went, and I gave up waiting for Civilai," said Bruce, "I decided to go ahead and cut all the extra scenes you've both been forcing on me. It's a lot shorter now."

"I wish to see the changes," said Siri.

"Right now, the movie is on hold," said Phosy. "We're putting our effort into your latest threatening letter. Bruce has read the note already, so we've drafted him into the team. We've got more important things to worry about than film scripts. This is getting serious. I've recruited my people to look into the case. I've made it a priority for the department."

"Any insights?" Siri asked.

"Well, it was obviously sent from inside the country," said Daeng.

"And the sender knows us and watches us," said Dtui.

"We talked to the people at the post office," said Phosy. "Nobody remembers seeing a foreigner buying stamps for a local delivery. Only airmail letters overseas. But of course he could have had someone local buy the stamps for him or procured them some other way."

"What about the writing?" Dtui asked.

Bruce put the two notes side-by-side on the table.

"I'm not a native speaker myself," he said, "but they both seem grammatically correct to me. Neat. Relaxed. He or she wasn't in a hurry."

"You think there's a chance it might have been written by a woman?" asked Daeng.

"Just saying it's not impossible," said Bruce.

"How are we doing with the list of journalists?" asked Daeng.

"The embassies just gave us copies of the standard application forms, the passports and their CVs," said Phosy. "A lot of them are on their first overseas assignments. If we're looking for someone bent on revenge for something that happened in the doctor's past, our choices are limited. There's only one old enough to have been around in Paris in '32. Dimitri Popov, Russian, sixty-eight years old. He was on the Pravda desk in Germany until the second war. Ring a bell, Siri?"

"No. I didn't go anywhere near Germany," said Siri.

"But no saying Popov didn't go to Paris," said Daeng.

"Why are the Soviets sending some feeble old journalist?" Dtui asked.

"They aren't going to spare someone with his own teeth for a dead-end mission like this, are they now?" said Bruce.

Siri cleared his throat loudly.

"If Civilai was here he'd beat the pair of you with his walking stick for disrespecting your elders," he said. "Compared to us lot, the Russian's barely out of diapers. But I don't think he's our man. His name doesn't ring any bells. Who else do we have?"

"Two Poles that covered our war with the French," said Phosy. "They fit the age bracket. Their names are Zielinski and Wisniewski. They would have been in Hanoi or on field assignments when you were in Vietnam."

"Don't forget this information came from their own CVs," said Daeng. "There were war correspondents who spent all their time overseas in bars and in various beds. They made up stories and the only excitement they had was what they wrote on their CVs afterward. We have to consider a lot of this data could be bogus."

"Anyone else?" Bruce asked.

"Just the one East German," said Phosy. "Ackerman. He was based in Hanoi during the war with America. Made a name for himself there. The embassy seemed quite proud of him. Made him sound like some sort of hero. It was a coup that they persuaded him to come to Laos of all places. They said he turned down more interesting offers."

"He's my favorite so far," said Daeng.

"Mine too," said Dtui.

"I don't know," said Siri. "I don't recall offending any Germans. I need to run all these names past my Dr. Watson."

"Who?" Phosy asked.

"Civilai," said Siri. "He's my facts and figures man. He could tell us if we met any of the journalists on the list. He has a remarkable memory for names."

"Madam Nong says he still has the runs," said Nurse Dtui.

"Well, that's very inconsiderate of him," said Siri. "If he didn't refuse point blank to accept my boundless medical experience, I'd ride over there to Kilometer Six and fill him full of aloe. Snails, indeed."

"Is somebody treating him?" asked Bruce.

"He swears by Dr. Porn," said Daeng. "He was on his way to see her when I had my medical appointment. He said she didn't find anything potentially fatal. Said he'd be right as rain soon."

"He wouldn't find a better doctor in this country than Porn," said Dtui. "Present company excepted."

Daeng laughed. Siri bowed.

"He says he prefers to visit a general practitioner because they make their decisions based on symptoms," said Daeng. "They're less likely to cut you open and take a look under the bonnet."

"After all these years he still sees me as a mechanic," said Siri.

"So until he's feeling better," said Dtui, "what do we do about the men on our shortlist?"

"I'll arrange translators for those that need them and have a talk with them," said Phosy.

"But, you know, we're really limiting ourselves," said Bruce. "We might not be dealing directly with the man who made the threat. He could have hired someone."

"I'm not so sure," said Daeng. "The notes seem personal."

"Then a relative?" said Bruce.

"That's the most likely," said Siri. "A vengeful son . . . grandson."

"Then it could really be any one of the sixty-four journalists here," said Daeng.

"I can't interview all of them," said Phosy. "And don't forget, we only have threats so far. No dead bodies."

Daeng said it was superstition, but Siri believed that talking about the dead increased the odds of encountering them. Fate had a wicked sense of humor. He immediately reached for the amulet beneath his shirt, but it was too late. Standing beyond the half-closed shutter was Phosy's deputy, Captain Sihot.

"Evening, all," he said.

"What is it?" Phosy asked.

"There's been a . . . an accident," said the captain.

"Anybody . . . ?"

"Two," said Sihot.

"I knew it," said Siri.

"I'm working sixteen hour days already," said Phosy. "Can't you just take care of it?"

The captain thought about it.

"No," he said.

The morgue at Mahosot Hospital had been opened for the night. It had the smell of a plastic bag that had once contained stale pork sausages. The two bodies were laid out side-by-side on aluminum dollies. A half circle of non-matching people stood staring down at them. Siri recognized the new Minister of Justice, a short army general by the name of Sing; Comrade Sikum who had taken over as head of the Public Prosecution department following the execution of his predecessor; Bjorn, the disagreeable Swede from the previous evening; the Australian ambassador and his translator; and a man in short trousers with a fishing net over his shoulder. Finally, there was Comrade Intara, the head of protocol assigned to the Ministry of Foreign Affairs and the coordinator of the journalists' visit. It was he who spoke first.

"Phosy, you have to do something about this," he said.

"I don't yet know what this is," said Phosy.

"I think I can tell you," said the Swede. His fluent textbook Lao felt overly fussy but it was understandable to all but the Australian. Phosy stepped up to the tables. He recognized the two men: the journalist scholar Marvin and the photographer Jim.

"I met you with these two last night," he said. "What happened between then and now?"

"Like these two here, I passed up the opportunity to visit the model cooperative this morning," said Bjorn. "No offence to the minister or the Lao government. I had a migraine and one of my Swedish colleagues agreed to take notes for me. I woke up late but in time to catch these two at breakfast. They were excited because they had, what they called, an adventure planned. They said they'd met an old friend who could get them access to the old Silver City, the nickname of the American OSB storage facility out past That Luang. It's where the Americans left behind the things they didn't have time to smuggle over the border when they were thrown out in '75.

"Jim had heard a rumor that one of the CIA boys had a 1952 red Ferrari that was locked away in a warehouse in Silver City. That car has developed something of a cult reputation among the Western press. Did it or did it not exist? Their contact confirmed that it was still there. When I met them at breakfast they were on their way to see it."

"I have to point out," said the protocol officer, "that Silver City is out of bounds. Access to the area is forbidden. I cannot think how this mysterious contact was able to obtain keys for the sheds."

"It wasn't guarded?" Phosy asked.

"There was no need. As I say, it was locked."

"Right."

"Then how did they drown?" asked Siri. He was leaning against a cabinet behind the group. They all turned around.

"How do you know they drowned?" asked the minister.

"It's not raining and they're wet and they're dead," said Siri. "Didn't need a medical degree for that one. Of course, I suppose one of you might have hosed them down before putting them on display, but there are other little telltale signs like froth around the nose."

The minister coughed. "I don't think Mr. Bjorn needs to be here for the further discussion," he said. "Thank you for your evidence."

The Swede huffed, obviously angry to have been dismissed so curtly. He glared at Siri before leaving the room.

"Then my question is, at what stage of their adventure did they happen to drown?" said Phosy.

"It appears that not only was the Ferrari still there," said the prosecutor, "but there were several cans of fuel—enough to fill the tank."

"And despite all the limitations we placed on the visiting journalists," said the protocol man, "these two gung-ho cowboys decided to take their stolen car for a drive. This, I must say, is exactly why we were against inviting anyone from countries with overly free presses. They think they can say and do anything they please. They adhere to no discipline whatsoever."

The Australian ambassador continued to smile and nod even though his interpreter said nothing.

"I'm assuming they lost control and drove into a river," said Phosy.

"A fish pond," said the man with the net. "I was lucky I wasn't standing four meters to my left. I'd just cast my net, pulled the draw string and felt the tug of a carp when this red monster leaves the road, takes off from the bank and flies into the water."

"And . . . ?" said Phosy.

"That was it," said the fisherman.

"You didn't go and help?"

"Can't swim."

"How deep exactly is that fish pond of yours?" Siri asked.

"Three or four meters at its deepest, I'd say."

"Then why didn't they open the door and swim to the surface?" asked Siri.

"Don't know," said the fisherman. "I was expecting something like that, but all I see is bubbles. I go to the local cadre's house and tell him, and, well, here I am and here they are. All a bit of a funny day really."

"How did you get the bodies out?" asked Phosy.

"The cadre sent his boys down," said the fisherman. "They smashed the windshield and dragged them out. They couldn't get the doors open."

"Hmm," said Siri.

Phosy turned to Captain Sihot. "Is anyone raising the car?" he asked.

"No," said Sihot.

"Where did this happen?" asked Phosy.

"Kilometer forty just past Ban Donhai."

"Okay, I want you to go out there and organize that. Make sure the cadre doesn't claim it as a souvenir. Bring it back here."

"We should get Dtui to start on these two," said Siri.

"Start on what, exactly?" said the minister.

"Determining the cause of death," said Siri.

"Obviously they drowned," said the prosecutor.

"I agree," said Siri, "but unless they were on some crazed suicide pact, two healthy, mentally astute men do not drive at speed into a pond and sit there waiting to drown."

"Well, you and your people are certainly not performing an autopsy," said the minister.

"We're not?"

"They're foreign citizens," said the prosecutor. "They were driving an old, poorly maintained vehicle. They had a terrible accident caused by their recklessness and they died. The Australian government would like their citizens returned as soon as possible."

The ambassador's interpreter awoke from his mute slumber and hurriedly summarized the prior conversation. The ambassador affirmed that he would take responsibility for the repatriation of both bodies. All was settled. The minister ordered the bodies to be locked in the morgue freezer before collection the following day. The officials filed out of the room, leaving Siri and Phosy.

"Anything you can do without cutting them open?" Phosy asked.

"I could take some samples. Do some tests. But I don't actually know what I'm looking for. If they were poisoned or stoned out of their minds, I'd need to get to the stomach. I think the car will tell us more than the bodies at this point."

Phosy stared at the doctor. "The second letter," he said.

"I know."

"It said there may be one or two collateral victims who fall outside the parameters of his mission. Do you think this could be his demonstration? The mysterious killer showing us what he's capable of?"

"In that case he'd be someone with access to Silver City or friends in high enough places to get him into the warehouse," said Siri.

He looked down at the photojournalist. The poor man had survived wars, yet here he was defeated in peacetime.

"Last night he said something about meeting up with an old acquaintance," said Phosy. "Marvin didn't want him to talk about it. I wonder if it was the friend who got them access to the warehouse. And I wonder if it's the person we're looking for. Perhaps he wasn't expecting anyone to recognize him, and he had to silence the two of them before his cover was blown."

"That's an awful lot of wondering," said Siri.

"He asked about you."

"Who did?"

"Jim. He said one of the Swedes was looking for you."

"That couldn't have been our man," said Siri. "He'd already found us."

"Perhaps someone was trying to warn you."

"This is too much conjecture for one old fellow to take on. Why didn't you mention this when we met today?"

"I don't know. You kept disappearing. I didn't have a chance."

Siri walked around the dollies and went over the chain of events in his mind.

"What do you suppose the Swede was doing here this evening?" asked Siri.

"Witness? Apart from the mysterious contact person, I suppose he was the last to see these two alive. He was the only one who knew what their plan was."

"But how would any of this crowd know that unless he volunteered the information himself?"

"I'll find out who it was that invited him," said Phosy.

"All right. But first things first. I'll start work on these two and see what I can find without leaving wounds. You follow up with the Ferrari and get someone to interview the other journalists. It won't be easy but see if you can find someone who hates me."

CHAPTER TEN
Hanoi, 1972

I remember the night of Hanoi Jane very clearly because it followed the first afternoon of Hanoi Hilton Henry. Both of these events, in their own way, made me think about misperception. I'd been without Boua for seven years already, but being without her was very much the same as being with her during those final years. She'd taken on the burden of hammering communism into the heads of the peasantry. She'd begun to show the signs of addiction. She'd never taken drugs, but she was so high on righteousness she could no longer listen to those of us who were witnessing her mental decline. She was untreatable. She was a total fool for a hopeless cause. Her suicide was not the most tragic event in her life.

The war we thought we'd already won raged on. But now the enemy no longer shouted insults in French from the trenches. Overnight the Tricolor had rearranged its colors, and we awoke to the sounds of Janice Joplin and The Doors. And the weapons were grander and more efficient, the budget ballooned and the motive for killing us was no longer merely to pillage. They were here to stop us reds from taking over the world. We all knew, of course, that if our new American minders hadn't stepped up to the plate, we would have flooded the planet with failed cooperatives and incompetent officials. But we had a weapon more effective than the B-52s, which could level a village in tenths of a second, and more slick than Agent Orange, which could strip a hillside and anyone standing on it, and more cunning than the bombies that burrowed into the soil and would blow the legs off buffalo and inquisitive children for decades to come.

We had heroin.

Boua wasn't the only one in Vietnam who'd lost all sense of right and wrong. My surgeon friend in Paris had been right. By late '71 there were already 560,000 heroin addicts in the US. Most of the product came via the Golden Triangle of Burma, Laos and Thailand. Seventy-five percent of urban crime was fueled by this addiction, and Nixon had called for a war on drugs. The CIA Indochinese opium policy had found its way back home.

A quarter of American troops in Vietnam were using heroin. Thousands were addicted, and the bad news for the gentlemen in Congress and the generals in their Saigon offices was that heroin made more sense to the reluctant soldiers than they did. It was a universally available brain tranquilizer. Any soldier could buy it on the roadside near the bases where young boys sold it along with snacks and soft drinks and cigarettes. The Vietnamese army was shipping and distributing it so nobody was afraid of getting caught. We in the north were being bombed to hell and back, but we were defeating the enemy one brain cell at a time.

That didn't make much of a difference to us on the ground in those days. I don't know how many young men and women I'd put back together as best I could. I'd cried with each failure. I'd drunk with officers who would be dead the next morning. Ours wasn't an army of guerilla soldiers. These were shopkeepers and farmers and teachers in uniform, and they were no less terrified of being in the jungle than the young American boys from the Midwest. But whoever it was there in the rain and the muck, they asked the same question. Down through the elephant mahouts of Hannibal, the foot soldiers of Kublai Khan, the Germans and English in the mud of the Somme—they all wanted to know the same thing: "What in God's name are we doing here?" But no matter what god you asked, you'd not get your answer because no god has ever seen any sense in war.

Which is all a long detour on the way to telling my story. You've probably worked out how it started. I was sitting at a table in front of the Metropole Hotel, which had recently rechristened the Reunification. There weren't many roadside bars in Hanoi back then. North Vietnamese had better things to do than lounge and booze. But there were some. There was a tourist trade of sorts. Curious foreigners came to see what it was like to party in a war zone. There was the Vietnam-American Friendship Association for one, shipping in anyone willing to pay their exorbitant prices. So there were cafés and restaurants and the odd bar, and there was me at the only occupied table at the Metropole that morning.

"Anyone sitting there?" came a voice I'd been expecting to hear.

I turned to see Civilai in full North Vietnamese Army dress uniform. His hair had retreated even further from his brow and he looked, I don't know, hardened. In his left hand, he held a rattan mango-plucker, which, from a very long distance, might have looked like a tennis racquet. I stood, kissed his cheeks and shook his right hand.

"That's the best you can do?" I asked.

"Do you know how hard it is to find a tennis racquet in war-torn Hanoi?" he asked.

"Sit down before someone asks you to harvest mangoes," I said.

He laughed and sat and looked around for a waiter. There was a greater chance of seeing a penguin stroll along Ly Thai To.

"How long are you in town?" he asked.

"Just long enough to pick up supplies. I head back to Vieng Xai on Thursday."

"Then I'm lucky I got to see you," he said.

"Always a pleasure. Why are you dressed like a postman?"

"It's . . ."

A waitress, obviously attracted by the uniform, came running out of the hotel. She had a permanently troubled scowl but pretty eyes. Civilai ordered four glasses of Cognac. She only had rum. He ordered Bacardi. She only had Saint James. He asked about beer. It wasn't cold. We settled for Saint James but ordered cola to take the taste away. That was warm too. The lengths we went to for a little alcohol buzz.

"And?" I said.

"And what?"

"The uniform."

"Right. It's the latest from Peking. Our allies want us to look stylish at the handover ceremony."

"Who's handing over what?" I asked.

"They're convinced that, with all the anti-American war demonstrations in the States and the obscene amount of money they're spending on eradicating us, it'll be over by next year."

"Haven't they been saying that for fifteen years?"

"Yes, but now we have uniforms so it's serious."

"Marvelous. I look forward to it."

The troubled waitress returned without a tray for some reason. They'd probably been requisitioned for the war effort. Instead she nuzzled the four full rum glasses, one bottle of cola and an ice bucket against her modest breasts. The bucket contained actual ice, which surprised us given that nothing else was cold. But we didn't bother to ask why. Those were hardship days. In her mouth she had the bill, which she handed to me. Perhaps the man dressed as a civilian was expected to pay for the soldier out of gratitude. Civilai grabbed it from me.

"Had a bit of luck in a card game last night," he said.

I didn't put up a fight. Even with ice and cola, the drinks were as bad as we'd expected. People passing in front of the hotel looked at us as if we were actors in some production that didn't need a camera.

"So," I said.

"Yes?"

"Any luck?"

"Six months since our last meeting and you want to start our reunion with a favor?"

"Yes. Did you do it?"

"In a way," he said. "But there's a catch."

"Any catches are acceptable if she said yes."

"She said yes."

I was so happy. I'd never wanted more to throw myself

at Civilai and rain kisses down on him. Naturally, I didn't. I merely nodded and said, "That's nice."

"But the catch is a rather large one," he said.

"Do I have to perform erotic acts with a member of the central committee?"

"Not unless you want to."

"Then there's nothing I wouldn't agree to," I told him. "Name it."

"Four American prisoners are to be released before the end of the year as a gesture of peace."

"After years of torture?"

"We prefer to call it 'custody with discipline.' In most cases it was just confinement. But over the years there may have been the odd renegade camp director with sadomasochistic tendencies. And there were factions that kept their own downed pilots like pets. It was hard to monitor all the jails."

"How long were these four locked up?"

"The longest was seven years."

"Seven years in a bamboo cage?"

"After a brief probationary period, they were all moved to one- or two-star accommodation. Some were quite comfortable."

It was one of my many sore points about our Viet Minh neighbors.

"Civilai," I said, "imprisonment should be punishment enough. Anything else is just gratuitous. Cruelty makes us look ignorant."

Civilai finished his first glass. The rum tasted better the more we drank.

"I don't want to get tangled up in this discussion again," said Civilai.

"Your average downed pilot has nothing more to tell you than—"

"Siri!"

". . . than you already know," I said.

"They've been bombing us for fifteen years," said Civilai. "Them and their Hmong puppets in Laos. They fly in. They press their button. They kill. They go home, have a nice meal and get drunk. They wake up the next day with a hangover and do it all over again. With their technology, it's like spraying ants. They're up there in their airplanes, and they have a pleasant flight over unspoiled jungle scenery, and they locate the village they've been instructed to liquefy, and they do as they're told. There's no accountability. They switch off all human dignity. When we shoot one down and a man survives, he carries the responsibility of all those who came and went before him. He needs time to be aware of what he's done. We give him time to think until he understands that it's not about targets; it's about families."

"So you want me to meet these four and assess whether they feel enough remorse?"

"No, I want you to go into each cell with a small medical team and make sure they're healthy. Treat whatever needs treating. Fix whatever's broken. And put together a brief medical report for them to take home. But while you're examining them, I want you to be yourself and joke and laugh and listen to their stories."

"Isn't it a bit late for that?" I asked.

"For what?"

"Basic love and kindness."

"It's never too late," he said. "But if you think it's too demanding . . ."

"You'd really blackmail me?"

"You said there's nothing you wouldn't agree to."

He gave me one of his looks and I gave him one of mine.

"I'll do it," I said. "But only because I've been looking forward to this evening for weeks. If I have to play Tom Dooley to earn it, I'll play the part. When do I meet the pilots?"

"Whenever you're free. They're at Clinic Twelve."

"Really?" I said. "The clinic behind the fuel depot?"

"That's the one."

"Do you think the B-52 pilots know that's where we're keeping them?"

"They should. We've leaked enough information about their whereabouts and we weren't subtle. Even the CIA should have understood."

We worked our way down our second glasses of rum. I could feel my intestines smolder.

"You do remember I don't speak English?" I said.

"Don't worry. It's all taken care of," he said. "And one of the pilots speaks Lao."

"How did that happen?"

"He was held by a militia group in Bolikhamxai for over five years. He learned it from his captors. See how accommodating we can be to our guests? Free language classes."

We decided against ordering another drink as I had to stock up on medications and that involved getting things signed. Those Vietnamese loved to get things signed. We stood to leave.

"Have you got time for a movie or two before I go back?" I asked.

Hanoi had an impressive network of living-room film

nights back then. Nobody dared congregate in numbers in a cinema for obvious reasons. So some bright spark had set up a smuggling route to bring up movie reels from Saigon. And they all had Vietnamese subtitles courtesy of the CIA propagandists. They had a department just working on translations. Nice of them.

"I'll see what's playing," he said. "And tonight, I want you on your best behavior."

"I can't think of what you mean," I said.

"Good-looking unattached older man, together with a strange woman in a hotel room. I'm afraid the temptation might be too much for her."

He handed me the mango plucker. "Here, take this. You might have to fight her off."

I still have that mango plucker somewhere.

I decided to get the airmen out of my schedule as quickly as I could, so I arranged to be there that afternoon. I arrived at Clinic Twelve at 2 P.M. The medical team Civilai promised comprised an unsmiling but naturally beautiful nurse in military uniform, an armed guard for our protection and a boy. He couldn't have been more than fourteen years old.

"Comrade Doctor," he said, "I'm Hung Lan, your interpreter."

"Hello, Little Comrade," I said. "And how did you get stuck with this job?"

"I excelled in languages in elementary school," he said. "I was recruited by the National Institute of Interpreters."

"I'm impressed," I said. "But aren't you a little young to be fraternizing with the enemy?"

"I am qualified and competent," he said. "But I admit

I was surprised to be chosen for this important mission ahead of my seniors."

I wasn't. This had Civilai written all over it: smart kid, beautiful nurse, senior Lao surgeon with a great sense of humor. He was showcasing communism. When the fliers were back home in front of the cameras they'd fondly remember the last people they met in Hanoi and forget the seven years of misery.

"Perhaps they aren't all bad," they'd say.

The nurse gave me the results of the pilots' blood, urine and stool tests. As you'd expect after years in the jungle there was a parasite orgy going on inside them. According to their medical history, two had made it through malaria. Three had survived dengue. One was currently still enjoying its effects. There was diarrhea and skin disease but, as far as I could tell from the records, nothing terminal. Or, at least nothing that would kill them in the next three weeks. And that was evidently our goal, to get them safely into the hands of American doctors who we could later blame if the pilots all keeled over on US soil. I doubted they'd ever be free of nightmares even when the physical symptoms were taken care of.

I gave each of the young men a thorough physical, noted breaks and bruises and sprains and scars the way a car rental shop might note down scratches and dents. The first three pilots were respectful and displayed an unexpected sense of fun. They joked through young Hung Lan who seemed more than capable of finding the right linguistic tones and textures. I bantered in battle-hardened black humor, and they responded with anecdotes from years behind bars. They weren't yet confident enough to criticize or blame. They'd start a story then stop, shake their heads, smile and think of something nice to say about their captors. They were still in enemy territory.

I tried to imagine what years in a cell might do to me. Would I become some other Siri? One that I didn't like? And how would I stop my mind from crusting over? What would I have to do to hang on to my memories, my knowledge, my sanity? And I'm sure it was that doubt about my own self-control that led me to leave Henry till last. They'd warned me about him. He'd spent five-and-a-half years in a bamboo cage in a remote, inaccessible area in the north of Laos. He'd been flying air support for a bombing mission over Vietnam, and his aircraft had been hit by random small-arm fire that brought him down. He broke his arm when he parachuted into the jungle and hit his head. He walked for a week, disoriented, ill, fatigued and was finally captured by a rebel militia unit. These were no regular PL troops—more a band of hill tribe bandits who sold themselves to whichever army offered the best deal.

The standing order from central command with regard to captured prisoners of war was to send them on to Vietnam via established prison camps, eventually to end up in the Hanoi prison network—known by foreigners as the Hanoi Hilton. But Henry never left the rebel camp. The commander of the group, a battered warrior of many campaigns named Yiw, was proud of his pet airman. He invited friends over to see him and poke sticks at him through the bars of his cage. He humiliated the American and starved and punished him when he thought his prisoner was showing disrespect. He was clearly certifiable.

But when Commander Yiw was off in the mountains, Henry befriended his captors, mostly young boys charged with preventing his escape. He learned Lao from them.

They brought him herbal medicines and natural poultices and tended his wounds until the next assault. They were every bit as afraid of their leader as Henry was, but they felt sorry for the man in the cage. Perhaps the most remarkable thing about this story was that Henry wrote a book during his years in captivity. The guards found him paper and pencils and he documented his experiences. When Yiw was in the camp, the manuscript lived in a plastic bag buried in the dirt beneath Henry's cage.

Yiw was killed in battle, probably no less than he deserved, and his second-in-command adhered to the protocol of the Pathet Lao and sent Henry to Hanoi. His only possessions were his dog tags, a shirt and shorts, a bamboo flute and reading glasses, all in one cloth shoulder bag. And sewn into the lining of that bag was his completed manuscript. The only reason I knew all this was that Hung Lan, my interpreter, had read it.

During his four months at the Hanoi Hilton, Henry had visitors. Some were priests who had refused to join the Catholic exodus south. Some were fellow American servicemen who had repented for their sins and apologized for their actions against the Viet Minh. But some were tourists. Visiting incarcerated POWs was on the itinerary. Curious foreigners were escorted to the jails where they could ask questions and take photographs. And it was to one of these visitors that Henry entrusted his manuscript. The tourist, afraid she might be arrested, owned up to the collusion and handed the script to the tour guide. Hung Lan was asked to read and summarize the text. He told me the highlights. It would have made a splendid movie.

I'd expected Henry to be friendly like the others. But he was not. He refused to speak English through the interpreter. It felt odd to be conversing with him in Lao. He had a strong, confusing accent and wasn't nearly as fluent as he thought he was. It shouldn't have worried me. He was a foreigner who had gone to the trouble of learning my language, and he'd been through a horrific experience, but I felt uncomfortable with him. I didn't want to dislike him, but I found it impossible to engage. And there were other things that worried me.

Despite the conditions he'd lived in for so long, he'd somehow avoided most of the parasites currently gorging on his countrymen. He'd had a bout of dengue some time back, and there was some liver damage that may have been a result of hepatitis, but apart from that he was in pretty good shape. He even had a belly.

"So what are you saying?" he asked.

"Just observations from the point of view of a doctor," I said. "I've always been fascinated by how different people react to hostile environments. As a foreigner, you wouldn't have any natural defenses against conditions in the jungle. Yet you've somehow been able to counter all the usual enemies of the human body. How did you fight off insects and treat their bites? How did you make sure the water you drank was decontaminated? How did you survive?"

My medical team sat around us in the cell obviously frustrated that they had no idea what was being said. I was already fond of Hung Lan—he's probably a rich property tycoon by now—but I liked being free of my interpreter.

"You do know I don't have to answer any of these questions?" said Henry.

"I know."

"But I tell you, Older Brother, I earned the respect of those savages."

I wasn't that fond of being his older brother, and I wondered whether I'd be able to respect anyone who called me a savage. He launched off into a narrative I felt he'd practiced beforehand.

"Despite my horrible injuries, when they found me I put up a fight," he said. "I took them on, hand-to-hand, fought to what I thought would be my death. Once they had me in the cage I constantly tried to escape. Bravery was what jungle fighters expected and respected. They saw me as a real man. They wanted to be like me. I could tell they had no respect for that bastard Yiw. He was cruel to everyone. So when he was away, they treated my wounds using natural remedies that had been passed down through generations. They gave me medicine and balm to prevent illnesses and keep the mosquitoes at bay. I learned their language very quickly. I have a knack. They were in awe. Soon, I was like their brother. They loved me. But they were scared shitless by what the commander might do if he found out we were allies. So I put up with it, played along so my captors wouldn't get into trouble. It's all in the book."

"Right," I said. "The book. You don't seem very upset to have lost your manuscript."

He winked. I had a problem with winking too. I took it to mean he had a plan B. I wondered if he'd left a copy with his close friends at the border. Great foresight, that, to make two copies of a manuscript written in pencil in extreme conditions. I assumed the village didn't have a Xerox. Either way, he seemed very confident.

I conducted my standard physical tests while he described some of the torture he'd endured. He had a number of recent bruises that he put down to "misunderstandings" with the guards at the Hilton although nobody recalled having cause to beat him up. His broken arm had healed beautifully, and he had a messy scar on his head that would have benefited from sutures that were obviously not available. A torn ligament that he said was caused by being dragged behind a buffalo cart by the ankle had left him with a limp. I had no X-ray to check that. Suddenly, and unexpectedly, he switched to English.

Hung Lan jumped to his feet. "You're going to pay for this," he said.

"For what?" I asked through the interpreter.

"The traumas your people have caused me," he said.

"We're letting you go," I reminded him.

"So?"

"So, I suggest that until you're on the plane, you feign a little gratitude and save your complaints. It's not too late to give your ticket to someone else."

He gave me a dirty look and in him I saw the ugly Dr. Siri I'd probably have become after five years in captivity. I'd probably be intolerable after five months. When we left the room, I spoke of my concerns to my team and assigned them some tasks. I had time before my date that evening to pay visits to two old friends.

Bao Ninh was at his desk at the department of statistics at Hanoi University. He'd been collating data since the beginning of the war. The Vietnamese loved collating and recording. He had records on everything from pelicans being shot accidently by antiaircraft fire to tanks sinking without a trace beneath the mud of the monsoons.

From there I still had time to stop by the office of General Xuan of the People's Army of Vietnam. Being a field surgeon, I often had the good fortune of saving the lives of important people. Xuan was in his office and alive only due to the fact that I'd removed half a ton of shrapnel from his chest. He was a man who greatly appreciated being alive. We shared a jug of coffee and some reminiscences, and I left him with homework I knew would be completed thoroughly.

I returned to my dorm, changed into clothes that looked exactly the same as the ones I'd taken off but were cleaner and took a bicycle *samlor* back to the Reunification. I was an hour early. The interior bar had come alive since my earlier visit. If I'd taken a photograph I doubt anyone in the world would have guessed the setting was a bar in a city that was about to be bombed to oblivion. Attempting to describe the international crowd there that evening would have been like identifying extras in a Fellini movie. I wanted to ask where all the freaks had come from—how they'd got there—why they'd bothered. But I had to rehearse my speech. I had my notes on a napkin. I didn't know how long we'd be alone together. She spoke French, I heard, so we could communicate without an interpreter. But I wanted to hit the right tone. It went something like this:

"Boys in their twenties in America are calling themselves 'veterans.' I'm sixty-eight. I've spent thirty-odd years fighting for something that I have eventually come to believe in. That, is what a veteran is. Those boys returned with the medals they'd been awarded for being wounded and they called our war 'The biggest nothing in American history.' And that hurt and offended me. You made a one-act appearance in a fifty-act play, and you killed more of us than were murdered in the entire century before and you called it nothing. And when it's all over for you, when the white-water flow of money abates and your leaders find something sexier to support, we'll still be here fighting for our lives against the next tyrant, or poverty, or nature. And by then you will have forgotten us. That's what I want your Hollywood to tell everyone. Tell them it's only *nothing* for you. For us, it's survival and hope."

That was going to be my big finish. I could perhaps squeeze out a tear or two and make my voice crinkle a bit and do my bulldog long-jowled expression. She'd give me a glass of whisky to make me feel better and . . . well, as Civilai said, one thing would doubtless lead to another.

The wobbly bottomed secretary found me in reception and led me up the staircase to the fourth floor and what they jokingly referred to as the "royal suite." A queue of ten to twelve people stood at the end of the corridor, and the secretary placed me at its tail. But before I'd taken a step forward, the hotel siren sounded. Some in the queue panicked and ran. Others, like me, held their ground. There was a policy for air raids. We'd all been shown the nearest bunkers and been directed to areas like schools or hospitals that were supposedly only hit by accident. There were a lot of accidents those days.

And then the door to the suite was thrown open, and a small scrum of people directed by a hotel official passed us in the hall headed for safety. Jane Fonda was at the rear, propped up by a large man in a baseball cap. She seemed smaller than I remembered her from *Cat Ballou.* She was wearing jeans and a sweatshirt rather than her silver space suit, and her hair was mousy brown. In her natural state she was even more naked than Barbarella. I noticed she held a ballpoint pen in her hand. She spotted me at the end of the queue and pulled away from her minder. I was holding the serviette with my speech notes. She smiled, took it from me, turned it over and signed it. She smiled again, said something I didn't understand and followed the entourage to the hotel bomb shelter.

There were no bombs that night. They'd be raining down in force soon enough during Operation Linebacker II, which made a mess of the northern capital and killed a lot of people. We all remarked later how limited the imaginations were of the men who came up with the name. Surely they couldn't have run out of sports references. But Jane and her team left the next morning without my message to Hollywood. I had her autograph and I cherished it until one day when I had the flu and thought it was a tissue. It was the nearest I'd been to a movie star. She'd smiled at me.

So, as there'd been no romance in the royal suite and I still had a tank of adrenaline, I put all my energy into my next interview with Henry. I seem to recall there was me, Civilai, General Xuan, the child interpreter Hung Lan and a CIA liaison person who was supervising the orderly release of his pilots. I can't remember his name. Two guards escorted Henry to the canteen. Something in the way he walked told me he was confident this was to be his release day. We sat him down and he smiled only at the CIA guy, who didn't smile back. As I was technically the lead attorney, I spoke to the prisoner in Lao, and Xuan translated into Vietnamese, which Mr. CIA seemed to understand. It was messy but it worked.

"Henry," I said. "I've been learning a lot about you."

He looked confused.

"I was able to trace the records back to the day you crashed," I continued.

"June 1966 flying an F-100," said Henry, smiling.

"They never did find your plane," I said.

"Lot of jungle out there," he said. "It may never be found."

"Perhaps because we're looking in the wrong place," I said.

"Once my instruments short-circuited there was no way of being sure where I was," he said. "Like I say, there's a lot of unoccupied land out there."

"Lot of river too," I said.

He looked at me for the first time.

"What's that supposed to mean?" he said.

"It means that a North Vietnamese radar unit plotted your course that day and had you a hundred kilometers off your designated route on the west of Bolikhamxai. You were over the Mekong when the blip disappeared."

Henry looked at the men in front of him and realized for the first time that this was not a handover committee.

"What is this?" he said.

"Your plane wreckage was not found in the jungles of Bolikhamxai because you put it down in the river a hundred kilometers west."

"Bullshit," said Henry.

"It's undoubtedly still there," I said. "But we'll have to wait for the war to end before we go scavenging. You parachuted, not into hostile Laos, but, as you planned, into Thailand."

Henry spoke not one more word that day. He just glared angrily into my eyes as I untangled his lies.

"You'd had enough of this war and the mindless killing," I said. "And you wanted to get out of it. We can all understand that. And, what better place to escape a war than Thailand? Pretty women. Low prices. Nobody asking questions. I'm not sure where you'd put down the roots to this new life, but it's unlikely you'd go to Udon Thani with its secret American airbases we all know about. You'd avoid big cities. There was always a chance you'd be recognized in the bars. I'm guessing you buried your parachute near the river, changed into civvies and jumped on a local bus to somewhere like Ubon Ratchathani. You had money saved—probably already set up a Thai bank account. And it seemed back then you could probably live off your savings forever.

"Not a lot of difference between northeastern Thai language and Lao," I said. "You probably married a local girl who taught you the language in a feminine kind of way, and you got confident because everyone understood you. But you aren't that good. There are differences between Isan Thai and hill-tribe Lao. In fact, I doubt you'd find a band of hill-tribe rebels fluent enough in Lao to be able to teach you anything. Yours is the Lao of Thai bars and yours is the body of the soft life. Whatever maladies you picked up were treated at the local hospital. Those last bruises and scrapes were probably thanks to you running head first into a wall or punching yourself in the face."

The early evening mosquitoes were flocking around the onlookers planning a sundown assault, but the audience was rapt and I was the star. Nobody else spoke.

"In the beginning, I imagine you had no intention of returning to the West," I said. "You were safe and you were happy. You had your secret Nirvana, but you were young and illegal. And there was a world out there you hadn't seen. You became dissatisfied, and your money ran out. Your banana farm and your lychee plantation and your pig pens or whatever you thought might make your fortune, they all failed and you were left dissatisfied and frustrated. You needed to get back to America. But how do you do that when everyone believes you're dead? The Central Command listed you as MIA. There was only one way to come back with dignity. You'd read about other US fliers imprisoned for years. The ones that made it back home had options and probably received a pension. But you had a bigger idea. You wrote about your fictional incarceration in a full-length manuscript. You could see movie and TV rights at the end of the tunnel.

"Someone you met in the north of Thailand knew about a gang of thugs on the Lao side that rented themselves out as mercenaries for the PL. My friend the general here knows about them. Their commander had recently shot himself whilst as drunk as a cellar rat, and his gang was in need of guidance and money. So you headed up there with your manuscript and you made a deal. You handed over what little money you had left and promised them a share of the fortune you'd be making from your book. All they had to do was say they'd kept you a prisoner for almost six years under orders from their boss. Then they march you to the nearest legitimate PL camp and drop you off. It was a brilliant plan. You knew the Viet Minh were bringing all the MIA together in Hanoi for an eventual handover. What were a few months of discomfort in the Hanoi Hilton compared to the alternatives?

"The book was a clever idea too. You were aware it might have been discovered but if it was, it would make you stand out from the other prisoners. Perhaps the Vietnamese would feel remorse for your cruel treatment over the border. Perhaps they'd respect you for your many attempts to escape. If it was successfully smuggled out by the tourist it would have been an immediate hit Stateside. But if it wasn't, that was fine too because—and I'm guessing this last part—your wife had the original, probably resplendent with dirt and bloodstains. All she had to do was post it anonymously to the US embassy in Bangkok with a note that a deserter had brought it to Thailand. You couldn't fail either way."

We'd left Henry alone in a cell that morning. He'd been exposed as a fraud so all of his dreams of back pay and compensation and book and film royalties, of one day getting a visa for his Thai wife, of being repatriated as a hero, that was all gone, thanks to me. The Vietnamese and the CIA fellow patted me on the back as we walked away, and I might have gloated just a little and Henry probably noticed that.

Civilai and I sat on the front porch of a small house over in Ba Din that evening talking about Hanoi Hilton Henry. We were waiting for a showing of *The French Connection* with subtitles. It was R rated but we had IDs.

"Why did you first doubt him?" Civilai asked.

"I don't know," I said. "There's what you see and what you perceive. Jane's perception was that I was an elderly fan desperate for an autograph."

"Which wasn't so far off the mark."

"I was more perceptive. I sensed there was something wrong with Henry. Unlike you in your penthouse suite and endless rounds of cocktail receptions here in the capital, I've been living in the jungle on and off for the past twenty years. Nature leaves scars. Some medical conditions are unavoidable, especially if you're in the open air and unprotected. But he looked too . . . too hale and hearty. If he'd been tortured as he claimed, why were there so few historical wounds? And some lies are obviously lies. His arm had been broken as he said but not from parachuting from a plane six years ago and left untreated. There was little evidence of trauma. The bone had clearly healed when he was a child and had continued to grow. The break was at least twenty years old. It was arrogant of him to think we wouldn't have qualified people here who'd notice things like that. I thought if he could lie about that, what else was he lying about? The liver disease could have been a result of hepatitis, but I have a nose for alcoholism."

"It takes one to know one, little brother."

I didn't think a lot about Henry for the next few months because I was too busy getting bombed by Nixon. Christmas was celebrated in style with the heaviest bombing raids since World War Two. Hanoi took the brunt of it. For the first time, the hospitals had more civilians being put back together than military personnel. There was something desperate about the attacks, like a boxer down on points in the last round coming into the ring with a machete. And it did promise to be the beginning of the end. I was back in Hanoi for New Year's, and I found a Christmas card in my mail pouch. I have no idea how it got there. It began pleasantly enough with the words *Season's Greetings* in glitter on the front. But when I opened it, the message became a little less agreeable:

To you and your loved ones. With nothing but unnatural death to look forward to. I shall kill you all. I'll be seeing you, Siri Paiboun. I promise you that.

CHAPTER ELEVEN
Mindless Assassin of the Century

"So, there are our three top contenders for mindless assassin of the century," said Daeng. "If the line in the first note, *I have already deleted one of your darlings*, refers to your lovely Boua, that would rule out contestant number three. Boua died in '65. You destroyed Henry's life in '72. Have you had any other loved ones bumped off since then?"

"Not including dogs?" asked Siri.

They heard a mournful howl from the street.

"No," said Daeng.

"Then I can't think of any," he said.

"What about the bread woman?"

Siri stared at his wife. They were together at a table, straightening aluminum spoons and forks. The cheap rubbish from China tended to curl up after a few months of sweaty palms.

"The bread woman?"

"You should have known I'd find out."

"What's to find out? We had one date and that was a disaster."

"You liked her enough to ask her out. Tell me about her."

"Really? All right. The bread woman, a.k.a. Lah, is, as far as I know, alive and well and baking baguettes with her sons. When I was still at Mahosot, Civilai and I would get our lunch from her cart and sit and eat on a log beside the river. Damn, I should really go and see how Civilai's doing. He's been bedridden for two days. I'll go in the morning and force some doctoring on him. I know if it was serious, Dr. Porn would contact us; she's looking after him, but a second opinion can't hurt."

"We can take him a bottle of something to cheer him up," said Daeng.

"Did Phosy say anything else about the journalists?" Siri asked.

"He ruled out the two Poles because they didn't arrive in the country until two days after we found Ugly's letter. And the Russian died of old age six months ago. He was replaced at the last second by someone much younger."

"That only leaves the East German," said Siri.

"Phosy talked to him. He was certainly in Hanoi when you were there and you might have met up with him in the caves at Vieng Xai. He wrote some pieces from there, being careful not to give away the location."

"Anything about me?"

"He claims never to have heard of you."

"Then we have to learn as much as we can from our two dead ones," said Siri. "Apart from the fact that they unquestionably died of drowning, I didn't see any signs of violence. The tall one hit his head, probably on the dashboard. That might have been enough to knock him out. There were no seatbelts. The photographer's airways were clogged. I'm guessing he suffered from allergies. I doubt that was serious enough to kill him."

Daeng looked up and sniffed.

"What is that smell?" she asked.

"I'm boiling chicken bones in the back garden in a tin drum," he said.

"What on earth for?"

"I'm afraid I cannot disclose that information."

"If you are planning to serve them with my noodles, it's very much my business."

"Goodness me, no. You can't eat them. They're old."

"Where do you get old chicken bones?"

"At the dump," said Siri. "Ugly dug them up for me. He's a natural. We managed to recover some thirty kilograms of the things."

"Thirty . . . ? That's disgusting. How did you get them back here?"

"I hired a bicycle *samlor*. It stank the thing up completely. It'll have to be fumigated. I had to ride the bicycle along behind him with a peg on my nose. I gave him a nice tip."

"And you're really not going to tell me what it's all about?"

"A man has to have a hobby that's all his own, Daeng. Can you watch the drum for me? Keep the fire going for another couple of hours?"

"Why? Where are you going?"

"I told Phosy I'd take a look at the red Ferrari," said Siri. "It just got back."

The Ferrari had finally been dragged from the fish pond and towed to the city behind a tractor. It was parked looking a little sorry for itself in the police parking lot. Phosy and Bruce were standing in the shade of a maiden's breast sandalwood tree when Siri arrived on his bicycle, followed shortly by Ugly. Captain Sihot was standing guard.

"Sorry I'm late," said Siri. "Bending spoons. Boiling bones. You know how it is. Time got away from me."

Phosy and Bruce stepped up to the car.

"We've been over it once," said Phosy. "We just needed your coroner's insight to take another look."

"Has anyone interfered with it since it went in the water?" Siri asked.

"No," said Sihot. "I accompanied it all the way home. Nobody's been anywhere near it apart from our police mechanic, and I was with him the whole time."

"And what was his conclusion?" asked Siri.

"He said the brakes and the steering were in great shape for an old car. Somebody obviously loved it and took care of it. He said he doubted it left the road due to some mechanical malfunction. He did offer a sort of explanation as to why the two of them couldn't get out. The lock latches were rusty. You couldn't open the doors from the inside. You'd have to wind down the windows and open them from outside. But with the pressure on the glass from the water it would have been hard to open them."

"Were the latches tampered with?" Siri asked.

"Didn't look like it, Doctor. Just natural rusting over time."

"I doubt anyone could have planned to have the car leave the road exactly where it did," said Bruce.

"That's right," said Sihot. "It's got all the signs of an accident."

"But what made the driver leave the road at all?" said Phosy.

"Drugs?" said Siri. "Booze? Speeding? Asleep at the wheel? Without an autopsy, we'll never really know."

"Was there anything inside?" Bruce asked.

"There's a bag behind the driver's seat," said Sihot. "We didn't touch it. There were beer bottles on the floor, so it's pretty obvious they were drinking. I think the driver just lost control."

"They seemed to have a very impressive tolerance for alcohol from my memory," said Phosy.

While he fished out the bag, Siri walked around to the front of the Ferrari and looked through the broken windshield.

"That's odd," he said. "There must be a dozen mimosa leis hanging from the rearview mirror."

"What's odd about that?" said Bruce. "A couple of old Lao hands want to go for a drive in the countryside. They remember the old days when everyone hung flowers inside their vehicles to keep the road gods happy."

"But that's exactly it," said Siri. "The old days. There's nothing on the road but military and government vehicles these days. Nobody sells leis anymore. Where would they get them from?"

"Temples still make them for festivals," said Sihot.

"When there's a fair they prepare them but not before. They don't have spare leis laying around just on the off chance someone wants one."

"The journalist welcoming committee," said Bruce. "They handed out leis at the airport."

"That was over a week ago," said Siri. "These are still pretty fresh."

"Why are we so hung up about flowers?" asked Sihot.

"It's called brainstorming," said Siri. "You just say things for no apparent reason until you accidentally stumble upon a truth. It's like politics."

Phosy had recovered a black camera bag from behind the seat. He got into a coughing fit from the fumes.

"Sihot, don't let anyone smoke around here. The interior stinks of petrol. The tank must be cracked."

"I'll get the mechanic to empty it," said Sihot. "Can't afford to let petrol evaporate in this day and age. It's hard to come by."

Phosy laid the bag on the ground and unzipped it. It contained three very expensive looking lenses, several sodden packets of film and one plastic bag with a day's supply of marijuana with soggy papers.

"These boys were serious," said Bruce.

"It was a bit early in the day to get stoned," said Phosy. "There's no paraphernalia in the front seat. Just the beer bottles."

"And more important than what's in the bag," said Siri, "is what isn't in the bag."

"Right," said Phosy. "I doubt a photojournalist would go on a trip without his camera. He'd be prepared for unusual sights. He'd have it with him on his lap or over his shoulder."

"The cadre swore his boys didn't take anything from the car or go through the foreigners' stuff," said Sihot. "But I'll go see him again. Those professional cameras are expensive. A year's salary for some of them."

"Have them go back into the pond too," said Phosy. "See if anything got dropped when they dragged out the bodies."

With cloths over their mouths and noses they conducted one more thorough search of the car interior but found nothing of any relevance. They agreed that the most-likely cause was that they'd been drinking and lost control of the car. Phosy drove Sihot to the station and took Bruce home. The Aussie had moved out of the guesthouse and was living with a relative until he could find a place of his own. It was on the way. He asked to be dropped off at the end of the lane so he could get some snacks at the roadside stall. The chief inspector offered to put Siri's bicycle in the back of the jeep and give him a ride to the restaurant but was reminded that Ugly wouldn't be able to keep up with them. And, besides, it was a cool, overcast evening, and he could take a leisurely ride along the river.

As Siri negotiated the dirt track in front of the Women's Union, he noticed that there was plenty of activity inside. From the doorway he could see that Dr. Porn was still at her desk. He wondered if she ever went home. Very few doors were locked in Vientiane, and, like Siri, most householders couldn't remember where they'd put their keys for safety.

He pushed open the front door and called out, "It's only me."

Porn's office still had no door of its own. She looked up from the logjam of files on her desk and seemed relieved to have a distraction from her bureaucratic combat.

"Siri, you old goat," she said. "Come in."

Even before he reached the desk she had a cup of tea poured for him from her thermos. They exchanged a warm handshake that told of many years of friendship and cooperation.

"How are the eyebrows coming along?" he asked.

It was a standing joke that only he found funny. Porn had shaved her eyebrows for a brief period as a nun and they hadn't grown back.

"I always dream that your mentioning them again and

again will be motivation enough for them to make a comeback," she said. "How are you, good doctor?"

"I'm sparkling," he said. "And you?"

"Tired," she said.

"Work?"

"Family."

"You have a family?"

She laughed.

"Yes, it comes as a surprise to me too."

"You never talk about them."

"It's my policy to keep my private life private. I stay here as long as I can every evening, so I don't have to deal with domestic issues. But you aren't here to listen to my woes. How is your blockbuster film progressing?"

"I think we're on hold for a while until we can sort out a few other issues."

"Then that's not why you're here?"

"No. I have two other matters to discuss," he said. "Firstly, how good are your contacts in the camps?"

"The refugee camps?"

"Yes."

"How good do you need them to be?"

"Let's imagine that I have a commodity that I would like distributed amongst a certain faction of the camps' residents."

"What is it?"

"I can't tell you yet."

"Is it legal?"

"Absolutely."

"Religious connections?"

"You really think I'd be proselytizing at my age? No, it's a good thing. Call it a gift. Would you be able to distribute it?"

"Is it bigger than an elephant?"

"Smaller than a house lizard."

"Then I think I can. For you."

"Excellent. I'll have all the details for you beforehand, I promise."

"And the other matter?"

"Right. I have a friend."

"You do?" she looked surprised. "When did that happen?"

"*Touché.* This friend is exhibiting certain, what could be called symptoms. And as a doctor I am concerned because the symptoms suggest to me a condition—one that I have been expecting for some time."

"Siri, you aren't the type of doctor who needs a second opinion. Why are you telling me? Treat him!"

"I'm not his doctor."

"Who is?"

"You."

Porn blew on her tea even though it wasn't that hot.

"And you think I've misdiagnosed a patient of mine?" she said.

"I hope not."

"Then you'll have to tell me his name. I'm full-time here at the Union. I have very few patients these days, and they're only at my house some evenings and during the weekends. If I'm making bad decisions because of overwork I need to know about it. What's his name?"

"Civilai Songsawat."

She sat up straight then laughed again.

"Civilai?"

"Yes."

"Our Civilai?"

"The one and only."

"Siri, I haven't seen Civilai as a patient for three years."

"You didn't see him last week after Daeng's physical? He was arriving at your house as she left. He said you gave him a clean bill of health. Told him he was in great shape. Just had a touch of diarrhea."

"I did examine Daeng, and, yes, Civilai did arrive as she was leaving. But I didn't examine him. He brought me homemade scones and we chatted for twenty minutes until my next patient arrived."

"You're not his doctor?"

"No. He insists you've been his doctor for so long he would never dream of seeing anyone else. He said it would be a betrayal. I daren't interfere."

"The lying bastard," said Siri. "He's not once let me examine him."

"Why would he lie about something like this?"

"Because he's a stubborn old bastard. Because he knows he's sick and doesn't want to worry anyone. He's too proud to let anyone take care of him."

"What symptoms have you seen?"

"Loss of appetite, nausea, bruising, and he's been hiding his jaundiced eyes behind dark glasses hoping I wouldn't notice. He's been in bed for a couple of days with his supposed diarrhea. I believed he was getting treated by you. If you'd considered it serious I was sure you'd get in touch with me. I should have—"

"Do you have transportation?" she asked.

CHAPTER TWELVE
Let Me Get This Straight. You're Dead?

It was certainly the worst movie Jane had ever made. It was in competition for the worst movie made by anyone. But Siri believed that no man, having watched Barbarella groaning through her ten-minute orgasm in the excessive pleasure machine, could have avoided milking the goat when he got home. It was blatant soft-porn sci-fi and he and Civilai were disappointed that she'd agree to make it. But that didn't stop Siri from putting up a *Barbarella* poster in the mobile ward to cheer up the injured soldiers.

And here he was piloting the throbbing pink 41st-century spacecraft, looking through the windshield at a blackboard dotted with fairy lights that was supposed to be the universe. And supposedly floating in that two-dimensional space at the end of a rope was Civilai in a Chinese postman's uniform.

"What are you doing out there?" Siri shouted. "You're ruining the scene."

"The scene ruined itself," said Civilai without the benefit of a microphone. "Will you stop trying to rescue this movie and its low budget special effects? Here I am supposedly in space with no oxygen tank, and I'm dangling rather than floating. With Jane in the driver's seat, nobody noticed the scenery. But you . . . ?"

"What exactly are you doing in my dream?" Siri asked.

"Not a dream, Siri. This is the reality. You speeding out to Kilometer Six on the back of Dr. Porn's motor scooter, that's the dream. You with a heart thick as sticky rice, tears streaming down your face, that's the dream."

"This feels like one of Auntie Bpoo's mind tortures," said Siri.

"No. Sorry. Bpoo's off in her trailer sulking. I don't know what you said to her, but it really upset her. She's wearing a football kit, boots and all. So you can't blame her. She has nothing to do with this scene. This is just your imagination and me, old pal."

"And what's the moral?" Siri asked.

"There has to be a moral?"

"Usually."

"Oh, I don't know," said Civilai, attempting to cut the rope with a nail file. "How about, 'All good things come to an end.' I like that one. Or, there's always, 'Don't trust people who drink too much.' Which reminds me, I'm supposed to warn you and Daeng to cut down on the rice whisky intake. I know there's a canary's chance in a jet engine that you'll take any notice of that. I certainly wouldn't."

"So, let me get this straight. You're dead?"

"Brilliant."

"How does it feel?"

"Death?"

"Yes."

"It feels like . . . I don't know. It feels like I'm a part of the big it."

"A part of what?"

"Mass."

"I don't get it."

"Well, you know when they take the unexploded ordnance to the smelting works and melt it all down and it sort of blends together and you can't tell what was a bombie and what was a wok because it's all one? Well, that's what this is except there are no unexpected explosions. You can't tell a tree from a Boeing 747 from a toothbrush. It's all a big *blancmange.* I was going to do the tennis racket gag to give you a laugh, but there are none over here. Or, at least, they're no longer identifiable. Shame. It would have been a good exit line."

"We had some good times," said Siri.

"A million of 'em, but let's steer clear of clichés, shall we?"

"Are you scared?"

"A little bit."

"I'm sorry you had to go first."

"A bit sooner than the universe had in mind, but we'll be together soon enough."

"Thank you for making this easier for me."

"What are friends for?" said Civilai. (Although he vehemently denied having said it.) "All right. You get back there to your devastation and grieving, and I'll catch up with you on the set of a much better movie sometime soon."

The nail file severed the rope and the backdrop became a long, stretched-out lava lamp display and Civilai was sucked into it. He shouted, "Wheeeeh."

And he was gone.

Dr. Porn's fifteen-year-old motor scooter sounded like a Harley Davidson in the silent compound. The heavily armed guards at the gate had been undecided as to what to do, so they waved the bike through. Elderly Party members and their wives tended to look alike after seventy. You could never be too cautious. The lights were all on at Civilai's house. Porn stopped in front of the gate. Madam Nong was on the front steps hugging her knees. Sitting beside her, mirroring her actions, was Rajhid, the crazy Indian. He was dressed, which seemed appropriate, and his hair was greased up into a point like a pencil. How he knew . . . how he got there . . . what he was thinking, nobody would know. But he was there.

Madam Nong seemed not to notice the motor scooter until it was silent. She looked up to see Porn and Siri looking down at her.

"You'll want a drink," she said.

Her face was ashen but dry. Her skull seemed to have grabbed at her face and pulled it tight.

"Where is he?" Siri asked.

"In bed," she said. "I'll get him for you."

It was a line so common to her lips she didn't even realize she'd said it.

Dr. Porn sat on the other side of her and put an arm around her shoulder. Siri stepped over them and took off his leather sandals before going into the house. He walked through to the bedroom. Civilai's body in Muay Thai boxing shorts and an *Apocalypse Now* T-shirt lay comfortably on the mattress. There was no question that he had a smile on his face. There was a chair beside the bed.

"Anyone sitting there?" Siri asked.

There was no objection so he sat beside his friend. In the films you only had to pass your palm across the eyes to close the lids. In reality you had to poke and prod and wrestle the bastards shut. So, even though it was a little bit creepy, Siri left the eyes open. They were as yellow as mustard. There was nothing to say. On the bed was a body that had once belonged to a great man. It was empty of soul and mind now, so there was no point in engaging it in conversation. There'd be time for that later.

Siri looked around the tidy bedroom. A glass cabinet with crockery and an unused tennis racket. Framed photographs on the dresser: Civilai and Nong in their sixties and their forties and back and beyond. The colors fading into memory until there were only pastel ghosts in ghostly locations. One photo of Siri and Civilai each shaking a hand of the last governor general of Indochina, a bogus smile of gratitude on his bloated face. One photo of the two couples: Siri and Boua, Civilai and Nong, black and white, a professional picture from a man who made a living from his art—the Eiffel Tower looming over them, the date, 1931. And Siri realized his hands were wet and noticed the steady drip from his cheeks but could not stop it and did not want to. He heaved the tears up all the way from his chest like an old pump emptying a flooded basement. He groaned out each spurt. Nobody came to investigate.

And when he was dry and silent he continued his study of the tidy room. And his eyes rested upon the bedside cabinet and a single pill box and the handwritten label attached to it:

Dr. Porn Chaisak Clinic. December 1st, 1980.

CHAPTER THIRTEEN
Begone the Boulangere

Death to the Oppressors was postponed if not abandoned completely given the circumstances. There was a cremation to arrange, and the greatest challenge was to relieve the Politburo of the responsibility of organizing a state funeral for an ex-Politburo member. Nong and Siri and all who loved Civilai, and Civilai himself, wanted a quiet, intimate ceremony so they could say goodbye in their own way. No cavalcade. No trumpets. No insincerity. No long meaningless wait.

Daeng had kept close to her husband these past two days, watching his smiling eyes, hearing his witty banter with the customers. Even when Mr. Geung and Tukta returned from their vegetable honeymoon and resumed their duties at the restaurant, Siri stuck around, wiping tables, washing bowls, hanging thirty kilos of blanched chicken bones on the lines in the back garden. But he didn't leave the building through the front entrance in all that time. It was as if the road outside might drop into the river at any moment.

On the third day after the Ferrari deaths, Phosy and Sihot arrived at the shop. It was the eve of the grand ceremony of the fifth anniversary of the republic—what Siri had begun to refer to as "the second biggest nothing." The news of the two dead journalists had been met with sadness in the West, but, given the recklessness of their accident, not much respect. The obituaries mentioned their wild pasts as if it were inevitable they'd have sticky ends. "It's how they would have wanted to go." No mention that perhaps they didn't want to go at all. Articles leaned heavily toward apologies to the Lao for spoiling their celebration. The bodies were sent to Australia and the case was closed.

"Is he in?" Phosy asked.

Daeng was presiding over the usual madness of noodle primetime.

"He's upstairs," she said. "Try to get him out into some fresh air, will you?"

"Do you think he can handle any more bad news?" Phosy asked.

"I don't know what he's thinking or feeling," she said. "It's as if he's inside a big puzzle, and he's trying to think himself out of it. He's certain one of the stories from his past has sparked something here in Vientiane. He's sure the death of the journalists is connected to the two letters and the man who sent them. But now that Civilai's death is a part of it too, he can't seem to rest until he's worked out the how of it."

"Well, Daeng, what I have to tell him isn't going to make him feel any better," said Phosy. "I think you should come up and hear it too."

She delegated noodle duties to her returnees and followed the detectives upstairs. Siri had formed a sort of nest in the skirt room and had notes all around him as if he were trying to solve a gigantic riddle. They went with him to a room at the back that contained nothing other than themselves.

"The bread woman," said Phosy.

"Lah, I was afraid of that," said Siri.

"What about her?" Daeng asked.

"She died on the second," said Sihot. "Apparently of natural causes."

"That's it," said Siri. "She died on the second. The journalists—the collateral victims—died on the fifth. Civilai died on the eighth. This is it. This is the threat realized."

"We've already had the paranoia conversation," Daeng reminded him.

"Oh, Daeng," said Siri. "How can this be paranoia? He's following up on his threat but he's making it look like natural causes. Look at the victims. Look at the order. And you're next."

"I'm afraid it's become impossible to ignore," said Phosy. "Daeng, I need to put you somewhere."

She laughed. "We have some empty cupboards in the skirt bank room," she said.

"You know what I mean," said Phosy. "We have to send you somewhere safe so I can work this out."

"I think that's a splendid idea," said Siri.

"You do?" she said.

"Yes."

"Siri, for the benefit of our guests here, can you tell us what happens when we arm wrestle?" said Daeng.

Siri blushed."I don't see that as . . ." he began.

"There's a point," said Daeng. "What happens when we arm wrestle?"

"You beat me."

"Once or twice?"

"I have an old war wound," he said. "A bullet . . ."

"Always, Siri," said Daeng. "I always beat you. So what chance do you think you and your policemen friends here have of dragging me to a safe house and having me squeeze pimples off my backside while you stumble around trying to find the man who wants to kill me?"

"Daeng, this is no laughing matter," said Phosy. "He's causing people to die."

"Then you'll just have to catch him before he causes me to be one of them, won't you?" said Daeng. "And if the cogs are indeed already in motion as he said, it would appear he's already infected me with his evil magic. So there's really no point in my going anywhere."

There followed the type of silence that comes from hitting a wall of obstinacy. Siri rebounded.

"Phosy," he said. "I have to do an autopsy on Civilai."

They looked at the doctor as if he were suffering from dementia.

"Isn't it obvious what he died from?" said Phosy.

"I need to be sure."

"He's your friend," said Phosy.

"He's not anything anymore," said Siri. "He's dead. All I have there in the morgue is his slowly decaying flesh. But that meat can speak to me. People are dying in the order predicted and I want to know how he's killing them and how to stop him."

He didn't mention the box of pills he'd recovered from the bedside cabinet, nor the words "sooner than the universe had in mind" that had stuck with him since his conversation with Civilai's spirit.

CHAPTER FOURTEEN
Reunion at the Morgue

The reunion at the morgue was not a joyful one. The welcome mat at the entrance made nobody smile. Mr. Geung was too busy sweeping and scrubbing to respond to Dtui's half-hearted jokes. And Dr. Siri had spent the last two hours with Civilai's widow convincing her there was something to be gained by cutting open her husband. It was only because of Civilai's respect for Siri that she finally agreed. That and the promise that the doctor would only go ahead with the autopsy if he found evidence of suspicious circumstances during his postmortem examination of Lah, the bread woman. Of course, Siri knew there was suspicion. He just had to be clever enough to find the explanations. He held only contempt for coincidence. Four deaths, six days apart, all predicted by the letter writer.

He pulled up three chairs beside the corpse of the bread woman and he, Dtui and Mr. Geung sat there like hospital visitors.

"Before we start," said Siri. "Let's plan our tactics. Let's begin with the hypothesis that our nemesis was responsible for the deaths of the two journalists. In his letter he made it sound random, that he'd just kill someone as a show of his intentions. But what if it wasn't random?"

"You mean he had a reason to kill them?" said Dtui.

"One of them had met someone he knew," said Siri. "Perhaps our friend hadn't planned to kill them, but they recognized him from the old days. His cover, whatever that was, was blown. He had no choice but to do away with them."

"You don't think it was an accident?" said Dtui.

"Before I went to see Madam Nong, I stopped off at the police car lot," said Siri. "I took my boy wonder, Geung here, with me."

Mr. Geung snorted through his nose and laughed.

"As you know, Mr. Geung's senses are more active than my archaic system," said Siri. "We took a look at the Ferrari. Geung's nose led him straight to the mat under the driver's seat. He pulled it out and there were three puncture holes in the floor. The petrol had been drained but he could still smell that the holes went right through to the tank. Someone had deliberately made those holes so the fumes would fill the car."

"Why?" asked Dtui. "To make an explosion?"

"No," said Siri. "That was my first guess too. But there wasn't much chance they'd ignite the fumes unless they lit a bonfire in there."

"The killer wants them to-to-to breathe it," said Geung.

"Exactly right," said Siri. "As the temperature rose, the fumes would have filled the car. They wouldn't notice because there was a much stronger smell there."

"Flowers," said Geung.

"Someone had put together a whole bunch of leis and hung them from the rearview mirror. Jasmine in a confined space tends to overpower other scents. If they'd smoked their weed they might have noticed the subsidiary smell of petrol fumes because grass tends to heighten the sense of smell, but they didn't. They drank beer. One of the bottles had been re-capped. I had Geung take a sniff."

"I could s-s-smell rotten egg," said Geung. "Like, like antibiotic."

"And why would anyone put antibiotic in a bottle of beer?" Siri asked.

"Beats me," said Dtui.

"Some antibiotics deaden the sense of smell temporarily," said Siri. "So, what if the killer gave them the leis and the beer to see them off on their journey. But also to make sure they didn't notice the petrol fumes?"

"But why?" Dtui asked.

"I couldn't do an autopsy on Jim, the photojournalist, but I did notice he had sinus problems. I guessed he'd had allergies. If his condition was chronic and he didn't have access to medication, the fumes could have been enough to kill or at least incapacitate him. He's drinking, driving too fast on bad roads in a car without seatbelts. He has an attack. It either kills him outright, or he drives into a tree or a house."

"Or a pond," said Geung.

"The killer couldn't have planned for both of them to die," said Dtui.

"It didn't matter if only Jim had recognized him," said Siri. "Perhaps they'd met in the war, stationed at the same press corps. I don't know. But he got lucky. The two of them ended up in a lake and both drowned. And anything Jim had told Marvin about the reunion drowned with them. Our killer had cleaned up."

"And he could use the deaths to show he was serious," said Dtui.

"And capable," said Siri.

"How did the k-k-killer man know about the ah, ah . . . ?"

"The allergy?" said Siri. "That's a good question. If they'd worked together it wouldn't have been much of a secret. If Jim used an inhaler it would have been noticed."

"Any of the journalists here for the festival could have seen him use it," said Dtui. "And they didn't recover an inhaler from the car wreckage."

"It could have floated away," said Siri. "We'll get Phosy to ask around when we're done here."

"And what are we looking for with your girlfriend Madam Lah," Dtui asked.

"Any evidence that the death wasn't natural."

"It wasn't," said Geung.

Mr. Geung, either under the influence of Siri and his spirits or through some innate Down syndrome sub-ability, had certain senses that reached into the realm of the dead. His intuition was rarely wrong.

They'd talked to Lah's sons. The only existing condition they knew of was her insomnia and, for that, she'd been taking herbal magnolia bark for years. But they recalled that recently their mother had heard reports on Thai radio and had switched to pharmaceuticals. They didn't know where she acquired them or how much she used. They gave Dtui all the drugs from their mother's medicine cabinet in a plastic bag. There was nothing to be learned from the containers. Only one had a label and that was for heartburn powder. Another two or three pill boxes were unmarked and a large bottle with only a centimeter of liquid inside had a handwritten sticker that said: *Two glasses before bed.*

Siri recognized the pills in one of the boxes. China was flooding the market with its cheap versions of European drugs, and they made their products look as much like the originals as they could. The drug was a variety of benzodiazepine commonly prescribed for insomnia, and, in certain cases, for depression. By itself it presented no danger. With alcohol it could be fatal. But, according to the sons, their mother drank alcohol rarely and in moderation.

There were no obvious signs of drug abuse. In fact, as they foraged inside the bread lady, Dtui commented that the woman was in great shape internally. They took samples and Dtui and Geung retreated to the lab. The days of guesswork and comparative color-chart tests were behind them. The Soviets had funded a room with equipment and chemicals to test the fluids and flesh. Only Dtui could read the directions and instructions, and, without her, the room remained locked.

Siri sat under a tree with the chemistry lab goats and drank sweet coffee and ate sticky buns—the specialty of the Mahosot canteen—and waited for news.

"You were right about the benzodiazepine," said Dtui. She sat beside the doctor on a pile of tractor tires. "High concentration but not enough to kill her."

Mr. Geung joined them on the grass, greeting the goats by name.

"Anything else?" Siri asked.

"We don't have results from blood and urine," she said, "but we did an analysis on the contents of the bottle the boys gave us. Some sort of liquid morphine. Again, a high concentration and mixed with something sweet. I guess it was to take the taste away. Geung sampled it. He said it was like a milkshake."

"Yummy," said Geung.

"Lucky it wasn't poison," said Siri.

He thought back to his days there at the hospital. To their lunches on the river bank. To Lah, and her handmade baguettes and pretty smile. And he recalled one week when she was away at the Soviet hospital, a small operation on a rather aggressive mole. She said it had been particularly painful because she had a low tolerance for opiates and had refused pain killers.

"That's how he got her," said Siri. "The combination of the opiate and the psychoactive drugs on an elderly woman. It would have shut down her central nervous system. And if he got the doses right he could have timed it to within a day of his schedule."

"So, someone knew about her intolerance," said Dtui.

"Must have," said Siri.

"Somebody's playing God," said Geung.

His stutter had become less pronounced since his marriage.

"Exactly," said Dtui. "He's blurring the line between natural and unnatural death. But how can he have access to everyone's medical history? A colleague talking about his allergies is one thing, but Lah was a Lao bread maker with no foreign contacts and a life that was limited to a few city blocks. How does he find out . . . ? Siri, she must have been seeing a doctor."

Siri knew Dtui would arrive at that conclusion soon enough. He still had Civilai's medicine bottle with Dr. Porn's label in his pocket. He'd known the doctor since he arrived in Vientiane and he respected her. He'd trusted her with his secrets. He didn't want to believe she'd have a role in this macabre drama but nothing in those odd days of Lao noir was out of the question. Only one thing could vindicate her.

Siri jumped to his feet and the goats scattered to the ends of their tethers.

"All right, team," he said. "Let's get back inside."

"Are you sure you're up for this?" Dtui asked.

"He'd have expected it of me," said Siri. "When I next see him, he'll be complaining about the rust on the scalpels and the coldness of the dolly under his arse. No pleasing some people."

Dtui probably took that as a comment designed to lighten the mood, but Siri knew it was true.

Mr. Geung had placed a hand towel over Civilai's face and it helped. The comrade's eyes, despite hours of manhandling, had refused to close. It was as if the old fellow was keen to see what had finally defeated him. They were surprised to see the scars of at least two bullets and one long, poorly stitched wound from a knife or machete. And that was only the front. Siri knew a politician would invariably have more knife wounds in his back.

He left the Y incision to Dtui and even before she was down to the navel all three of them stepped back in horror. The liver looked like someone was smuggling an over ripe durian inside him. His spleen was bloated and fatty deposits sat here and there like clouds on a break. Thick bands of fibrous tissue tried, to no avail, to hold everything together. But, most importantly, there was congealed blood. Lots of it.

"This happened too fast," said Siri.

"What do you mean, Doc?" Dtui asked.

"If he'd been bleeding like this he wouldn't have been

able to function for months. He certainly wouldn't have been sipping Hundred Pipers last week and annoying everyone and acting out scenes from our film. A week ago, Civilai was himself, albeit dying slowly from cirrhosis. Then, almost overnight we have the glasses to hide his jaundiced eyes and the loss of appetite and the bruises and the trips to the bathroom to throw up. It was as if he went from ignoring his condition to freefall and death."

"You think it was accelerated to fit into the killer's timetable?" Dtui asked.

"I think we need to see what's in his gut," said Siri.

At that point the temperamental air-conditioner let out a rare puff of cold air, and the hand towel on Civilai's face lifted and wafted away like a magic carpet. Siri found himself staring into those jaundiced eyes and returning that cheesy grin.

"You bastard," he said.

Siri sat at his desk and again left the analysis to Dtui and Geung. In his heart, he knew what they'd find. Someone had given Civilai anti-coagulants. If they tested the jar in Siri's shoulder bag they'd find Aspirin or Warfarin or some such. And again he'd return to the same three questions: How did the killer learn of Civilai's condition, why would Dr. Porn prescribe him something potentially lethal, and why did she lie when she said she hadn't been treating him at all? Was she doing him a kindness? Did he go to her office and ask for something to end the pain? She was surely too professional to agree to that and there was still a lot of pain to be had in bleeding to death. Siri had no choice now but to tell Phosy of his findings and have the lady doctor brought in for questioning.

"Are those tears, boss?" said Dtui from the office doorway.

"My face leaks from time to time," said Siri. "It's the old pipes."

"Time to switch over to PVC," she said.

"What have you got for me?" he asked.

"It's conclusive. What's your guess?"

"Aspirin?"

"Ibuprofen."

That afternoon, while Siri was at the morgue, the third letter arrived. Bruce was upstairs tinkering with the Panavision. He was the only one who still believed their film would be made. It seemed to give him a purpose for returning to his homeland. What else would he do? Daeng held out the envelope to him. It had the same odd combination of stamps attached to it. He didn't take it from her.

"It's to Dr. Siri," he said.

"He's not here."

"We should wait."

"Open it," she said, then threw in a half-hearted "please."

Reluctantly, the young man took the letter and tore open the envelope. He read it through silently first and sighed. He looked into her eyes and she nodded. He translated.

"My dear Dr. Siri," he began. *"I'm sure you can see that the countdown has begun. Loved ones A and B have kicked the proverbial bucket. Loved one C is already under my spell and there's nothing you can do about it. Grief would kill you eventually, I suppose, but I don't have time to wait for that. You'll be following*

close behind, doctor. And my promise to you will be consummated and I will be able to breathe again. Fare thee well, you shit."

It wasn't until later that night that Daeng showed Siri the letter and told him what it said. They were on a grass mat on the bank of the river drinking Daeng's own homemade rice whisky with wild apricot juice. That minor fruity addition made it feel more medicinal. Less likely to kill them. The mosquitoes had apparently tired of Lao blood and were off in search of foreign journalists. The moon was hopping from cloud to cloud. It reminded Daeng of the bouncing ball in song lyrics but the only music was from the cicadas and the frogs.

"So, if I'm next," said Daeng, "what existing condition is he going to exploit?"

"I've been racking my brain," said Siri. "You're so annoyingly healthy. Your tail's not even long enough to strangle you."

She knocked the top of his head with her fist.

"Why doesn't he just shoot me?" asked Daeng.

"What?"

"If the objective is to wipe out your loved ones because you directly or indirectly ruined his life, why not get it over with as quickly as possible? He has a limited time. Guns and various explosives are readily available for a small fee. He could have just wiped us all out in a couple of days and honored his threat. Why the show?"

"What are you saying?"

"I'm saying he's gone to all this trouble to make a point. He's doing to you what he thinks you've done to him."

"Used natural causes to kill someone?"

"Something to do with a physical condition that was

aggravated because of something you did or didn't do? I don't know. He's playing God because he thinks that's what you did. You made him lose face or made him poor or put him in jail, where he picked up a disease. I don't know. You need to go back over those three threats and find out what happened to the men you incensed."

"How do I do that?"

"Has bereavement really left you so empty of ideas? The French have released their records on their involvement in the colonies. Their reports are on public record. It shouldn't be that hard to locate a major incident that occurred during the last few days of French control in Saigon. And our good friend, Seksan, acting caretaker-cum-ambassador at the politically clogged French embassy, has a lot of time on his hands. I'll send him over some noodles and see what he can do."

Siri smiled. Daeng was at her most desirable when she was organizing. Nobody did it better.

"Now, as for the Americans," she said, "I'm sure they can tell you what became of long-nose Henry once they found out he was a fraud."

"We still don't speak English," he reminded her.

"Which would have been a problem before the gorgeous, speaks-fluent-Lao, movie star Cindy came on the scene. They don't have a single thing to do at the US embassy. I'm sure she'd be delighted to thumb through a few files, especially if you were leaning over her, breathing onto her neck."

"You'd trust me alone with her?"

"I know your fancy: mature, slightly overweight and armed."

"That's true. She could never compete. What about Paris?"

"As you are one of the few residents of 1932 Paris still alive, I think we need help from someone with a good memory. And I reckon we'd have a chance with the oral history traditions of the Corsicans."

"And where do we find a Corsican at this time of night?"

"How about this for a suggestion," said Daeng. "We stroll ten minutes down the road to the Nam Poo fountain, where we will find the open-air bar of Dani and his Lao wife."

"Dani's a Corsican? I thought he was Serbian."

"Dani's father was a pilot with Air Opium in the glory days of trafficking. I'm sure he could help us with some history, and, if we're good, with a cold pitcher of beer."

"Dr. Siri," she said. "What a nice surprise to see you here."

"They told me this was a famous hangout for foreign diplomats," said Siri.

The bar at the Nam Poo fountain was popular with foreigners even though the fountain never spurted and the beer was never cold enough to please everyone. When Siri arrived they saw Cindy drinking with a handsome young Asian man built like an athlete. It was dark, but he had sunglasses perched on top of his head. She let go of his hand when Siri arrived and didn't introduce him.

"How's the film going?" she asked.

"On hold," said Siri.

"Yes," she said. "We heard about Civilai. You and he were very close."

"We were brothers."

"I'm so sorry."

"Thank you."

He didn't feel a lot of sincerity coming from her direction. She was clearly drunk and impatient to get back to her liaison.

"I was hoping you could find me some information about a pilot who was shot down over Vietnam in '66."

"Much of our records are still classified," she said.

"This one should be open enough," he said, and told her about Henry. He kept it brief because he felt he was intruding. She threw back a tall rum and Coke and signaled to the waitress for another while he spoke. He got a feeling her Grace Kelly looks wouldn't be accompanying her into her forties.

"We all have to go to the parade tomorrow," she said. "But I'll see what I can find after."

"I appreciate that."

He nodded at the young man who merely glared back, and he went in search of Daeng on the other side of the fountain. They were in the middle of the city but there were no street or shop lamps around, so he used the table candles to light his way. He almost missed his wife, who was sitting at a shadowy table with Dani and Chanta, the owners of the bar.

"Siri," said Daeng. "We may have some good news at last."

"I don't know," said Siri. "There was something uneasy about her."

He was sitting in front of Phosy's desk at police headquarters telling them about his brief encounter with Cindy the night before.

"And perhaps she had something to be uneasy about,"

said Sihot who was leaning against the wall behind his boss.

"Why's that?" Siri asked.

"I was talking to the Swedes last night," he said. "One of them said he saw your friend Cindy talking to Jim the photographer the night before he died."

"That would have been after Dtui and I talked to them," said Phosy.

"You think Cindy was the mysterious contact?" Siri asked.

"They're sure to have spare keys for Silver City at the embassy," said Phosy.

"You'd think we'd have been smart enough to change the locks," said Sihot.

"There were no keys on the bodies," said Phosy. "So, whoever tampered with the car had to be there to wave them off and lock up."

"The embassy has its own guests turning up for the parade today," said Sihot. "They were given leis at the airport when they arrived. They have a supply."

"So, she gets there early," said Phosy, "fills the tank, punches the holes in the floor, puts up the flowers and leaves the doors open until the Australians get there. They're already on cloud eleven from whatever they'd been ingesting the night before, so they're not completely tuned in. She joins them in a few sips of beer and off they go."

"It's not impossible," said Siri. "And Jim, wanting to document everything, insists on taking her photo. So, somehow, in the confusion of the departure, she makes sure the camera doesn't travel with them."

"I don't know," said Phosy. "I don't think a photojournalist would be separated from his camera that easily."

"The Swede said everyone was aware of Jim's allergies," said Sihot. "He's been using an inhaler for years. He bought a fresh one the day he arrived in Vientiane. Always liked to have a spare in case of emergency."

"So, where were the inhalers?" Siri asked.

"They didn't see any at the pond," said Sihot, "but they were looking under the water. Inhalers would have floated. I sent someone to talk to the fisherman, see if he caught anything plastic."

"Did you find out why the Swede was asking about Siri?" Phosy asked.

"Something about writing an article for a French magazine," said Sihot. "The life of an Ancienne graduate fighting against the French. We have no way of checking whether that was true or not."

"Oh, so close to stardom," said Siri.

"Look," said Phosy. "I'll be leaving all this with you two. I have to attend this damned stupid parade at That Luang and listen to a National Day speech moderately altered from every other National Day speech I've ever sat through. At least I can take some files and sign stuff. Siri, how are the arrangements for the funeral going?"

"The Party's having its state funeral on Friday," said Siri. "It's symbolic so they don't need a body. Or, at least they won't be getting one. They're not having Civilai lying in state, although he'd really get a kick out of it. Not that it would matter if he were there. The average villager couldn't identify a politburo member even if he had his name tattooed across his forehead. I doubt there'll be a cheer squad or women throwing themselves in front of the hearse. The actual funeral will be this evening."

"I'll be sending my people to both," said Phosy. "I want

photographs of the mourners and the gawkers. There's a good chance our killer will attend one or both of them. If he . . . or she, has put as much effort into all this as it seems, he or she will be there to admire his or her work. Siri, I don't want you or Daeng anywhere near the parade today."

"Oh, what a disappointment," said Siri. "Daeng will be devastated."

Despite the threat to his life, Siri rode his bicycle back to the restaurant with Ugly trotting alongside, without giving a thought to snipers or tossed grenades.

"You do know you started this whole mess?" Siri shouted. "What are you doing allowing a complete stranger to tie notes to your tail?"

Ugly's ears and tail drooped and he assumed a repentant expression all the way home. They arrived in time to find Daeng at a table with two Europeans. One was Dani, the owner of the Nam Poo bar. The other looked a lifetime older than Siri. The doctor pictured the old fellow lashed to the mast of a sailing ship for his entire life braving the storms and the baking sun.

"This is Dani's Uncle Joe," said Daeng. "He's visiting Dani and his family."

Siri shook the old man's hand. He had one hell of a grip. The experience was like putting your hand on a railway track and having a train run over it.

"Dani says he never forgets anything," Daeng added.

Joe sipped his coffee.

"Tell him," said Joe in gutter French. "Tell him I was there in Paris in '32 when the president got shot."

They'd obviously discussed Siri's request already.

"Tell him yourself," said Dani. "He speaks better French than any of us."

"What?"

"You tell him," said Dani.

"He's a Chinaman," said Joe.

"Try him," said Dani.

"You speak some?" shouted Joe.

"Only what I picked up from the whores on the old rue Bouterie," said Siri.

He'd never actually been to the old rue Bouterie and had never learned anything of value from a whore, but his comment had its desired effect. Joe looked at the doctor and laughed so hard he couldn't keep the coffee in his cup.

"Good luck to you," said Joe.

"I was in Paris in '32," said Siri.

"So Dani here tells me," said Joe. "You anywhere near the shooting?"

"I witnessed it," said Siri.

"You don't say," said Joe. "You don't say. Fancy that."

Daeng refilled his cup.

"They told me the Russian they arrested for the killing was just a patsy," said Siri.

"A madman," said Joe. "A drunken fool so high he had no idea why he was pumping bullets into the guy. It was all set up by the family. Doumer had two of the boys killed over there in Annam."

"Do you know why?" Daeng asked.

"All drugs," said Joe. "Those were nutty days. Drugs bring out the worst in people. The third brother, Marcel, he was sworn to avenge the death of his kin. He was there at the . . . I don't remember the name of the hotel."

"Rothschild," said Siri.

"That's it. That's it. He *was* there," said Joe pointing at Siri. "Marcel was there to make sure the Russian wasn't so out of it he'd miss the president and shoot himself. It all went great but Marcel got himself arrested somehow. I don't know how that could of happened."

"What became of him?" Siri asked.

"Not a lot, as far as I can remember. He was in jail for a week or so then the *gendarmerie* gave him some money for the inconvenience and sent him home."

"What?" asked Siri.

"As far as I remember," said Joe.

"Why?"

"Now, that's another story," said Joe. "He didn't shoot no one, did he? And there was a little matter of repercussions."

"About what?"

"Doumer had been the state representative for Corsica before stepping on a few heads and hitting the big time. There's those that say it was drug money that got him up there. They say he'd feathered his nest over there in Annam and brought the trade home with him. If Marcel had been formally arrested and charged, there would of been a lot of evidence leaked to the newspapers to that effect. The government was struggling to keep everyone happy during the Depression. They didn't want the presidency besmirched. And they had their assassin. They didn't need Marcel, did they?"

When the guests had left, Siri and Daeng went outside to sit on the two barbershop chairs that had arrived on the current one day and snagged in the weeds. Once they'd dried out they were surprisingly comfortable. Ugly lay between them.

"So, you didn't actually ruin Marcel's life," said Daeng. "A week in jail is hardly purgatory."

"I doubt he even remembered me when they let him out," said Siri.

They drank in the river air and considered Joe's story.

"It looks like we're just about to learn whether our crazed killer is behind door number two," said Siri.

Daeng looked up to see a short plump man riding a bicycle. In white chinos and a pink brushed-silk shirt, he was dressed more for cocktails than exercise. On the otherwise empty road he stood out like an Easter egg on wheels. Monsieur Seksan was French with Lao parents. But France wasn't ready for an ambassador to Laos of Lao ancestry. The compromise was that he could look after the embassy after diplomatic relations had broken down as a sort of high-level janitor. He showed his resentment of this slight by drinking all the wine in the cellar and damaging things.

He kicked down the bicycle stand and hurried toward the couple.

"I thought you were anti-exercise," said Daeng.

But the man sidestepped her question, barged into Siri, threw his arms around him and wept on his shoulder.

"I just heard," he said through his sniffling. "I'm sorry. I'm so sorry. So, so sorry."

He then repeated it all in French. It took them a while to calm him down. They sat him on one of the barbershop chairs and Daeng patted his hand.

"Give him the talk, Siri," she said.

"All right," said Siri. "Here we go. Siri and Daeng and Civilai were elderly people who had lived for many years in an area rife with weapon fire, tropical diseases and falling coconuts. There were any number of ways our three heroes could have been snuffed out. They may have leaned a little too heavily on alcohol from time to time to get through it all, but get through it they did. And by some miracle they stayed alive until ripe old ages. They knew the grim reaper of infinite patience was sitting on a stool at the end of the tunnel ready to claim their penitence. And so the first pin fell. It was unfortunate that Civilai left them. They'd miss him. Given the amount of booze he'd thrown down his throat over the years, they could hardly have been surprised. It would have been a bigger surprise if none of them died. No, Monsieur Seksan, a lifetime is more than enough."

And, with that, Siri pushed the Frenchman away from his damp shoulder and asked him what he was doing there. After a few seconds of self-gathering, Seksan took a deep breath and said, "Yes, let's all be brave about this."

Siri smiled at Daeng.

"Let's," said Siri.

"I found the records you requested," said Seksan. "Before our little diplomatic standoff, Paris sent the no-longer secret files referring to the last few days of our occupation of Indochina. The staff here locked the files in the strong room and didn't even get a chance to open the dispatch folders before they left. I took a look. Page after page of bureaucratic dross. But, as I'm blessed with having no distractions, I was able to dig down to the incident you mentioned."

"You found it?" said Siri. "Excellent. Did you see mention of Civilai and myself?"

The name Civilai sparked another emotional response from the ambassador janitor. It took a while for the dry sobs to clear.

"No," he said at last. "But they did mention the incident.

They wrote that French agents had uncovered a plot to steal valuable artifacts from the national museum in Saigon."

"Bastards!" said Siri.

"That army officers were involved and that they were court-marshalled and executed by firing squad whilst still on Vietnamese soil," Seksan continued.

"And the museum curator?" Siri asked.

"He was to return to France for a civilian trial. He was escorted by a French agent. On the ship home, according to the report, he pushed the agent to whom he was handcuffed overboard. The agent was a large man who couldn't swim and the bodies were never found."

"And then there was one," said Siri.

CHAPTER FIFTEEN
The Lightning Bug Angel

They'd chosen Hay Sok temple for a number of reasons. It was small and intimate and it had a history. Siri's first Vientiane house, before it was blown to bits by a mortar, had overlooked the temple grounds. He and Civilai had often sat at the kitchen window there and drank too much and finished one another's sentences. One night, Civilai had alerted Siri to a surprisingly large swarm of lightning bugs gathered around the main stupa.

"They're trying to tell us something," Civilai had said. "I feel this is a crucial moment in our lives."

Siri had been head down at the time, engaged in conflict with a wine bottle. He was holding it between his knees and gouging at the foil top with a corkscrew. He completely missed the significance of Civilai's sighting.

"I must be losing my touch," he said.

"It's incredibly beautiful," said Civilai.

"There was a time I could just rip these things off with two fingers."

"No, I see it," said Civilai. "I see the shape clearly now. It's an angel."

"I'm bleeding here."

"She's beckoning to me."

"They must be using some new alloy."

"I'm coming, my darling."

"I need a hacksaw."

"This is where I shall be laid when it's all over," said Civilai, looking down at his young brother spouting blood.

"What?" asked Siri.

"My cremation. It will be here."

"Then this will be the death of both of us."

"Siri, what are you doing?"

"I'm trying to get to the cork."

"There is no cork."

"Eh?"

"It's a screw cap, Siri. You're hacking through metal."

"Sacrilege," said Siri. "Since when did wine come in screw tops?"

"A present from Australia. You don't have to drink it if it offends you."

"Don't be ridiculous."

Siri hadn't seen the lightning bugs and he had to take Civilai's word for the angel, but he referred to it often. So it was decided that Hay Sok temple was where they'd barbecue old Civilai. And they'd do it at night because fire in the daytime always seemed like a wasted opportunity to watch the spirit take off. There was only one monk minding the temple, and it wasn't the same ghost monk Siri had once talked to. This was an ex-mathematics teacher whose wife had swum the Mekong to get away from him. He'd decided that becoming a monk in a city that had little respect for monks was preferable to giving chase. And it seemed fitting. They didn't want some religious fanatic telling them how their sins could be forgiven. Siri and Daeng were fond of their sins and they wanted credit for them.

It was just as well the math teacher didn't have a lot to say because the guests wanted Civilai on the bonfire and on his way so they could get to the wake. Despite the overwhelming sense of irreverence, there was a healthy crowd there to pay respect. In Bruce's bag of magic tricks there was a Super 8 home movie camera. He was entrusted with the task of filming everyone in attendance. If Phosy was correct, the killer was somewhere in the crowd. Siri didn't know everyone there but there were a number of old friends. He was hoping to see Dr. Porn and have her explain the tablets beside Civilai's bed, but there was no sign of her. Sitting around on the grass with lit candles dancing in the breeze were Madam Nong and Daeng; Crazy Rajhid in a white nightshirt; Phosy and Dtui with Malee on her lap; Mr. Geung and his bride, Tukta; non-Ambassador Seksan; the Swedes (although nobody remembered inviting them; Cindy and two others from the US embassy; the entire household of Siri's government residence still given over to the homeless; and an assorted collection of people who had felt Civilai's warmth and kindness over the years. There was nobody from the politburo.

To the math teacher's dismay, Civilai had written very simple instructions for his trip to the pyre: tell a couple of jokes, pour some accelerant on the body so it doesn't take all night to burn, and go get drunk.

"How can you celebrate his death with alcohol when it was alcohol that took him from us?" asked the annoying latest girlfriend of Mr. Inthanet, the puppet master.

"If he was run over by a bus, would you force the guests to find their own way to the temple on foot?" asked Daeng.

"If he drowned in the river would you tell everyone they couldn't bathe for a week?" asked Siri.

The bemused girlfriend scurried back into the crowd and Siri and Daeng performed their own version of a high five. Of course, Civilai would haunt them all for eternity if there was no booze at the wake.

Across town the fireworks had begun, marking the last leg of the journalist's visit and the end of the second biggest nothing. After an arduous ceremony at the stadium, seemingly endless speeches and an embarrassing display of military might, the guests would have been enjoying the last of the freebees. Those that could be bothered would have read the Xerox of Civilai's posthumous speech Siri had delivered to their hotels that afternoon. At least there would be one small belt of honesty for them to consider on their journeys home.

The firework show was limp compared to what they had seen at the Olympics, but the timing was perfect. Civilai's journey to Nirvana or heaven, whichever he best qualified for, was accompanied by whooshes and bangs and one or two "ooh" moments. As predicted, the whole thing was over in thirty minutes. Siri had brought a pack of sparklers and they caught the last flames of the pyre and waved them as Siri and Daeng sang Civilai's bawdy Lao version of "La Marseillaise." Siri had marshmallows and wooden skewers in his shoulder bag but decided at the last minute that only he and Civilai would see the funny side of that.

Daeng announced that everyone was invited back to the restaurant to drink a toast to their old friend. That afternoon, Madam Nong had driven to Daeng's in Civilai's yellow Citroën jam-packed with her husband's leftover bottles, so there was plenty to drink that night. The temple was only four blocks from the restaurant so very few of the guests refused the invitation. One of those apologizing was Cindy. She approached Siri with a large brown envelope under her arm. Ugly sniffed at her leg. She was clearly one of the police department's favorite suspects for the killings but Siri felt no fear. It was as if Civilai's death had made him not invincible but indifferent to attempts on his life.

"Dr. Siri," she said. Already she was slurring. "You asked me if I could find you information on the downed pilot. I was able to pull this file after the parade. It seems to me there are a lot of inquiries going on about the . . . I don't know, about the accidents? The journalists and now Civilai. You know? Perhaps if you could confide in me what you're looking for exactly, I could help. I have resources."

"So it seems," said Siri, holding up the envelope. "Perhaps after I've looked through this I'll have requests. Are you not going to join us for the wake?"

"I'm obliged to attend the closing ceremony, however briefly," she said. "Then I have to pack."

"Where are you going?"

"I'm on my way to Phnom Penh," she said. "This was just a temporary posting."

"You're fluent in Lao and they send you to Cambodia?"

"I speak a fair bit of Cambodian too."

"Multitalented."

"My offer of help still stands."

"You've only been here, what? Nine days?"

"Fourteen," she said, "but my work here is done."

"Two weeks? That's most efficient of you," said Siri.

CHAPTER SIXTEEN
The Wake

"Bruce, my boy, you don't have to film the wake," said Siri.

"It's like they say back home in Sydney," said Bruce. "You can make a bit of money filming a wedding, but you make a hell of a lot more filming the honeymoon."

Siri laughed and slapped him on the back. The restaurant was packed to the point where they'd had to move the tables out to the roadside so the guests could fit inside. Daeng had felt obliged to make noodles for everyone, but Siri had put his foot down. Instead they chewed on baguettes with assorted dips and salads.

"You think this gathering might degenerate into an orgy?" Siri asked.

"You never know, Doctor," said Bruce. "Sometimes you just have to point the camera and it makes things happen."

Daeng arrived, put her arm around her husband and asked to borrow him.

"Phosy and Dtui and Sihot are upstairs," she said. "We're looking at the US documents. You want to join us?"

"It's Civilai's wake," said Siri.

"He'll understand."

▫ ▫ ▫

They sat cross-legged on the floor in the skirt-bank room. With Malee asleep on a pile of *sins*, Dtui did her best to translate the relevant documents. There were a lot of them.

"All right," said Phosy. "Originally, I thought we were down to the last threat. We can pretty much discount the first—the Corsican in Paris. I'll get back to the second suspect later."

"What do you mean?" said Siri.

"One at a time," said Phosy. "We'll start with Henry in Hanoi in '72. The last contact you had with him was Christmas that year. He sent a Christmas card to you, Doctor. You picked it up on your next visit to Hanoi. What do you remember about that card?"

"Reindeer. Glitter," said Siri.

"Not helpful," said Daeng.

"Let me remind you," said Phosy. "The message read *'To you and your loved ones. With nothing but unnatural death to look forward to. I shall kill you all. I'll be seeing you, Siri Paiboun. I promise you that.'* Once the pilot had been exposed as a fraud, the North Vietnamese plan was to fly him to Saigon with the other three pilots and let the US military sort out the punishment."

"That's the last I knew," said Siri.

"The records we got from the US embassy start on December twenty-eighth," said Dtui. "Apart from a break for Christmas Day so the pilots could have some nice roasted chicken and a cold beer, Hanoi was spattered with ordnance for eleven days straight. As they couldn't leave, Henry was still in a cell at the clinic where you met him. The US bombed the fuel plant and missed. They leveled a suburb for four blocks in either direction. The clinic was reduced to rubble. One of the pilots was killed but not Henry."

"What happened to him?" Daeng asked.

"In the chaos of the bombing, thousands were killed, communication networks were destroyed and the surviving MIA pilots were forgotten and left to fend for themselves. Despite the fact that their country was raining bombs from B-52s on the Vietnamese, they gave themselves up to the authorities. I'm guessing they had no other choice. Henry wasn't amongst them. He'd fled."

"How could an American remain unnoticed in Hanoi?" asked Daeng.

"There were foreigners in Hanoi, even through the bombing," said Siri. "There were Eastern European advisors, press, tourists. All he needed to do was get a change of clothes."

"Even so, he wasn't about to walk out of Vietnam during the heaviest bombing of the war," said Phosy.

"But he could fly," said Dtui, flipping over the page. "The last entry in Henry's file is this mention of a group of American folk singers staying at the Reunification. While they were down in the bunker hiding from the air raids, someone broke into the room of a guitar player and stole his passport and air ticket as well as a large sum of money. When they noticed the robbery the next day it took forever to find someone to report it to. The Committee for Solidarity with the American People in Hanoi was obviously not quite as enamored of their American guests as they had been before the bombings. It would have taken some time to arrange replacement travel documents for the guitarist. But, that morning, a commercial flight left for southern China. On board, having successfully changed the date of his flight was someone claiming to be the guitarist. That same person made an ongoing flight to Bangkok. There's no firm evidence that it was Henry who stole the passport, but there was no trace of him in Hanoi."

"When I interviewed him he had a two-month old beard," said Siri. "He could have easily passed for a folk singer. I'm sure Immigration didn't look too closely."

"And that brings us back to his Thai family," said Daeng. "His plan had failed. He was still poor. But by now the Thai authorities would have been alerted to look out for him. The Americans were on his trail."

"If he was thirty-three in '72 he'd be forty-one now," said Phosy. "Even married to a Thai he'd need a passport to stay there all this time. He'd have to apply for residence every year."

"Or pay a local cop to keep his mouth shut," said Sihot.

"He couldn't take on the guitarist's ID because the passport had been reported stolen," said Phosy. "But it's Thailand. You can buy a whole new identity there."

"He'd need money for that," said Siri. "He stole some in Hanoi but not enough to start up a new life."

"I don't know," said Phosy. "He's a conman. He almost convinced two governments he was a POW. He's cunning. His type is never short of a money-making scam. He could get away with anything. He might be in Vientiane as a diplomat or a journalist or an aid worker. You never know."

"He'd still need documents to get into the country," said Daeng.

"Or a boat," said Sihot.

"All right, so what's the other news?" asked Daeng.

"What other news?" asked Phosy.

"You said there was information about the second suspect."

"The Frenchman, right."

"He drowned," said Siri.

"Presumably," said Phosy. "Again, no evidence. But following your suspicions I sent some men to your friend Dr. Porn's house. She's bolted. It looked like she'd packed in a hurry."

"Front door was open. Lights were still on," said Sihot. "Something had spooked her."

"Perhaps the fact that we were on to her," said Phosy.

"I don't believe Dr. Porn's involved in all this," said Daeng.

"Well, she's certainly hiding something," said Sihot. "Her motor scooter was gone. I couldn't find a passport. But I did talk to a neighbor. What do you know about your Dr. Porn?"

"Not a lot," said Siri. "I first met her here in '75. The Women's Union trusted her enough to give her a top position. I know she was with the resistance for a while."

"Did you know that she was in Saigon?"

"I don't recall her mentioning that," said Daeng.

"She was there for quite a while during the French occupation, evidently. Long enough to take a French lover."

It was then that Siri remembered where he'd seen the tube that had contained the original note. The one tied to Ugly's tail or one very similar to it had sat in a glass souvenir cabinet in Dr. Porn's office.

"This information is from the neighbor?" said Daeng. "Hardly a secret then."

"She was a bit sketchy on details," said Phosy. "I've called for the records from the Union. Evidently, the lover was multilingual. Spoke Lao."

"You don't think . . . ?" said Siri.

"Brokenhearted," said Sihot. "Her lover arrested and shipped to France. The thought of revenge the only thing keeping her going. I don't—"

Bruce and his camera appeared in the doorway. He was drunk and giggly.

"Afraid you have to either look soused for the camera or come down and poin the . . . join the party," he said. "People are leaving. No hosts. Bloody poor show."

"He's right," said Daeng. "There's nothing we can do tonight. Come, young Bruce. Follow me from guest to guest and I'll disclose their most intimate secrets for the camera."

"Bravo," said Bruce. "I'll have enough footage to produce my own documentary. In fact, that's a bloody good idea."

"Stay with Daeng," Phosy told Sihot.

"Not so close her husband will get jealous but near enough to take a bullet for her," said Siri.

The party was over and nobody had died. Siri and Daeng lay on a patch of grass at the river's edge, close enough to feel the spray from the water dashing against the rocks and getting whisked up on the breeze. They were holding hands and had been since they staggered down the bank. They heard a splash. Crazy Rahjid had abandoned his white nightshirt and was backstroking naked against the current. He should have been carried away by the force of the water but he remained, neither ebbing nor flowing, as if he were anchored.

"Will you have a wake for me?" Daeng asked her husband.

"No."

"Why not?"

"Because you're not dead."

"When I am."

"I'll be dead ten years before you, and I'll be in far too advanced a state of decay to think about all that organizing."

"He said I'm next, Siri."

"I know. You're not the type to worry about dying."

She sighed. "I just don't want to go without knowing who he was and how he did it. How sad will it be if our final mystery together remains unsolved."

"I'm afraid to say Dr. Porn isn't looking that innocent," he said. "Maybe it is solved."

"But so many questions are still unanswered."

Rajhid vanished below the surface of the water. He was something of an aquatic animal, but, instinctively, Siri and Daeng began to mentally count the seconds. Siri must have lost count because when the Indian reappeared near the far bank, the doctor had him under for an hour.

"Have you seen him?" Daeng asked.

"He's over there," said Siri.

"No, I mean, Civilai. Since . . ."

"Yes."

"You didn't tell me."

"Sorry. We had a bit of a chat the night he died. I disappeared in Dr. Porn's office when she went to get her motor scooter."

"Was he . . . natural?"

"He was suspended at the end of a rope with lava lamp effects all around him."

"No, I mean, did he seem different? Is the other world like an afterlife?"

Siri gave it some thought. "I don't think so," he said. "I mean we won't be lying there hand in hand in our halos sipping cocktails."

"But we can communicate?"

"Until eternity."

"Then that's good enough."

With the help of Rajhid, Siri and Daeng climbed the riverbank, crossed the dusty road and negotiated the challenge of the staircase to bed. Rajhid turned off the downstairs lights and closed the shutters. Daeng collapsed fully dressed—for now—on the mattress. Siri, always orally aware, went to the bathroom to brush his teeth. He smiled at himself in the mirror as the toothpaste dribbled down his chin. His teeth always seemed more desperate for a good clean when he was drunk, and he had time on his hands. He opened the medicine cabinet, which usually contained nothing but old razor blades and various balms and ointments for the elderly. But that night he saw four bottles he didn't recognize. Still brushing, he focused on the label of one of them. He was confused. He read it again and the brush dropped from his hand and into the toilet. He grabbed the bottle, ran into the bedroom and shook Daeng awake. She came to reluctantly and in poor humor.

"Look at this," Siri shouted, holding the bottle in front of her face. "Look."

She tried to focus.

"How many of these have you taken?" he asked.

"What?"

"How many?"

CHAPTER SEVENTEEN
Porn

By midday on Wednesday they had all the evidence they needed to convict Dr. Porn. All they were missing was the doctor herself. Phosy and his team had worked since sun up to put together all the pieces. The fisherman at Ban Donhai had caught two inhalers. The refills in both were empty. But the label on the newer one was clearly from the office of Dr. Porn.

The sons of Lah, the bread woman, recalled that their mother had obtained her benzodiazepine from Dr. Porn's surgery as well. The locked cabinet in Porn's office contained a bunch of keys that were labeled "Silver City/ USAID." And the final clue had been in Siri's bathroom all along. Since Daeng first started seeing Dr. Porn, she'd been prescribed methotrexate: 7.5mg to be taken once a week to treat her arthritis. It would have been far too difficult to explain how she had been cured of an incurable condition so she'd said nothing. She'd stopped off at the doctor's surgery and picked up her prescription from the housekeeper. Daeng didn't notice at the time, but the doctor had upped the dosage to 10mg a day. At least that was the amount handwritten on the label. That concentration would be fatal in a woman of Daeng's age. Daeng accepted and paid for the medication—but she had no reason to take it. So it sat there, unopened in the cabinet until Siri brushed his teeth the night before. The only element missing now was motive, and they agreed the French lover angle was now worth pursuing more than ever.

The morning noodle rush had not helped remove the pain that frog marched back and forth across the brains of Dr. Siri and Madam Daeng. They had the headaches they deserved.

"It's this," said Siri, as he dipped the tips of his old chicken bones in a pot of yellow paint. Daeng had sent Mr. Geung and Tukta on some unnecessary errand to stop their overly loud laughter. They regretted having promised Bruce access to their heads to complete his documentary, but at least he and his camera were silent.

"What?" she said.

"This is the reason we shouldn't drink," he said. "Not liver failure and death. Death is by far the better option. The hangover. That should be our incentive to give it up. Why do we persist on having mornings after, given how horrible they are?"

"No, I can't use any of this," said Bruce, switching off his camera and loading a new three-minute cartridge. "We're reaching the climax here. You have to focus. The world wants to know—"

"The world's watching your film?" asked Siri.

"Are you kidding?" said Bruce. "This could be compelling. You're about to tell the audience how you unmasked a killer. We need your thoughts. We need to know why a woman you trusted and liked should want you and your loved ones dead."

"But we don't know why," said Daeng. "I thought we were all friends."

"That's fine," said Bruce turning the camera back on. "That's the relationship we need to establish. But first, we need atmosphere. Something undeniably Lao. I know. Follow me."

Bruce settled on the skirt-bank room for background. He draped the *sins* elegantly and had Siri and Daeng sit cross-legged on the floor in front of them. They were concerned that his decision to have them drinking coconut water from actual coconuts was a little hokey. But Bruce convinced them Aussie audiences lapped up all that sentimental ethnic content. And they couldn't deny the cool sweet water was exactly what they needed to douse the cinders in their brains.

"I'll edit this all in the right order after," he said. "We'll get to the 'why' later. Let's start with what you think happened."

Their cameraman was far more energized than the old couple in front of him. He could obviously picture commercial success and personal fame. The more excited he became, the more pronounced his Aussie-tainted accent was.

"Start with the dead Australians," he said.

"One of the first things Jim did when he arrived here was buy a new inhaler refill," said Siri. "We're guessing he knew Porn from the time he lived here. I don't know if he contacted her, or if he bumped into her at the surgery. But it obviously screwed up her plans that she was recognized. Maybe he knew something about her background in Saigon. Hard to say until we find her."

"There's still a lot that doesn't make sense," said Daeng.

"Like what?" asked Bruce.

"Like why she'd be so stupid as to put her labels on all of her bottles and refills," said Daeng. "Either she wanted to get caught or she was sure nobody would notice. She knew, given the seriousness of his condition that Jim wouldn't survive an attack without his inhaler."

"What about Silver City?" Bruce asked.

"The Women's Union had keys for all the USAID buildings—I guess because there was a lot in the warehouses that could be used or sold. Although as yet, nobody has done so," said Siri. "Porn was here in the old CIA days, so she'd remember the famous Ferrari and know what a coup it would be for a journalist to get a ride in it. She had time and opportunity to puncture the tank and set up the leis. She couldn't have anticipated the pond. She'd have been hoping the car hit a tree or went over a cliff and caught fire, destroying all the evidence."

"And given what she did to Madam Lah and your dear friend Civilai, you still like her?" asked Bruce.

"It takes time to hate someone you love," said Daeng.

"If she did this—" said Siri.

"If?" said Bruce.

"All the evidence points to her, I agree," said Daeng. "But after a lifetime of experience, it seems like you should be able to judge a person. If you're totally wrong, it's as much a reflection on you as on her. Look, you know, Bruce, this has been a real drain on both of us. Why don't we give it a break now and come at it again when we're fresh."

"We're both buggered," said Siri.

"I completely understand," said Bruce. "Look, I've got two minutes left on this tape. How about I ask just two more questions and we'll call it a day?"

"Fair enough," said Siri.

"How was Dr. Porn planning to do away with you, Daeng?"

"She'd been treating me for rheumatoid arthritis for a couple of years," said Daeng. "She prescribed methotrexate. Originally, I was supposed to take it once a week. After our last appointment she changed the dosage to once a day."

Daeng yawned and leaned against her husband.

"And what's the problem with that?" asked Bruce.

"It's very toxic in high doses," said Siri. "Daeng has been known to have a drink every once and a while. That and methotrexate combined would have been enough to kill her."

"So, why isn't she dead?" asked Bruce.

Siri could barely keep his eyes open.

"All right, Son," he said. "Time for a nap."

He tried to stand but the room twisted.

"I said why isn't she dead?" asked Bruce.

He had raised his voice as if talking to the deaf. The camera was down at his waist. He was clearly angry that nobody was answering his question. Daeng's usual flashing light warning system was dull. Siri tried to lunge forward but his reflexes were shot. He looked at Daeng and—with the few facial features that still worked—they shared an expression of apology. The window shutter was open but they couldn't shout for help. The clouds outside grew cumbersome and heavy and dropped to the ground, followed by the sky.

CHAPTER EIGHTEEN
The Thai that Binds

"Oh, at last," said Bruce. "You know? In the movies I'd just toss a glass of water in your face and you'd splutter into consciousness. That was your third glass. I thought you'd had a heart attack, or I'd drowned you. For obvious reasons I didn't want to get the room too wet."

Siri was the first to come around. He could see the young man in a blur and hear his words, but it was as if he were in the audience watching a scene from a play. He blinked a few times to clear his sight. He and Daeng were lying on the floor back to back, tied together at the wrists with their ankles bound. He tried to speak but whatever the boy had put in the coconut water was powerful stuff. The Lao skirts had been piled around them a meter high and Bruce sat on the top of one pile like a mischievous elf. There was a scent of lighter fluid in the room.

"Yes, it was perhaps a bit stronger than it needed to be," said Bruce. "But I really didn't expect you to drink that much."

Daeng groaned.

"I'm not sure I'll have the time for both of you to regain your speech. I have a plane to catch this evening. At least your ears are working. Two weeks, just like I promised. Not as smooth as I'd hoped. It all started off so well too. Good fortune with the journalists, eh? Right on time. Civilai desperate for sleep popping the Ibuprofen I prescribed for him. And you, Lady Daeng, my only failure. So proud of yourself. But, Daeng, you should have gone with the drug option. Burning to death is so . . . icky. With all this antique cotton you'll go up a lot faster than Comrade Civilai, but it'll still be a wicked way to go. And it'll be a shame for you to leave this earth without knowing what the point was, right? So I'll chat for a little while, if you don't mind."

He was flicking the top of an engraved Zippo lighter open and closed and rolling the flint wheel with his thumb. Daeng stirred.

"I'll begin at the end. Or, a bit before the end because the end hasn't happened yet. Seksak who runs the Fuji Photo Lab did have a cousin named Keophoxai who went to study in Australia when he was ten or thereabouts and eventually became Bruce. That much is true. But it wasn't me. Theirs was a big extended family with more cousins and nephews and nieces than you could spray with insecticide. Your dear old friend Dr. Porn was his unpopular aunt. She'd gone off to fight the royalists, so she wasn't the most loved family member. But I'll get back to her later.

"The Australian embassy had language classes back then and Bruce was their brightest student. They arranged a scholarship for him, and he breezed through high school in Sydney, got into university and studied film production. Again, all true.

"And then, there's me. I'm Thai from the northeast so, technically and historically, I'm Lao too. I was a keen student but I came from a poor family and I didn't have any opportunities to study. My mother was a widow from a young age. My father got shot by the border patrol. Smuggling. I was the only son so I stayed home and worked the fields. We struggled. My mother went away to the town for a few weeks from time to time. She said she'd found work in a shop but I wasn't stupid. I could smell booze on her clothes and I knew what she'd been doing. But, good luck to her, was my philosophy. Better than starving to death. She was pretty then and we needed the money. When it ran out she'd get back on the bus. I got used to the system.

"Then, one day, and I'll never forget it, she came home with a *farang*—a white guy. She introduced him to me as Uncle Henry. He was tall. He had a blond buzz cut and phenomenal teeth—even and white like the man in the Darkie toothpaste ads. He said something I didn't understand and held out his hand to me. I didn't know what to do with it.

"Shake his hand, Dom," my mum said.

"Dom, that's me. So I grabbed his fingers and shook that hand the way you'd shake dust out of a mat. And they laughed. I didn't know why. But I laughed too. And that was the start of the happiest two years of my life. As he taught me English, I learned that Henry was a pilot and that he had a disease that stopped him being able to fly anymore. The US Air Force had given him money so he could retire. And he chose our house for his retirement. Nobody worked. The rice paddies dried up and cracked in the drought. The vegetables got overrun with weeds. We ate all the pigs so there were none to mate in the fall. But if we needed something we'd drive to the market in the old truck Henry bought and buy whatever we needed. It was as if the money would never run out.

"Henry bought a generator and fixed up our cabin nicely. There was nothing fancy. He didn't want to draw attention to us. There was no TV. Nothing that you'd call a luxury. But we were a happy family. Every afternoon Henry tutored me in whatever subject we could find books for. He always said I was the brightest kid he'd ever met. I ate up everything he said. I wanted to please him. He told me stories about his parents who were both university teachers who were short-listed for Nobel Prizes, and his sister who won the Miss California beauty title in 1967, and his brother who was working his way up to being the President of America. And my mum said that nothing would make her more happy and more proud than if her son could study in a real university and become a doctor.

"And I guess they decided that I'd go away to study. I hated the idea of being away from the house, but Henry convinced me that school wasn't a lifetime. That I'd . . ."

Siri coughed. "I don't . . ." he said in a breathy voice.

"Ah, good," said Dom. "Communication. It can never be overrated. But, right now, you can't interrupt me. I'm on a roll. I have a lot to say and the clock's ticking. You'll have your moment. Where was I? Right, he told me that in no time I'd be back with skills and a degree, and I could support my family and be someone important in the community. I told him I wanted to be a pilot like him. But he said that pilots just kill people and that I should be a doctor and help people instead. He said it would make my mother happy. And she was. After a life of abuse and struggle I could see that finally the spirits were on her side. I couldn't disappoint her.

"I travelled to Bangkok with Henry. We went to the Australian embassy. At the time I wondered why he'd want me to go to Australia rather than America. It was several years before I really understood."

Siri's senses were returning. First came his sense of smell. The lighter fluid wasn't on the skirts. It was on him. He felt Daeng's index finger tapping against his hand. Dom, the boy who was not Bruce, droned on.

"I took tests in Bangkok that were obviously designed for idiots. I was embarrassed at how easy they were. And the next thing you know I'm on a Qantas flight to Sydney. Then the blur. The classes. The bullying. The cultural explosion. The A grades, the distinctions and, wham, I'm accepted at Sydney University to study medicine. And the only thing that kept me centered through it all were the monthly letters from Henry. My mother couldn't write so I learned of their life through him. They were such happy letters in the beginning. Every semester, money arrived in my account to cover my study fees. I didn't socialize so my income was more than enough. My only two objectives were to graduate and go home.

"It was 1972 when I received the letter that changed everything. Henry's condition had deteriorated to the point that he had to go to Vietnam to see a specialist."

Siri tried to say something but the words crumpled together before he could organize them.

"Yes, Good Doctor Siri," said Dom. "I can feel your excitement. Because now is when you appear in this story. Daeng, my darling, this is the bit I want you to hear. The specialist was you, Siri, remember? Educated in Paris. Trained in tropical medicine. How could he fail to find you? As I was into my second year of study, Henry decided that I was ready to learn about his condition, echinococcosis. He described it in detail. It was a horrible, debilitating disease but it was curable. If Henry had come to Sydney he would have recovered. But he didn't. He found you instead. He was in your clinic for four months being treated for something erroneous. You withheld his letters to me during that time. He sent me no money because you were draining his account for medicine unrelated to his illness. He sent that same medicine to my mother who had the same disease. By then he was too sick to go to America so he returned to Ubon. And there he found that my mother had died in his absence. A disease that would have been cured if you had prescribed the correct medicine."

"All . . . bull," Siri managed at last. It was barely audible but the Thai was too engrossed in his own story to notice the interruption.

"Out of his love for my mother he stayed on at our house. Any time he wrote for the next year, he mentioned you in his letters. Your cruelty. Your incompetence. And every letter concluded with the same line: *'Siri Paiboun the fake Lao surgeon has done this to us. He has destroyed our family. He must atone. This is my final wish.'* I couldn't stand it anymore. The payments into my account stopped. I didn't have any money to return to Thailand or to continue my studies. I took a menial job and saved as fast as I could. In 1976 I received a letter from the village headman telling me Henry was dead. I had loved him even more than I loved my mother. Suddenly, I had nobody."

Siri coughed again and forced out the words, "Henry was a . . . a compulsive liar."

"Of course, Fake Doctor. What else could you say to protect your reputation? But me? I had been told I had to discontinue my studies. I had passed every course. I specialized in pharmacology. I was offered a post at a research laboratory. But by then I had a bigger ambition: to avenge the deaths of Henry and my mother. I befriended the Lao community in Sydney. It wasn't too hard to convince them I was one of them. They were quick to adapt to life in Australia. We spoke English together. Then, in '75 when the floodgates of refugees opened, I was already a respected member of the Lao welcoming committee. And through them I heard of your whereabouts, Fake Doctor. I learned where you worked and where you lived and who you loved.

"I learned about Dr. Porn in Vientiane who had a nephew studying in Sydney. His father had died and the boy was alone. I contacted him and became his friend—in a way. I hadn't yet formed my plan to—"

"You should just stop and listen to the stupidity you're talking," growled Siri. "None of it makes sense. I was in Hanoi. Why would a US pilot go to Hanoi for medical treatment in the middle of a war? And there is no echinococcosis in Thailand. He just selected the name from a medical dictionary. You—"

Siri fell into a coughing fit. The boy reached behind him and found his can of lighter fluid. He removed the cap and sprinkled the remainder of the liquid, not on Siri, but on Daeng. Her finger percussion became frenzied.

"Nearly done," said Dom. "A little bit more and we can all go on our respective ways. It turned out that Dr. Porn's nephew wasn't a great communicator. He rarely wrote home. Never sent photos. Even less often after his sad demise."

"You killed him too?" Siri asked.

"Not really," said the Thai. "It turned out he had a weak heart. I introduced him to cocaine: the heart-attack drug of choice. It was my first experiment with death by existing conditions. It was nothing like murder, you see. If I'd given him the cocaine and he didn't have cardiovascular disease, I'd have been doing him a favor. It's not at all like being a poisoner. I haven't directly killed anyone. If you feed your friend peanut butter sandwiches every day he'd thank you and scoff the lot and suffer no more than weekly stomach-aches. But, what if he was allergic to peanuts? Oops. It led me to look more closely at the sometimes lethal combinations of conditions and medicines. I got away with young Bruce's deliverance and nobody found the body. I adopted his ID. I started to communicate with the family in Laos pretending to be him. I'd learned the Lao alphabet when I was a kid. My Lao writing wasn't fluent but appropriate for a boy who'd spent fifteen years in Australia. Spoken Lao was easier. My village dialect was easy enough to adapt. I apologized for my slackness at not writing. Telling them how close I was to graduating. Saying I wanted to return to my homeland. I wrote to my dear Aunt Porn who was the family's black sheep: anti-royalist, registered Communist. Nobody else spoke to her. She wrote back to me. She was surprised I knew about her. It was like Pandora's box opened up in front of me. She told me all the gossip: about relationships, about the resources she had at her weekend surgery. I stole pharmaceuticals and sent them to her for her stock. We became close.

"I had Bruce's passport. We looked similar. I put on some weight and dyed my hair like him—he had this peroxide fixation—and we could have been twins. The family met me at the airport. They hadn't seen Bruce since he was ten so it wasn't hard to fool them. They wanted me to stay with them but I insisted on going to a hotel. I was waiting for Dr. Porn to invite me to stay with her. She lived alone so she was reluctant at first, but we soon became comfortable with one another, and I moved into her spare room behind the weekend surgery. I pretended to like her but she was sloppy. She wasn't one for security. Her filing cabinets weren't locked and the medicine cabinet was always open. I'd alter the labels, change the contents and she'd hand over the drugs that would kill her patients."

"Why the journalists?" Siri asked.

"See? I knew you'd be interested. I was planning to start my attack with the bread woman but there I am at the market and this guy comes up to me—this *farang*—and he says, "Bugger me, if it isn't little Dom." I recognized him from Ubon. It was Jim. He was one of Henry's drinking and toking buddies. He'd come to stay with us a few times when he was doing stories up country. I tried to convince him he was mistaken, but he'd watched me grow up. We'd played soccer together. I guess he had that photographer's eye that never forgot. The hair and the added weight didn't fool him. I guess my face hadn't changed that much. It really screwed up my plans.

"Porn had told me about the red Ferrari and Silver City. The keys were sitting there in her office cabinet. So I got the two Aussies all fired up about taking the car for a drive. I'd emptied the inhaler he asked me for, opened a couple of beers to see them off and dropped some antibiotics in the open bottles to deaden their senses to the smell of the gasoline. I'd arrived a couple of hours early to—"

"Boy," said Siri. "Henry had reason to hate me, but it had nothing to do with disease or misdiagnosis. Your mother's boyfriend was AWOL. He was a deserter and a coward and a liar."

The Thai threw the empty fluid can at Siri, and it caught him on the side of the head. The cut bled. Daeng's tapping grew frantic.

"I'd like to consider myself something of an expert now," said the Thai. "Take you for example, old man. You're the antidepressant type. If things hadn't gone wrong here I would have had dear Aunt Porn give you antidepressants from her stock. I'd already substituted her low dose with much higher potency pills. After losing those near to you, you'd be distraught. You'd pop paroxetine until they put you to sleep and made you care less. But you're also an alcoholic. You can't stop yourself. You'd mix booze and pills and whittle yourself down to nothing, and I wouldn't have had to do another thing. You'd have been on self-destruct. I'd just check for your obituary from time to time knowing you were spiraling down a toilet."

"How did you kill your aunt?" Siri asked.

Dom smiled. "What makes you think I killed her?" he asked.

"It's only logical," said Siri. "She wouldn't have just up and left. She wasn't the type. I'm guessing she found out what you were doing."

"The nosey cow went through my things. Found my real passport. With the Mekong pumping away at the rate it is she should be somewhere near Cambodia by now."

"So you aren't as clever as you thought you were," said Siri. "You're just a common or garden murderer. There's nothing smart about throwing an elderly lady in a river or setting fire to an old couple."

"That is your fault, Fake Surgeon," said the Thai. "And I'm in a hurry to get it over with. So if you'd just be kind enough to tell me why your charming wife here isn't dead in spite of a heavy overdose of methotrexate . . ."

"Yeah, you know, that wasn't clever either," said Siri. "That had nothing to do with existing conditions. Rheumatoid arthritis was never going to kill Daeng naturally."

"Whatever! Why didn't the medicine kill her?"

"Because she didn't have rheumatoid arthritis."

"Of course she did. I've been through her file."

"She got over it."

"People don't get over arthritis," said Dom.

"My wife did. She's remarkable. You should have considered that in your flawed plan. She has skills too. Did you know she can whistle?"

"What?"

"Whistle. She could whistle the eyeballs off a buffalo."

"What are you talking about?"

"Go on, darling," said Siri. "Show the foolish boy how loud you can whistle."

Daeng whistled. It was impressive but no world record.

Dom laughed and he flicked a flame from the Zippo.

"I've got better things to do," he said.

He reached behind him for the rolled-up newspaper and lit the end. It took a while to catch. Siri cocked his ear toward the door but there was no sound. He needed a few more seconds.

"How did you get the Ibuprofen to Civilai?" he asked.

"Didn't need to," said the Thai. A healthy flame had engulfed one end of the newspaper. "His wife came to the clinic regularly. She'd mentioned that her husband couldn't sleep. I put together a little pill box and delivered it myself when Civilai was away."

Siri heard a scamper of footsteps on the landing and

suddenly the confused face of Ugly appeared in the doorway.

"Hello, my friend," said Dom. "I hope this wasn't your backup plan. This dog's loved me from first sight. Sorry, boy. I didn't bring any cheese today. Amazing how many dogs are cheese junkies. They can't—"

Having looked at Siri and Daeng, who were suddenly screaming for help, tears pouring down their faces, Ugly ran full speed at Dom and buried his fangs in the back of his neck. It was the perfect attack spot. The victim couldn't punch or kick him away. Dom dropped the newspaper, which continued to burn, on top of the skirts which had yet to catch fire, and dragged the dog across the hill of fabric. Despite his prey swinging from side to side, the dog didn't let go. Dom screamed and cursed.

"This is stupid!" he yelled. "He'll get tired. There's nothing to be gained from this."

Siri and Daeng had pushed together into a standing position. Dom continued to scramble around on top of the *sins*, eventually edging closer to the old couple. Siri leaned forward, and, using their bound wrists as a pivot, Daeng left the ground and swung her legs through the air. Both feet connected to the Thai's head. The force of the blow shook off Ugly, but it also stunned the killer. Siri and Daeng stood breathing heavily in the cleared space in the center of the room. The newspaper continued to smolder, but the material in the heap was packed together too tightly to burst into flame. The Thai was out cold on the skirts.

"Nice one," said Siri.

He looked around.

"What do we do now?" he asked.

"I haven't thought that far ahead," said Daeng.

"How did you know Ugly would come inside?"

"Instinct," said Daeng. "Mine and his."

In the distance they could hear the squeak of the hinges on the dog door. Dom began to stir.

"Merde," said Siri.

The boy took a while to get himself oriented, but just as he reached for the Zippo, a dark figure appeared in the doorway—a dark, completely naked figure. Crazy Rajhid was much faster at assessing the situation than Ugly had been. He dived across the skirts, grabbed Dom's Zippo hand and wrestled him down. Ugly went for the ankle. But the attack seemed to unleash the beast in the intruder. He snarled and flailed and seemed to draw on a pool of strength from deep inside him. Rajhid weighed no more than a Wednesday. Dom threw him off, bouncing him against a wall. The dog got a kick for his troubles and fell into the central clearing where Daeng and Siri stood helpless, back to back. Someone downstairs was banging on the restaurant shutter. It was past noodle time.

Dom made for the rear window. It was narrow but open, and he was about to dive through, when Rajhid with his second wind made a flying rugby tackle at Dom's legs. The boy's chest fell heavily against the window frame. He tried to kick free of the tackle but what Rajhid lacked in bulk he more than made up for in adhesion. He now had an unbreakable grip. But the Thai still had the Zippo. He flipped it open, produced a tall flame and tossed the lighter in the direction of Siri. It landed at the doctor's feet and immediately ignited the slowly evaporating fluid. The flames engulfed one leg of his trousers.

Rajhid made the call. He let go of Dom, grabbed the nearest skirt, and threw himself at the fire. He wrapped the cloth around Siri's leg and smothered the flames. When Siri looked up, he saw that Dom was gone. Rajhid crawled to the window, looked down and shook his head. They'd lost him.

CHAPTER NINETEEN
Works Like a Charm

Almost a week had passed. The journalists had departed and the city went back into social hibernation. The border was still closed. At the market, for the equivalent of a dollar you could get a potato or a lifetime supply of marijuana. The appearance of cooking oil caused a stampede. In the end-of-year review, someone calculated that the country had fourteen thousand kilometers of road, most of which was impassable in the wet season. Another thousand cooperatives had folded and industry still comprised one percent of the economy. There were three unexploded ordnance incidents a day, many of them fatal. The schools still had no textbooks, and the teachers were being paid in rice because the budget didn't stretch to education.

Civilai would have had some sarcastic comment to make about it all. Nobody of any personal importance to him attended his state funeral. Even Madam Nong had to pull out at the last moment due to a touch of migraine. She was replaced on the bleacher by somebody who looked a little like her. A lot of photographs were taken and there was an article about Comrade Civilai in the *Pasason Lao* newsletter and a forty-minute special on Lao radio. But the live turnout was sparse and the sincerity shallow. Civilai had always spoken his mind and socialism wasn't cut out for such foolishness. That final speech had raised hackles throughout the Party.

Probably the most pertinent news of the week was that there had been no sign of the murderous Thai. The chicken ropes that crisscrossed Siri's backyard had broken his fall from the upstairs window. Where he went from there was anyone's guess. Once Phosy was alerted, every available policeman was on the streets looking for a plump young man, probably hiding his blond hair beneath a cap. He hadn't turned up for his booked flight on the day he attempted to cremate Siri and Daeng. He wasn't seen at any guard posts along the roads leading from the city. There were no sightings of him crossing the river. He'd just vanished. Neither had Dr. Porn's body been recovered. But the Mekong was a huge winding stretch of water with no end of crevices and gnarled roots to trap a body.

Siri and Daeng fell back into a routine. It wasn't the first escape from near death for either of them, but they weren't getting any younger. Survival was hard work and even a week after the incident they were drained. They couldn't get the scent of lighter fluid out of their nostrils. Both were philosophical about death and had no ambition to claim more life than they were owed. Daeng was probably as pleased to have preserved the antique skirt collection as she was to have preserved herself. They still had their lives thanks to a dog and a naked Indian and for that they would be forever grateful. But, until Dom was caught there could be no rest.

Siri had packed all of his chicken bones, each one exactly three centimeters long with a yellow stain at one end. He'd had no template for his design but decided it didn't matter. It was most certainly the thought that counted. Before her sad demise, Dr. Porn had arranged transport for his cargo to three refugee camps on the Thai side. Madam Khunthong, who had taken on the responsibility for this shipment, had called Siri into her office to have him explain once more what it was all about. She hadn't quite grasped the concept. Khunthong was a jolly, football-shaped woman with no chin and a high forehead.

"Tell me again what they are," she said.

"They are small lengths of chicken bone with dobs of yellow paint at one end of each," he said.

"And how many, in total, do we have here?"

"Twelve-hundred in each box."

"And we give them to . . . ?"

"One to every single man in the camps under the age of twenty-five," said Siri. "And a handful for families to hand out to single Lao men they meet in the countries they're accepted by."

"I'm assuming we don't tell them these are chicken bones."

"Absolutely not," said Siri. "These are ancient amulets blessed by generations of shamans. They should find a strong length of string and wear them around their necks. They're infused with magic. They are more powerful than even the most evil of night seductresses."

"Night seductresses?"

"That's what you tell them."

"But it isn't true."

"It doesn't matter."

"You want our people to lie to them?"

"Yes."

"I don't think I can tell them to do that."

"Madam Khunthong," he said. "These boys already believe lies, and those lies are killing them. A silly story becomes a rumor, which becomes a legend, which becomes a reality. Our boys are dying in their sleep, killed by malevolent spirits that take advantage of their naivety and susceptibility. Once you believe enough in something, it becomes real. Believe me. I have inherited a whole dimension through belief. These young men are afraid to go to sleep because, in their dreams, there lurks a woman who can suck out their souls. And in their sleeping hours she becomes real. And in their dreams she kills them. And they believe they are really dead. So they have no option other than to die. Here!"

He held out one of his bones.

"This is magic," he said. "It looks simple but it is blessed. It contains enough karma to ward off any evil spirit woman who walks the night. It's a false belief sent into battle a false belief."

She looked into his eerie green eyes.

"Are you sure this will work?" she said.

"I know it will," said Siri. "There's only one thing."

"What's that?"

"You'll have to charge for them."

She laughed.

"I knew it," she said. "Porn told me it wasn't a scam but I—"

"It's not," said Siri. "It only needs to be a hundred *kip* or a baby chick or some embroidery. It's a token. You can use whatever you earn for any projects you have running. But it can't be free, you see? Quite rightly, we Lao have learned not to trust anything free. For this to be credible it has to have a price."

◘ ◘ ◘

Daeng awoke with the sky as black as blindness outside the window. She turned around to see a familiar empty space on the mattress beside her.

"Siri, are you in the bathroom or in the other world?" she shouted.

There was no answer.

He was in the other world.

"You're a being of extremes," said Siri.

"I can't think what you mean," said Bpoo. He had finally shed the 'Auntie' skin. He was dressed in a man's three-piece-herringbone suit with a tie and flip-flops. He sat opposite Siri at a metal table in a conventional police interview room. One wall had a long mirror that would have been disappointing if it wasn't two-way.

"I suppose I'll have to take my own credit for getting you out of skintight lamé and unwalkable stilettos," said Siri. "But now you're overdoing the macho. I expect you to pull out your rubber hose and start beating a confession out of me. There's middle ground, you know? I'll probably miss your elaborate sets and rampant symbolism, but I'd be quite happy to meet you on the bank of the Mekong over a metaphorical baguette."

"Do you have a point?" said Bpoo. "I have a darts tournament in half an hour. What do you want?"

"What do I want?" said Siri. "I thought you summoned me."

"Doesn't work like that. I sense your desire to have a chat and I enable your crossing over."

"What? That's useful to know. I conjure up a desire and you appear? You couldn't have told me that a year ago? It feels more like the sort of relationship we're supposed to have."

"Do you have a question, Oh Master?"

"We still need to work on that sarcasm. Here's the deal . . ."

Siri told him about his chicken bone project and raised his eyebrows hopefully at the end.

"So?" said Bpoo.

"So, I was wondering whether you'd be able to . . . you know . . . bless the bones or something."

"Do I look like the pope?"

"Isn't there some mechanism over there to promote supernatural activity in inanimate objects? Sprinkle a little bit of fairy dust or something?"

"You really are bad at this," said Bpoo.

"You said this world exists in my subconscious," said Siri. "I want to explore the outer limits of our relationship. Like the homework I gave you during our last visit two days ago. I bet you haven't done it, have you?"

"You see?" said Bpoo. "You don't even understand what our relationship is. I am not your private detective. I lead you through the labyrinth of your mind; I do not find missing persons."

"So, you failed."

Bpoo made a furtive glance at the mirror.

"I'm not authorized to give such information," he said.

"Who's behind there?" Siri asked.

"It's just a mirror," said Bpoo. "I was just checking my hair."

"In that case, I desire to go home to bed," said Siri.

Bpoo hesitated.

"There is one thing I am at liberty to tell you," he said.

"Yes?"

He looked again at the mirror.

"The person you inquired about is not deceased."

CHAPTER TWENTY
Siri Down

"Tell me again how you coordinated the escape," said Nurse Dtui.

The noodle shop tables had been pushed together, and the usual gang sat around the large square. From left to right there was Dtui and the ever-snoozing Malee, Chief Inspector Phosy, Mr. Geung and Tukta, Siri, Daeng and a large Donald Duck balloon standing in for the absent Civilai. A late evening shower had brought out the fire ants in such numbers Daeng had been forced to close the shutter, turn off the lights and illuminate the table with two temple candles. It gave the gathering the air of a séance.

"We didn't exactly escape," said Siri. "We were just as tied up and incapacitated at the end of it all, but we did organize the whistle for Ugly and we got in one good kick."

"It's called the tap code," said Daeng. "It's like Morse Code for beginners. The POWs in the camps developed it when they were banned from speaking. It's alphabetical. You have a letter grid in your head and you count the number of taps you hear until you've spelled out a word.

One quiet night Siri and I developed a French language version."

"Why?" asked Dtui.

"You never know when you're going to be incarcerated and have your tongue cut out," said Siri.

"He's right," said Daeng, "You don't."

"So Daeng's there tapping away, and I'm doing my best to keep a count and concentrate and talk to a maniac at the same time," said Siri. "And after a very long time I realize my wife was putting our lives in the hands . . . the paws of a neurotic mongrel."

There came a muted howl from the street.

"I put a lot of faith in our dog," said Daeng. "I hoped he might sense our fear. He'd stood looking at the dog door many times, but I'd never managed to coax him inside. I guess a building's a frightening proposition for a dog that spent most of his life in the jungle."

"I hoped we'd built up enough gratitude points from all the meals and affection for him to break his rule just that once," said Siri. "Then I get the second plan tap coming through explaining the two-man Bruce Lee kick. But tapping's a painfully slow process so we hadn't really outlined the whole thing. And then it was too late. Ugly was there and we just relied on the warrior spirit to make it work. And there's Daeng flying through the air."

"Not bad for a woman with chronic arthritis," said Phosy. He'd read Dr. Porn's files.

"It was the sedative," said Daeng. "I could feel nothing below my waist."

"It hadn't occurred to us that Crazy Rajhid would be skinny enough to get through the dog door," said Siri, keen to get off the topic of arthritis. "But given his girth

I shouldn't have been surprised. He'd seen the noodle crowd gathering and heard the whistle and the shouts from upstairs. He leaped three garden fences to get here. He should get a medal."

"Where would we pin it?" asked Tukta.

She didn't say much, but what she did say usually hit the spot. They drained a lot of laughs out of that, had one more drink and found other things to laugh about. Then they had one more drink. All but Civilai, who was on water. Served him right.

"And why," asked Phosy, "did your stash of antique *sins* not go up in flames at the mere scent of fire?"

"Now, for that we have to congratulate our resident genius, Mr. Geung here," said Daeng. "In his role as keeper of the *sin* bin he took it upon himself to cover every contingency. As you may recall, we have already been victims of vandals and nothing would tickle the fancy of your average arsonist more than a room full of dusty cotton and silk. So he fire retarded them."

"How on earth would you go about such a thing?" asked Phosy.

"Borax," said Geung. "It . . . it's quite easy."

"Evidently, it's a sort of laundry additive," said Daeng. "You soak your natural material in it and let it dry and it makes it hard to ignite."

"Not exactly f-f-fireproof," said Geung, "but good enough."

"How do you know all this stuff?" asked Dtui.

"The spirits of the *s-s-sins* told me," said Geung.

They all laughed, even those who were sure it wasn't a joke.

"How about Dom's movie camera?" Daeng asked.

"It's on its way," said Phosy. "I'd like to take it myself but sometimes you have to trust the Thais to do it right. And I suppose this is as much their case as ours. It's okay. There'll be someone watching over them."

"I think the brief, euphoric life of another generation of flying ants is over," said Siri.

"Right," said Mr. Geung.

He hopped to his feet and hurried to pull back the screen. They needed the river breeze. Tukta turned on the lights.

"Where do you think he is?" Daeng asked.

"Dom?" said Phosy. "No idea. But I'm guessing he's back in Thailand. It's not easy for an outsider to disappear in Vientiane. He doesn't have any relatives or friends here. He's not the type that could survive in the jungle. All I can guess is that he found a boat and floated home."

"But he's not finished," said Siri. "Perhaps he'll reorganize and try again some—"

"Dr. Siri!"

Geung had dragged open the shutter and was standing in the entrance.

"Come," he said. "Quick."

Everyone rushed to the street. Ugly, unconscious, lay in a pool of blood in front of the restaurant. Siri went down on one knee and felt for a pulse.

"He's—" he began.

The crack of the rifle carried along the river in a watery echo. Everyone froze. Siri looked briefly at his wife then dropped to the ground. Daeng screamed. Phosy and Geung ran for the trees and used them as cover as they headed in the direction of the shot. But there was no more gunfire. They saw nobody.

▪ ▪ ▪

Under the glare of the electric light, Daeng, Dtui and Tukta carried Siri inside and into an alcove not visible from the street. They lay him down and he sat up straight away.

"Bring in the dog," he said.

Tukta returned to the pavement with a towel and scooped Ugly from the roadside as if he weighed nothing. She lay him beside the doctor.

"You sure you weren't hit?" Dtui asked.

"I think I'd know if I was," said Siri. "I only went to ground under orders. Good thinking, Wife."

"We needed the shooter to believe he hit his target," said Daeng. "Otherwise he'd have kept shooting. How's the dog?"

Siri was looking for a wound.

"He's been drugged," he said. "This is where all the blood came from."

He pointed at the tail, or what was left of it. The last six centimeters had been hacked off.

"A lot of blood," said Dtui. "Nothing fatal."

"Looks like Dom's forgiven Ugly for turning on him," said Siri. "Still couldn't bring himself to kill the beast."

Dtui went to check on Malee, who'd slept through the drama. Phosy and Geung returned.

"No sign of anyone," said Phosy.

"Not even Rajhid?" said Dtui.

"He's not exactly on the clock," said Daeng. "He could have an appointment with some dolphin up river for all we know. We're just fortunate to get him when we can."

"Will Ug-Ugly make it?" Geung asked.

"His wagging days are over," said Siri. "And he's never going to trust cheese again. But he'll be fine. Just a bit light-headed for a day or so."

CHAPTER TWENTY-ONE
You're on Candid Camera

The next two days flew by in a blur. The police checked every deserted building, every guesthouse. They rechecked the houses of anyone connected to the original Bruce, went through Dr. Porn's basement, even visited the few seedy opium dens that everyone denied existed. Once again, Dom had vanished. Still, Siri remained out of sight at his official government residence by the That Luang monument.

The missing camera belonging to Jim was retrieved from the house of Dr. Porn. Dom had obviously lifted it from the Ferrari before the journalists set off. Once developed, the film showed four very clear photos of Dom and the car and the journalists, taken on the morning of the day they died.

The handheld movie camera and twelve developed films arrived at Phosy's office from Thailand and with Dtui's help, the chief inspector went through every second, constantly pausing and replaying. But after no more than ten minutes it was obvious to both of them what had motivated Dom to act the way he did. That evening, Siri broke cover and cycled to police headquarters.

"Siri, what are you . . . ?" said Phosy.

"Is that what I think it is?" said Siri, nodding at the film projector.

"Why are you here?" asked the policeman.

"I know where he is," said Siri.

Dom was awoken by the rattle of a key in a metal lock. The echo bounced around the building like a disoriented bat. He took out a pistol and an M16 and climbed to the top shelf level of the storage facility. In the shadows of the hampers and heavy equipment he couldn't be seen from the ground. In nine days, this was his first visitor.

Apart from one red Ferrari, Silver City remained virtually untouched since the Marines locked it up in '75. They deposited the keys with the embassy, and, under duress, the embassy handed one of those bunches to the PL. But it was an administration without balls. Nobody dared make decisions. Nobody would commit a signature to an order. So, apart from a visit by the Russian circus performers who were forced to camp in the grounds outside, Silver City had been frozen in time. Officials made brief visits, an inventory was taken, but nobody removed anything. The doors were relocked and the keys deposited with the Women's Union. It was perhaps because those keys still hung in Dr. Porn's office that nobody thought to look there for Dom.

The main warehouse was a treasure trove of household goods, various electrical equipment and enough weaponry to launch a third world war. Dom had wondered why an aid agency would need so much military hardware. He'd made copies of the keys as soon as he realized their significance, and after his escape from the fake surgeon's restaurant he set up his secret command post slap in the middle of the city. From there, his plan had been to follow through on his threats and assassinate the widow first. But he'd let himself down again. He was no marksman even though that modern equipment came with manuals. All he had to do was get the target in his sights and squeeze the trigger. Or so he thought. He could see her in the crosshairs. He wasn't that far away. Yet somehow he'd missed the wife and hit the doctor. Better than nothing, he decided. He saw him go down. He saw them carry the lifeless body into the restaurant. He needed first to be sure Siri was dead, then he'd return and do away with the widow.

But now he had to lose this unwanted visitor at the storage facility. He crawled to a spot where he could see the entrance. Someone was there locking the door from the inside. He was dressed like a farmer. He wore a broad straw hat so he wasn't recognizable from above. He had a two-wheeled market trolley that held a cardboard box. Dom crawled to the edge of the stack where there was an uninterrupted view of the ground. The visitor had moved a small table into the space and placed it beside a large white industrial refrigerator. He opened the box and took out a compact movie projector. As there was only one of its kind in the country, Dom recognized it as the one he'd brought from Australia. The newcomer unreeled a long extension cord and plugged it into a socket on one concrete post. Dom remained silent, unseen but fascinated as the man turned on the projector and pressed a switch that produced a neat rectangle of light on the side of the fridge.

"Dom, I have some good news for you," shouted the man. The voice was familiar but a little distorted in the windowless chamber. Dom was shocked to hear his actual name.

"I should have realized earlier where you'd be," the man continued. "You could probably live here for the rest of your life. Plenty of survival rations to eat. Lots to entertain you. You won't be able to see the picture from up there but the volume's probably loud enough," he said. "Of course you'd know, seeing as it's your equipment, right? Hope you don't mind us borrowing this and the camera. If you do want to watch, feel free to come down. I'm not armed. All you'll see on the screen is a couple of drunks in a bar alcove talking. You should recognize both of them. One of them I think you took a shine to when you met her here. Our pretty blonde. The other's changed a lot since you last saw him but it should be quite obvious who he is."

The intruder pressed play, walked to the wall by the door and sat down on the concrete floor. He took off his hat.

Dom couldn't believe his eyes. The audacity. Dr. Siri—uninjured, unarmed and alone—was no more than thirty meters from him. It was as if the old man was giving him a second shot.

"You're either brave or stupid," said Dom.

"Bit of both really," said Siri. "I didn't tell anyone I was coming. I doubt they'd have let me be here alone if I did. All I ask is that you watch the film before you shoot me. You've got plenty of time. And it'll make things easier the closer to me you are, right? You're not much of a marksman. No offence."

Voices emanated from the projector.

"Better hurry," said Siri. "The show's started."

"What's to stop me from shooting you dead first and watching the tape after?" said Dom.

"Nothing, except then you wouldn't get the punch line, would you? And that's the best part."

Dom came down the ladder on the far side of the stacks and walked cautiously to the table. His gun was trained on Siri the entire time. He squinted at the screen. There were two people: a middle-aged overweight man with thinning hair and a beautiful blonde woman who looked quite drunk. He was holding her hand. The Thai recognized her as Cindy from the US consulate but couldn't place the man.

"No, Darling, you're a legend round the bars of Ubon," said Cindy. "Everyone knows you. I've heard a lot about how amazing you are. I bet you've got some great stories."

"You sure you aren't with the CIA?" asked the man. "'Cause if you are I'd have to shoot you."

"Do I look like the CIA?" she said.

He laughed and looked into her cleavage.

"You sure don't," he said.

"Recognize the man yet?" Siri asked.

"No."

"Imagine him fifteen years younger and ten kilos lighter."

"I don't . . ."

The truth hit Dom with the force of a stack of crates landing on top of him. He looked up at Siri, who raised his hands to the heavens and shrugged.

"It can't . . ." said Dom. "When was this video taken?"

"Three days ago," said Siri.

"That's not possible," said Dom. "It's just someone who looks like him."

"Stay tuned, viewers," said Siri.

"What have you heard?" said the man on the screen.

"Just some things that can't be true," said the blonde.

"Try me."

They were drinking Thai rum with ice and soda. The man was constantly topping up their glasses.

"They said something about you convincing the US government you were a POW for six years. It would be awesome if it was true."

He smiled and raised his eyebrows.

"No?" she said.

"Almost got away with it too," said the man. "I even wrote a book about my six years in captivity."

"You're kidding me."

"True as I'm sitting here," he said. "I was this close to a hero's welcome and a million-dollar movie deal."

"What happened?"

"Some shitty little Lao doctor is what happened. But I can't tell you any of that. It's kind of classified."

"Oh, come on."

"No, I shouldn't."

She topped up his drink and stirred in a cube of ice.

"Well, you sure know a way to a man's heart," he said. "Okay, I'll tell you. But it can't go any further than this bar, you hear?"

"Cross my heart," she said, making a finger X on one breast.

"All right," he said. "You see, I was quite a well-known anti-war activist in the States. I'd written a book and other stuff. I was invited to run for Congress on a peace ticket, but we had a plan. I was already a decorated pilot."

"You were a pilot? Wow!"

She squeezed his arm. He flexed his muscle.

"I enlisted so I could operate from inside the insidious war machine," he said.

"From minute five to minute eight you'll notice there was a lot of bull dung getting tossed around," said Siri. "It's not easy to separate the fact from the fiction. We only edited out his trips to the bathroom and our girl changing the cartridges. The rest is verbatim. But just bear with it. We make our appearances toward the end."

Dom was stooped over the screen, the gun limp at his side. He didn't react to Siri's comment.

"To cut a long story short, I stole an airplane," said the man. "An F-100. I flew it away from the war zone and landed it in a Communist controlled area. Of course, I disabled it so the enemy wouldn't use it against my brothers. I hiked a week to the border. I'd broken a leg landing it, but I had jungle training. I knew how to lash it and tolerate the pain."

"So where were you for those six years if you weren't in a POW camp?"

"Here," he said. "I shacked up with a Thai whore and her mental son—as a front, mind you. And I continued to fight for our pacifist cause incognito from a village in Ubon. I had to come in to the bars and spend time here, earning the trust of servicemen and journalists and learning their confidential information. I'd pass on this intelligence to the anti-war movement in the States. I knew them all. Jane Fonda was a close friend. She came to visit me here several times. We had

a sort of . . . fling. She was serious but I didn't need all that baggage."

"I'm jealous," said the blonde.

"No need, Honey. I've got plenty of loving to share."

"So you were like a real spy," said the girl.

"I was a master of disguise," he said. "I could change identities overnight. I have a knack for convincing people I'm somebody else."

"Give me an example," she said.

"Well, languages and accents. I can do accents. Australian's one of my best. I remember I took the whore's son to Bangkok and got him on a scholarship to Australia by convincing the embassy he was the top student in my school in Ubon. I didn't have a school but I had all the fake paperwork to say I did. And I had an Australian passport I'd stolen from some drunk here. Even the Aussies thought I was one of them."

"And they accepted the boy to study there?"

"They were desperate for kids from the third world who could speak English to meet their quota and they had a lot of funding for education."

"Did the boy know he was there under false pretenses?"

"He had no idea. I told him the money was from me, but I didn't have to pay a penny. It was all Colombo Plan funding."

"Why send him to Australia and not the US?" said the blonde.

"Why not what? Send him Stateside? You seem like a clever girl. You've probably worked out I'm persona non grata *in America these days after all my agitation. They'd never let me back in without throwing me in jail. But the Aussies have a family reunion visa. The boy goes*

to school, gets residence and I can apply to join him there as his legal guardian. I faked that document too. I can go anytime I like. Just got a little bit tied down here with, you know, business."

"You're a real conman, aren't you?" she said. She was leaning against him. Another shirt button had popped open.

"What went wrong with the POW scam?" she asked.

"It was my last chance to get back into the US legally," he said. "As a hero I could convince them they were wrong about me stealing the plane and operating undercover. I was a week away from getting on that flight. I was having a final medical. I'd spent four months in a sort of up-market prison camp in Hanoi. I figured it was worth the inconvenience. I grew a beard and let my hair sprout wild. I got the shit bitten out of me by insects. I ran into a few walls, collected some grazes and bruises. And I picked at the food they gave us so I'd lose weight. After those four months I looked the part. Could have convinced anyone, I thought. But then this smart-assed little bastard Pathet Lao doctor comes and examines me. He decides I'm not sick enough. Haven't been ravaged enough by diseases.

I mean, shit. All he had to do was sign a release, god damn it. They should have been happy to be rid of me. But, no. This guy wants to do the full Edgar J. Hoover investigation to make himself look good to his Vietnamese bosses. He lied about a bunch of stuff, but they believed him and bumped me from the flight. Tried to get me into CIA hands. But I escaped."

"You remember his name?" she asked.

"I'll never forget it," he said. "Fake Doctor Siri

Paiboun. His name still comes to me in nightmares. But I've fixed him."

"How?"

"I set the mental son on him. I have to tell you there was always something scary about the boy. He was crazy about me to the point that he'd have done anything I told him to. In fact, he was clingy. Deranged, I'd say. I told him me and his whore mother had a disease. Got it into his head that Paiboun was responsible for us dying. She's not dead either, the mother. She's still putting it out there for old geezers. I see her slumming around the bars some nights. The boy was easy enough to stir up. I arranged for his scholarship to be cancelled, blamed Fake Dr. Siri for that too. So I knew he'd be pissed, knew he'd find a way to get revenge on behalf of his dead mother and dear old Uncle Henry. He promised me in the last letter I got from him. That's when I 'died' and left him in vengeance limbo. The guilt would have been too much for him not to go through with it."

"Ah, I hear my name," said Siri. "You must have got to the meat in the sandwich. We're not far from the end."

Dom's weapon was on the ground beside him. He was leaning with both fists on the refrigerator, blocking half the picture. The bar conversation continued.

"So, what have you been living on all these years?" the woman asked.

"I'm surprised you haven't heard," he said. "I run a very profitable import-export company here in Ubon. Made quite a fortune off of it. Of course, I'm still very active in the international peace movement."

"There really is no end to you, is there?" said the blonde.

"Look, this is a bit embarrassing," he said. "I've left my wallet in the Benz. Could you get this and we'll go somewhere quieter."

"Sure," she said.

"You're staying at the hotel, right?" he asked.

"Yeah."

"What say we get another bottle and burn off some calories over there?"

"Sounds peachy," she said. "But, hey. Do you mind if we take those two guys sitting at the end of the bar?"

She nodded in that direction. The man followed her gaze.

"What?" he asked.

"Yeah, we kind of came together," she said.

Two Western men in casual clothes appeared in the picture, grabbed Henry by the arms and stood him up. Their heads were all out of the frame now.

"What are you doing?" said the man.

"First I'll retrieve my camera from my overnight bag and make sure it's working."

The woman approached the camera. The picture went dark briefly then returned. She was holding the camera now and pointing it to another table where two Thai men sat drinking beer. They made V signs.

"If they could speak English," she said, "those two plainclothes Thai police gentlemen would probably say, 'You're under arrest.'"

"On what charge?"

"Where should we start?" she smiled. "You've just confessed to a dozen illegal things you really did, and

another dozen that you probably didn't do. We've traced several postal scams back to you already. But we can start off with immigration violations and work our way up to inciting murder. That should keep us busy."

Siri got to his feet and stretched his stiff old back.

"Good show, eh?" he said. "I'll leave it up to you to sort the mushrooms from the toadstools in that salad, but I think you've got the gist of it. He had no connections to the peace movement. That was a story he perfected to explain why he'd been there for so long. But even if every word he spoke was a lie, you can surely see how you and your mother fit into his world of fantasy. And perhaps he really believed all the garbage he said. Dementia works in odd ways. He was never a successful businessman. He taught English—made just enough for his next drink. It seems his world pretty much existed in the postal service. In his apartment they found begging letters and applications and scams. They found some letters to you he hadn't sent. They all asked for help with money."

"This is all a setup," said Dom. "You put this all together to mess with my mind."

He reached down for the gun.

"Don't do it," came a voice, and the building echoed with the sounds of gun hammers cocking behind him. While Siri had kept Dom engaged, Phosy and a few select officers had entered through the rear door and taken up positions.

Dom laughed.

"I had you in my sights, you know?" he said.

"I know," said Siri. "But secondhand revenge is rarely effective. You were carrying someone else's vengeance.

Those few seconds it took to step into your stepfather's shoes were enough to throw off your timing."

"I don't believe that was Henry on the film," said Dom.

"Yes, we thought that would be the case," said Phosy. "That's why we've arranged for a family reunion."

"With Henry?" said Dom.

"You're under arrest in Laos which probably won't be a lot of fun for you," said Phosy. "Our prisons aren't the most hospitable. So we've arranged a happy moment for you to take to jail with you."

"Our American colleagues were delighted to hear of Henry's whereabouts. He's been on their wanted list for a long time. Our friend Cindy was only too pleased to join our sting operation. They've transported your daddy to the US consulate here before flying him down to his own oblivion via the embassy in Bangkok," said Siri. "His dream of being repatriated will come true, but I think he'll be admiring the land of the free through barred windows for a very long time."

EPILOGUE ONE

"Hey, Say," said Monh, "not putting on your stockings tonight?"

Say and Monh and two other Lao were in a corrugated tin hut in Bangkok. They'd worked on the site till it was dark. Then they ate instant noodles and went to bed, too exhausted to listen to the radio or look at pictures in magazines. That's the way it was seven days a week, and, for Say with his nightmares, it had been hell. He'd nearly died in an accident a few weeks before. He'd been so exhausted he almost fell from the thirty-fifth floor of the unfinished building. Monh had grabbed him at the last second. It was because of this that his relatives at the camp had sent him the charm. It was ancient, that much was obvious. It was yellowing with age. His mother told him it had belonged to a great shaman. It hung on a simple string and weighed no more than a bubble but it contained great magic.

He'd worn it the day it arrived, and for the first time in a year he didn't see her in his dream—the succubus. She didn't taunt him. Didn't attempt to seduce him. The next night he left off the nightdress but wore the stockings. He dreamed about fields and chickens and friends from the old days. She was afraid of the charm. He knew it. And tonight he'd be leaving off the stockings, and his roommates wouldn't mock him again.

Because Say had the power.

EPILOGUE TWO

"It's quite mundane, isn't it?" asked Daeng.

"What is?" asked Siri.

"Life without an assassin breathing down your neck."

They were on the veranda at the French embassy enjoying one of Civilai's leftover bottles of Merlot. Seksan, the not-French ambassador, was in the kitchen frying up another batch of crêpes. The moon was just an unconvincing smile in a tar sky. Ugly had reverted to form and remained on the pavement beyond the barbed wire–garnished wall. Like Daeng, he continued to wag a tail that only he could see.

"How did they get along?" she asked. "Fraudulent father and homicidal son?"

"Phosy said they were together for five minutes before the boy attempted to garrote Henry with his belt."

"Families. What can you say?"

They looked at the inflatable Fred Flintstone punching bag that sat at the head of the table. He hadn't touched his drink.

"Still not talking to us, Civilai?" said Daeng.

"He'll get over it," said Siri. "I haven't spoken to him

about the whole murder thing yet, but I imagine he'll be more angry at being a victim of a lie than at being dead."

"It's another one of your biggest nothings, isn't it?" asked Daeng. "America believing their war was justified. Laos believing we have something to boast about. And this, a young man fooled by a pack of lies."

"People are basically stupid," said Siri. "We're easy to dupe. Nobody asks for proof anymore. A lie told with confidence is indistinguishable from the truth."

The scent of sweet crepes frying reached their nostrils.

"Any other news from police HQ?" Daeng asked.

"No sign of Dr. Porn's body," said Siri.

"I'm glad she wasn't involved in all this," said Daeng.

"She kept quiet about her past but now that the files have been released it appears she was in the same business as you."

"Noodles?"

"Subterfuge, deception, insurgency, revolution, counterintelligence, spying."

"It's good for a country girl to have interests other than sewing," said Daeng.

A strong breeze cut through the embassy garden and Fred Flintstone rocked back and forth.

"See?" said Siri. "Civilai always did appreciate a good joke."

And as the evening wore on and the warm air currents mingled in the embassy grounds, Civilai danced with his trademark lack of coordination, and Siri smiled in his direction, and they told stories about the old fellow that would have been farfetched . . . were they about anyone else.

Continue reading for a preview of the next
Dr. Siri Paiboun Investigation

The Delightful Life of a Suicide Pilot

CHAPTER ONE
Every Body Has a Story to Tell

There was a myth. Not a ghostly urban legend that might cause little children to wet their beds, but a disturbing notion nevertheless. It was likely begat from the mischievous storytelling of a doctor not unlike Siri Paiboun, the ex-national coroner of the People's Democratic Republic of Laos, who was known to smudge the lines between fact and fiction. The myth went something like this: after you're dead, your hair and nails will mysteriously continue to grow. Any qualified physician would snigger at such a thought. But no matter how unlikely the possibility, there were those who swore to have witnessed such a phenomenon. And all those doubting so-called "experts" needed to do was to take the key from beneath the welcome mat at the Mahosot Hospital morgue in Vientiane, let themselves into the cutting room, and slide out the only occupied freezer tray. And once they pulled back the sheet they would see for themselves. Comrade Thinh still sported a fine head of hair that was just a little too long to be called respectable. His nostril hair, on the other hand, had sprouted remarkably since his arrival on the slab. It was currently a good six centimeters long. Mr. Geung, the lab assistant, had already combed it into a neat mustache and was certain that before too long, there would be enough for a goatee.

Comrade Thinh's corpse had been in the morgue for almost a week with nothing to do but nurture this nasal display while his wife and his mistress argued their respective cases for taking the corpse home. It was fortunate for Thinh that he was dead because the two women were loathsome creatures. He'd probably inflicted a broken neck upon himself to be rid of them. The decision was currently in the hands of an ad hoc council composed of members of the Vietnamese Central Committee, naturally, all men. That it should be under consideration by such a lofty team was a testament to the importance of the deceased and the potential ramifications of sending him off to the wrong pyre.

Dr. Siri was no longer connected with the morgue in any official capacity. His lot now lay behind the portal of his wife's noodle shop, where he sat between shifts at a rear table with a cup of coffee and a book, any book. His illegal library had been destroyed some years earlier, and 1981 Laos was not a world hub of literature. The one bookshop had five Lao translations of Soviet Communist rhetoric, a shelf of official reports, and a three-year archive of the weekly edition of the *Passasson Lao* newsletter. The rest of the space was occupied by dusty sports equipment and stuffed endangered creatures with marbles for eyes and the terror of that final chase frozen on their faces. But once you have a reading habit it's a bugger to shake off. No love nor money could produce a Proust or Victor Hugo in Vientiane, so Siri read the minutes of the last Central Committee conference and the proposal for the next three-year development plan. And, of course, he read and reread the script of his motion picture that would never make it as far as the silver screen. He yearned for something creative and stimulating to enliven his dull days. As is often the case, a strong-enough yearning was just enough to tweak fate into action.

He had promised never to set foot in the morgue again but there was something about postmortem nostril hair growth that was far too tempting to pass up. As soon as Mr. Geung arrived for his evening noodle shift and passed on the news of the body in the freezer, Siri was on his bicycle and peddling in the direction of Mahosot with Ugly, the thrice-almost-dead mongrel, trotting along behind. There were no cars on the road. A recent survey had suggested there was a total of fourteen thousand motor vehicles in Laos. Eleven thousand had no access to gasoline because the scant offerings were monopolized by the government. Children were growing up bemused by these four-wheeled, moss-covered monuments in front yards.

It was a balmy evening that followed a balmy day at the end of a balmy month. The hot season lurked beyond the mountains of Vietnam, awaiting its cue to bake the Lao capital, but until it made its entrance the calm evenings brought out a procession of girls and boys doubling up on bicycles like amusement park duck targets hoping to be hit with a smile or a nod. They pedaled so slowly it was inconceivable the momentum was enough to hold them upright. Siri had invented the word "ertia," which was a microscopic step up from "inertia" and perfectly described flirtatious cycling. He shamelessly teased the girls he passed and they pretended not to hear him. But there was no disguising the small curl of lip, the flutter of eyelashes. No woman is deaf to a compliment.

The morgue door was ajar. Siri left the bicycle and Ugly in the shade of a nipplewort tree and kicked off his old leather sandals in the foyer. He passed the office where he'd sat many hours trying to make sense of ancient French forensic pathology texts and entered what was called the cutting room. There, leaning over the freezer tray, were Chief Inspector Phosy and his wife, Nurse Dtui. They looked up mid-chuckle.

"Ah, Siri," said Phosy. "I didn't think you'd be able to stay away."

"I've spent too many happy hours staring into offal to give it all up completely," said Siri.

"Have you seen this, Doc?" asked Dtui. She was pretty and slightly more rounded than usual. He refrained from asking her if she was pregnant just in case she wasn't.

"I hope you aren't making fun of the dead," said Siri.

He joined them and couldn't hold back a guffaw of his own when he saw the corpse. Mr. Geung had fashioned a splendid mustache; it was true it had outgrown a Poirot and was approaching the realm of a Fu Manchu. Siri tugged on it to be sure it wasn't a practical joke. It held firm.

"Well, I've seen some things," said Siri, "but this takes the prawn cracker."

"Do you think there's any connection between the nose hair and the death?" Phosy asked playfully.

"Not for me to say anymore," said Siri. "Whose case is it?"

"Dr. Mot announced the cause of death," said Dtui.

"Ah, then we'll never know for certain," said Siri, no fan of the current coroner, a recent returnee from the Eastern bloc. As Siri often said, it was a miracle he'd graduated after studying in a language he couldn't speak. He did have a certificate suggesting he was qualified to perform autopsies.

It was framed and hanging on his office wall beside a similar certificate claiming he was proficient in porcelain glazing.

"And what brings you both here, apart from the obvious sideshow?" Siri asked.

"I was asked to investigate the case personally," said Phosy.

"I thought they'd strapped you behind a desk."

"They let me out every now and then for delicate matters," said the policeman.

"What's delicate about this?" Siri asked. "I heard from my inside source that your man here had too much to drink and fell off a cliff. What Mr. Geung couldn't tell me was why all this warrants so much attention."

"And that all comes down to who he is," said Phosy.

"Who is he?"

"Does the name Bui Sok Thinh ring a bell?"

"Not a tinkle."

"He was the son of Bui Kieu."

"Still nothing ringing in my ears."

"Perhaps he was after your time," said Phosy. "He's one of the richest men in Vietnam."

"I thought we'd obliterated wealth," said Siri. "Did something happen to communist dogma while I was napping?"

"The inevitable happened, Doc," said Dtui. "It's the same here. Lots of good intentions but no money. A few years of failed cooperatives and natural disasters and there's no budget for infrastructure. So we fall back on good old cronyism. We call the rich guys back from lifelong banishment overseas, borrow a few billion here, make a few deals there."

"Ooh," said Siri. "Your wife's grown horns."

"She's bored with being poor, I think," said Phosy. "She's waiting for me to accept my first graft so she can buy a refrigerator."

"I feel that refrigerator will be a long time coming," said Siri.

"That's what I try to tell her."

"Never mind, Dtui," said Siri. "You're still comparatively young. It's not too late to find yourself a sugar daddy."

"No hope there," said Dtui. "Sugar daddies like them wafer thin with silicon breasts."

"Sounds awful," said Siri. "Give me a good old-fashioned naturally buxom girl any day. But back to hairy nose here. Did he get a share of his daddy's wealth?"

"They sent Thinh to Italy to study during the war. His family had a lot of mandarin money to invest in Europe. Thinh made a fortune in war profiteering. When Uncle Ho took over Vietnam the Viet Minh found themselves short of funds so they started courting the Bui clan. Thinh brokered a deal for the Italians to drill for oil in the gulf of Tonkin. Thinh ran the company. The income from that amounted to a large chunk of the country's GNP."

"And how do you go from that to a cold slab in a foreign country?" Siri asked.

"He was very high-profile in Hanoi and he liked to get away and relax when he had a chance. He had a soft spot for our very own Vang Vieng; peaceful, beautiful scenery and nobody knew him there. He'd fly the family helicopter down. He had a hidden chalet in the hills. He liked nothing more than to hike up to the karsts with a few bottles of very expensive wine in his pack, sit on a ledge, and watch the river. Simple pleasures. In the early days he'd take his wife. I'm told she is a sow of a woman as well as the daughter of a Vietnamese politburo man. She soon tired of those hikes and he soon tired of asking her. He took himself a younger girl to be his minor wife and she was in better shape. Didn't mind the trekking. They'd sit on the ledge and drink to Mother Nature . . ."

". . . and probably play a few rounds of paper, scissors, stone," said Dtui.

"I tell you, Madam Daeng and I never tire of that," said Siri.

"Thinh could have had his choice of beautiful, loose women to be his mistress," said Phosy. "But he was apparently a glutton for punishment, and he selected a plain, opinionated girl who was the daughter of a Viet Minh war hero. I hear she has the temper of a rabid Chihuahua. She's claiming that the major wife was with him on his last trip to Vang Vieng and that she pushed him off a ledge when he was drunk. The wife laughed off that allegation and countered that it must have been the mistress who accompanied Thinh to the mountain and killed him."

"Why do we think either of them had to be there?"

"A goat herder saw this Vietnamese man hiking there last weekend. He was with a woman. Too far away to identify her."

"And what's to be gained by killing him?"

"The first wife stands to inherit a hell of a lot," said Phosy. "If she's convicted of murder, the money will go to the minor wife. And the concubine's father happens to be on the board of directors of the drilling company. He'll no doubt be pushing for an inquiry."

"Any children?"

"No."

"Other siblings?"

"Apparently not."

Siri looked around at the morgue he'd worked in for five years. In that time, it had been refurbished first by the Chinese, then by the Soviets, but it still looked neglected. The air conditioner wheezed. The corpse carts limped like old supermarket trolleys. Not even Mr. Geung's "Twelve Puppies to Make You Laugh" wall calendar could inject any passion into that old building. Siri walked to the freezer that had not contained Comrade Thinh and fought with the handle for a few seconds as always. Inside were the jar of water and four tumblers. Mr. Geung always left them there just in case the morgue had visitors. They didn't see a lot of use. Naturally, there was no ice. The freezers got their name from a short-circuiting accident following which Nurse Dtui and Daeng had spent several hours attempting to thaw out a body with the aid of kettle steam and a two-bar heater. The equipment had frozen nothing since. Siri poured his guests a glass of cool water each and returned to the matter at hand.

"All right," he said, "even if one of the women in his life was there, how do we know he just couldn't stand them anymore and stepped off the ledge to be rid of them?"

"Everyone who knew him swears he's the last person on earth who'd commit suicide; fun-loving, over the moon with the Italian project. He even seemed fond of the women in his own way. No business pressure. No political bullying. He loved his life."

"Yet here he is," said Siri. "Dtui, why didn't you do the autopsy?"

"I'm just a nurse," she said.

"A nurse with a deep knowledge of forensic pathology," Siri countered.

"But no certificate on my wall," said Dtui. "Not even in porcelain varnishing."

"I'll print you one," said Siri. "It seems all you need these days is a bit of paper with one illegible signature at the bottom."

He pulled back the sheet that covered the corpse.

"Look," he said. "Dr. Mot didn't even bother to cut our friend here open."

"Said it wasn't necessary," said Phosy. "Said it was obvious the victim had died from multiple injuries sustained whilst bouncing off rocks on his way down the cliff. Said the empty bottles proved that he was so drunk he probably didn't feel it."

"May I?" Siri asked.

"Go ahead," said Phosy.

Siri turned the corpse on its side and studied the back.

"No handprints, no bruises, no indication he was hit with anything," he said. "It is possible he stepped up to relieve himself, took one pace too many, and peed himself to death."

"Then why would the wives deny they were there?" Dtui asked. "They could have explained what happened and there'd be no evidence to say otherwise."

"Unless it wasn't one of them," said Phosy.

"Good thinking," said Siri.

"I'm wondering whether he went to Vang Vieng alone last weekend, met a local girl, and took her up into the mountains," Phosy continued. "She might have panicked when he made advances and pushed him away."

"Even if it was an accident, she'd still have given birth to a buffalo from the shock of it," said Siri.

"No way she'd admit to being there," said Dtui.

"And Vang Vieng's a small community," said Phosy. "They'd set up a force field around one of their girls."

"You wouldn't even get to talk to her," said Dtui.

"Unless we could convince her we know it was an accident," said Siri, lowering the corpse onto its back.

"How would we go about that?" Phosy asked.

"I have no idea just yet, but every body has a story to tell if you just show a little patience. Do you suppose our intrepid Dr. Varnish has exhausted all his autopsy skills?"

"He said there's nothing more to be learned," said Dtui.

"Then he wouldn't mind me tinkering a little."

"I doubt he'd notice."

"Splendid. Then I shall return tomorrow at dawn with my tool kit and my faithful lab assistant."

CHAPTER TWO
My Friends Call Me Toshi

Dr. Siri arrived at the noodle shop a little too early to beat the evening rush. Diners had already filled the small open-fronted restaurant but they weren't there for the Mekong views. They'd come to enjoy the best noodles in the capital. Government workers in khaki or white shirts had eaten away the frustrations of another day of paperwork and inefficiency. Lady teachers in stiff cotton *phasin* skirts had kicked off their uncomfortable shoes beneath the tables and sighed off another day of explaining how Marxist-Leninism had affected the shifting of the tectonic plates. Karl and Vladimir had been a busy pair since '75.

Standing on the uneven pavement was a scrawny man dressed as a farmer but wearing a splendid post office helmet from the old regime. He never entered the restaurant unless invited by Siri himself.

"Comrade Ging," said Siri. "I've told you, you really don't have to get permission to go inside."

"Oh, I'm not here for food," said Ging as always. "Just doing my duty delivering mail. Officials of the Lao Postal Service do not request or expect remuneration for doing something of which we are proud."

There was no mail delivery service in Laos. Letters were either sent to post office boxes or to a large *poste restante* sack, much of the contents of which would never be claimed. There were as many postal workers slitting open and censoring mail as there were selling stamps, and customers could never be sure of what subversive material their mail contained. Comrade Ging sold stamps. But on his breaks and after work he would don his helmet, wrap a homemade post office armband around his boney bicep, and deliver unopened mail to residents he knew would show their gratitude. Madam Daeng's noodle shop was one such place.

"Do you have something for us?" Siri asked.

"I do." Ging smiled, reached into his back sack, and pulled out a parcel the size and shape of an Omo washing powder packet. He nodded and handed it to Siri. "And with that, I'll be on my way."

Siri was tempted to let him go but he knew his wife would berate him for doing so. And it was nice to have mail delivered.

"Perhaps you'd be kind enough to join us for a meal," said Siri.

"I . . . I don't think I'll have time."

"Madam Daeng would be pleased if you could spare a few minutes."

"Well, I . . . All right, then. To keep Madam Daeng happy," said the man, walking triumphantly into the restaurant. He removed his helmet and found an empty stool. Mr. Geung welcomed him by name and Geung's wife, Tukta, served him without asking what he wanted. In fact, after forty years in the postal service, all he really wanted was respect.

"What's that?" Daeng asked her husband. She was bent over the noodle trough. The steam wafted around her like a dream sequence but she never seemed to work up a sweat.

"Parcel," said Siri, heading for the stairs.

Daeng could have repeated her question but a simple eyebrow raise stopped him in his tracks.

"Feels like a book," said Siri. "Heavy. Ging just dropped it off."

"That's very nice for you," said Daeng, ladling out four bowls with the deftness of a conjurer. "But don't you think our customers could use a bit of *maître-d'* ing?"

"Darling, your noodles sell themselves. They don't need promoting."

"After a day of dealing with bureaucracy our customers appreciate a little sympathy and a few laughs. We aren't just a noodle shop. We're a wellness agency and you are the doctor of compassion."

"But I . . ."

"The book can wait."

The book waited until 8 P.M., when the customers had all returned to their overcrowded homes, the tables were cleared and clean, and Mr. Geung and Tukta were back in their room talking to the baby that wouldn't be born for another six months. Everyone was aware that the odds were stacked against a woman with Down syndrome producing a healthy child. And when the father also had Down syndrome those odds tumbled into infinity. But, like Dr. Siri, Geung had friends in other dimensions and he'd been shown their daughter in a dream. Geung said she looked a little like Sarinthip Siriwan. Siri pointed out that it would be a most difficult birth considering the size of the Thai actress. The couple laughed at that for a week.

"So, are you going to open it?" Daeng asked.

"I was wondering what the chances are that it's a bomb," said Siri.

They were sitting on the riverbank sipping their after-noodle rice whisky cocktails. The lights of Sri Chiang Mai on the Thai side were all out; probably another power cut. The Thais were renowned for creative wiring. So, with the moon yet to make an appearance, the darkness was thick: like staring out over a landscape of tar. Daeng got to her feet.

"Where are you going?" Siri asked.

"You don't expect me to sit beside you if it's a bomb, do you?"

"I don't know. It could be romantic, splattered across the Mekong together, our parts floating side by side to Cambodia."

"There's nothing romantic about dismemberment, Siri. I'm off to the ladies' room. You can open it while I'm gone. I'll listen for the bang."

Guided by the single lamp in the shop behind her, she scampered up the bank. Not bad for a seventy-year-old. Siri took his penlight out of his top pocket and held it between his teeth—teeth that he could still proudly call his own, all thirty-three of them. From the same pocket he removed a Soviet army knife and flicked open a blade. He sliced through layers of thick masking tape and removed an inner skin of brown paper. Inside that was a plastic bag followed by several layers of Thai newspaper and another plastic bag, all taped securely.

When Daeng returned, Siri was sitting in a pile of assorted wrappings, holding a somewhat smaller parcel in his hands.

"We used to play that when we were children," she said.

"Play what?"

"You give someone a gift and by the time they've unwrapped it there's nothing inside."

"How cruel you were," said Siri. "No, I feel I'm almost down to the meat. Just one more layer of tissue paper and . . . there."

At last he found what was most certainly a book of some kind. The cover was made of a sort of skin; leather perhaps. It was dotted with a dark mold and smelled rancid. He opened it carefully but all he found were blank pages.

"Hmm," he said. "That's odd."

He turned the book to what should have been the back and there on the rear cover were two small Chinese-looking initials branded onto the skin. He opened it to the back pages, where he was met by line after line of neat handwritten text.

"Chinese?" said Daeng.

"Japanese."

"Can you read it?"

"I'm afraid not. I picked up the numbers when we were in the underground and the Japanese were threatening to invade. Thought it might be useful for recognizing times and dates in captured documents. But I didn't get around to the letters. They don't use the same date system as us. It starts with the reign of the current emperor and that began in . . . 1926. So the number here is probably Showa Eleven. I'm assuming this is a diary and it starts in 1937."

"And there I was thinking I only married you for your body."

"It's a two-for-the-price-of-one package, Daeng. No extra cost for the genius."

"So, 1937? Japan's at war with China," said Daeng.

"This starts July seventh."

"Stop showing off."

Siri flipped through the pages, right to left.

"It's beautifully penned," he said. "Someone's obviously put their heart into it. Every page neat and precise. Not a crossing-out or a smudge; not so much as a wine stain. There's a week or two between each entry. And it looks like the writing gets more confident. Much stronger. It's as if the writer's gouging the ink into the paper. And I . . ."

"What?"

"Daeng. Look at this."

She leaned over the page.

"Well, I'll be," she said.

The Japanese text ended halfway down the page and was replaced with the date 12/30/1940, in Western numerals, and the Lao sentence *My name is Kangen Toshimado (咸元利圓)*. The Lao lettering was childish but it was legible, and to Siri's eyes, it seemed to introduce a sudden burst of fun: a hibiscus sprouting suddenly in a cabbage patch.

"Our Comrade Toshimado's learning Lao," said Daeng.

Siri turned the page and there was Toshimado agreeing with her.

I am studying Lao, he wrote.

A week or two had passed in diary time but he'd obviously been practicing his lettering. Daeng turned the page and read the entry for 1/6/1941.

I am Japanese. I am a major in the Imperial Army of Japan. I am thirty-four years old. My friends call me Toshi.

With every page they turned, the Lao language seemed to spread like a virus over the paper. On 1/24/1941 he attempted his first full page. There were mistakes here and there but they all suggested that Toshi was enjoying his journey through this new language. He wrote about traveling across the Lao countryside with his friend and eating and drinking local delicacies. He threw it all down on the page, hang the consequences. Suddenly, after three years of beautiful but disciplined Japanese text, his words had flamboyance.

The penlight was made in China so neither of them was surprised when the feeble beam gave up the ghost. It was a sign of the times. Soviet donations were ugly and almost indestructible. Chinese donations looked like the originals but didn't work, yet the donors still believed the third world should be grateful.

"Let's go inside and read some more," said Daeng.

"A riddle first," said Siri. "Why do you think someone would send me the diary of a Japanese soldier?"

"Because they knew you were desperate for reading material?"

"I admit it will be fun to read but they've gone to a lot of trouble to get this to me in one piece. My guess is that there has to be a point."

"You sure there isn't a letter in there?"

"I didn't look."

He held up the diary by the spine and, recklessly, fanned through the pages. At first nothing happened. Then a single page came loose. It was caught briefly in the lamplight from the shop as it surfed a breeze. It was almost impossible to follow its course but it was clear to both of them that it was headed in the direction of the river. Before it could hit the water it was out of sight.

Other Titles in the Soho Crime Series

STEPHANIE BARRON
(Jane Austen's England)
Jane and the Twelve Days of Christmas
Jane and the Waterloo Map
Jane and the Year Without a Summer
Jane and the Final Mystery

F.H. BATACAN
(Philippines)
Smaller and Smaller Circles

JAMES R. BENN
(World War II Europe)
Billy Boyle
The First Wave
Blood Alone
Evil for Evil
Rag & Bone
A Mortal Terror
Death's Door
A Blind Goddess
The Rest Is Silence
The White Ghost
Blue Madonna
The Devouring
Solemn Graves
When Hell Struck Twelve
The Red Horse
Road of Bones
From the Shadows
Proud Sorrows

The Refusal Camp: Stories

KATE BEUTNER
(Massachusetts)
Killingly

CARA BLACK
(Paris, France)
Murder in the Marais
Murder in Belleville
Murder in the Sentier

CARA BLACK CONT.
Murder in the Bastille
Murder in Clichy
Murder in Montmartre
Murder on the Ile Saint-Louis
Murder in the Rue de Paradis
Murder in the Latin Quarter
Murder in the Palais Royal
Murder in Passy
Murder at the Lanterne Rouge
Murder Below Montparnasse
Murder in Pigalle
Murder on the Champ de Mars
Murder on the Quai
Murder in Saint-Germain
Murder on the Left Bank
Murder in Bel-Air
Murder at the Porte de Versailles

Three Hours in Paris
Night Flight to Paris

HENRY CHANG
(Chinatown)
Chinatown Beat
Year of the Dog
Red Jade
Death Money
Lucky

BARBARA CLEVERLY
(England)
The Last Kashmiri Rose
Strange Images of Death
The Blood Royal
Not My Blood
A Spider in the Cup
Enter Pale Death
Diana's Altar

Fall of Angels
Invitation to Die

COLIN COTTERILL
(Laos)
The Coroner's Lunch
Thirty-Three Teeth
Disco for the Departed
Anarchy and Old Dogs
Curse of the Pogo Stick
The Merry Misogynist
Love Songs from a Shallow Grave
Slash and Burn
The Woman Who Wouldn't Die
Six and a Half Deadly Sins
I Shot the Buddha
The Rat Catchers' Olympics
Don't Eat Me
The Second Biggest Nothing
The Delightful Life of a Suicide Pilot

The Motion Picture Teller

ELI CRANOR
(Arkansas)
Don't Know Tough
Ozark Dogs

MARIA ROSA CUTRUFELLI
(Italy)
Tina, Mafia Soldier

GARRY DISHER
(Australia)
The Dragon Man
Kittyhawk Down
Snapshot
Chain of Evidence
Blood Moon
Whispering Death
Signal Loss

Wyatt
Port Vila Blues
Fallout

Under the Cold Bright Lights

TERESA DOVALPAGE
(Cuba)
Death Comes in through the Kitchen
Queen of Bones
Death under the Perseids

Death of a Telenovela Star (A Novella)

DAVID DOWNING
(World War II Germany)
Zoo Station
Silesian Station
Stettin Station
Potsdam Station
Lehrter Station
Masaryk Station
Wedding Station

(World War I)
Jack of Spies
One Man's Flag
Lenin's Roller Coaster
The Dark Clouds Shining

Diary of a Dead Man on Leave

RAMONA EMERSON
(Navajo Nation)
Shutter

NICOLÁS FERRARO
(Argentina)
Cruz

AGNETE FRIIS
(Denmark)
What My Body Remembers
The Summer of Ellen

TIMOTHY HALLINAN
(Thailand)
The Fear Artist
For the Dead
The Hot Countries
Fools' River
Street Music

TIMOTHY HALLINAN CONT.
(Los Angeles)
Crashed
Little Elvises
The Fame Thief
Herbie's Game
King Maybe
Fields Where They Lay
Nighttown
Rock of Ages

METTE IVIE HARRISON
(Mormon Utah)
The Bishop's Wife
His Right Hand
For Time and All Eternities
Not of This Fold
The Prodigal Daughter

MICK HERRON
(England)
Slow Horses
Dead Lions
The List (A Novella)
Real Tigers
Spook Street
London Rules
The Marylebone Drop (A Novella)
Joe Country
The Catch (A Novella)
Slough House
Bad Actors

Down Cemetery Road
The Last Voice You Hear
Why We Die
Smoke and Whispers

Reconstruction
Nobody Walks
This Is What Happened
Dolphin Junction: Stories
The Secret Hours

NAOMI HIRAHARA
(Japantown)
Clark and Division
Evergreen

STAN JONES
(Alaska)
White Sky, Black Ice
Shaman Pass
Frozen Sun
Village of the Ghost Bears
Tundra Kill
The Big Empty

STEPHEN MACK JONES
(Detroit)
August Snow
Lives Laid Away
Dead of Winter
Deus X

LENE KAABERBØL & AGNETE FRIIS
(Denmark)
The Boy in the Suitcase
Invisible Murder
Death of a Nightingale
The Considerate Killer

MARTIN LIMÓN
(South Korea)
Jade Lady Burning
Slicky Boys
Buddha's Money
The Door to Bitterness
The Wandering Ghost
G.I. Bones
Mr. Kill
The Joy Brigade
Nightmare Range
The Iron Sickle
The Ville Rat
Ping-Pong Heart
The Nine-Tailed Fox
The Line

MARTIN LIMÓN CONT.
GI Confidential
War Women

ED LIN
(Taiwan)
Ghost Month
Incensed
99 Ways to Die
Death Doesn't Forget

PETER LOVESEY
(England)
The Circle
The Headhunters
False Inspector Dew
Rough Cider
On the Edge
The Reaper

(Bath, England)
The Last Detective
Diamond Solitaire
The Summons
Bloodhounds
Upon a Dark Night
The Vault
Diamond Dust
The House Sitter
The Secret Hangman
Skeleton Hill
Stagestruck
Cop to Corpse
The Tooth Tattoo
The Stone Wife
Down Among the Dead Men
Another One Goes Tonight
Beau Death
Killing with Confetti
The Finisher
Diamond and the Eye
Showstopper

(London, England)
Wobble to Death

PETER LOVESEY CONT.
The Detective Wore Silk Drawers
Abracadaver
Mad Hatter's Holiday
The Tick of Death
A Case of Spirits
Swing, Swing Together
Waxwork

Bertie and the Tinman
Bertie and the Seven Bodies
Bertie and the Crime of Passion

SUJATA MASSEY
(1920s Bombay)
The Widows of Malabar Hill
The Satapur Moonstone
The Bombay Prince
The Mistress of Bhatia House

FRANCINE MATHEWS
(Nantucket)
Death in the Off-Season
Death in Rough Water
Death in a Mood Indigo
Death in a Cold Hard Light
Death on Nantucket
Death on Tuckernuck
Death on a Winter Stroll

SEICHŌ MATSUMOTO
(Japan)
Inspector Imanishi Investigates

CHRIS McKINNEY
(Post Apocalyptic Future)
Midnight, Water City
Eventide, Water City
Sunset, Water City

PHILIP MILLER
(North Britain)
The Goldenacre

MAGDALEN NABB
(Italy)
Death of an Englishman
Death of a Dutchman
Death in Springtime
Death in Autumn
The Marshal and the Murderer
The Marshal and the Madwoman
The Marshal's Own Case
The Marshal Makes His Report
The Marshal at the Villa Torrini
Property of Blood
Some Bitter Taste
The Innocent
Vita Nuova
The Monster of Florence

FUMINORI NAKAMURA
(Japan)
The Thief
Evil and the Mask
Last Winter, We Parted
The Kingdom
The Boy in the Earth
Cult X
My Annihilation
The Rope Artist

STUART NEVILLE
(Northern Ireland)
The Ghosts of Belfast
Collusion
Stolen Souls
The Final Silence
Those We Left Behind

So Say the Fallen

The Traveller & Other Stories
House of Ashes

(Dublin)
Ratlines

KWEI QUARTEY
(Ghana)
Murder at Cape Three Points
Gold of Our Fathers
Death by His Grace
The Missing American
Sleep Well, My Lady
Last Seen in Lapaz

QIU XIAOLONG
(China)
Death of a Red Heroine
A Loyal Character Dancer
When Red Is Black

NILIMA RAO
(1910s Fiji)
A Disappearance in Fiji

MARCIE R. RENDON
(Minnesota's Red River Valley)
Murder on the Red River
Girl Gone Missing
Sinister Graves

JAMES SALLIS
(New Orleans)
The Long-Legged Fly
Moth
Black Hornet
Eye of the Cricket
Bluebottle
Ghost of a Flea
Sarah Jane

MICHAEL SEARS
(Queens, New York)
Tower of Babel

JOHN STRALEY
(Sitka, Alaska)
The Woman Who Married a Bear
The Curious Eat Themselves
The Music of What Happens
Death and the Language of Happiness
The Angels Will Not Care
Cold Water Burning
Baby's First Felony
So Far and Good
(Cold Storage, Alaska)
The Big Both Ways
Cold Storage, Alaska
What Is Time to a Pig?
Blown by the Same Wind

LEONIE SWANN
(England)
The Sunset Years of Agnes Sharp

KAORU TAKAMURA
(Japan)
Lady Joker

AKIMITSU TAKAGI
(Japan)
The Tattoo Murder Case
Honeymoon to Nowhere
The Informer

CAMILLA TRINCHIERI
(Tuscany)
Murder in Chianti
The Bitter Taste of Murder
Murder on the Vine

HELENE TURSTEN
(Sweden)
Detective Inspector Huss
The Torso
The Glass Devil
Night Rounds
The Golden Calf
The Fire Dance
The Beige Man
The Treacherous Net
Who Watcheth
Protected by the Shadows
Hunting Game
Winter Grave
Snowdrift

HELENE TURSTEN CONT.
An Elderly Lady Is Up to No Good
An Elderly Lady Must Not Be Crossed

ILARIA TUTI
(Italy)
Flowers over the Inferno
The Sleeping Nymph
Daughter of Ashes

JANWILLEM VAN DE WETERING
(Holland)
Outsider in Amsterdam
Tumbleweed
The Corpse on the Dike
Death of a Hawker
The Japanese Corpse
The Blond Baboon
The Maine Massacre
The Mind-Murders
The Streetbird
The Rattle-Rat
Hard Rain
Just a Corpse at Twilight
Hollow-Eyed Angel
The Perfidious Parrot
The Sergeant's Cat: Collected Stories

JACQUELINE WINSPEAR
(1920s England)
Maisie Dobbs
Birds of a Feather